A WOLF'S HONOR

THE KINCAID WEREWOLVES #2

L.E. WILSON

EVERBLOOD
PUBLISHING

le@lewilsonauthor.com

Print Edition

Publication Date: January 17, 2017

Editing: Julia Ganis, JuliaEdits.com

Cover Design by Coffee and Characters

ISBN: 978-1-945499-47-0

To my friend, Isabel.
For holding my hand in blurb hell with me, and everything else
you do.

We call them faerie. We don't believe in them. Our loss. ~
Charles de Lint

Werewolves were far more terrifying than vampires. It is probably the idea of seeing the human within the beast and knowing you can't reach it. It might as well be a great white shark. There is no sitting down and discussing Proust with it, which the traditional vampire model seems to leave room for. You can have a conversation. ~ Glen Duncan

CHAPTER 1

This is no' goin' tae end well.

Marc Kincaid rose to his impressive height from the park bench he'd been lounging on. He eyed the threesome of sizable Lycan males sauntering toward him at typical southern speed across the front lawn of the Texas Capitol building. He sighed heavily, and wished they would hurry it the fuck up.

He silently reviewed what he was planning to say to them, calculated the risks of saying this and not saying that, and prayed the hellish heat didn't make them ill-tempered. He just needed them to listen for a few minutes. But even from this distance, one look at their stony faces and he was more certain than ever that this was naught but a mistake. He was wasting his time.

But it was what his alpha wanted, and he'd agreed to try. Cedric hadn't been pack leader for this long without knowing what he was doing.

As they neared, Marc's eyebrow rose at their wannabe

cowboy ensembles: button-down shirts with rolled up sleeves, well-worn jeans, cowboy boots, and large brimmed hats slung down low on their foreheads. He half expected to hear jangling spurs and see stalks of hay sticking out from between their teeth, and was almost disappointed when he didn't. He couldn't quite keep the smirk from his face as he wondered if they all gathered round the campfire every night and planned what they were going to wear the next morning so they would all match.

They even had giant silver buckles on their belts, even though Marc knew for a fact that not a one of them had ever ridden a bull. Bucking chute or not, there was no way an animal would allow any of their kind to get close enough to be able to climb onto its back. The poor thing would break its wee neck trying to escape first.

Arms hanging at his sides in a deceptively relaxed pose, Marc discreetly cracked his knuckles one by one, then wiped his sweaty palms on his jean-clad thighs. He wasn't nervous. Quite the opposite, actually. His wolf was well under control, which was how he liked it, and this meeting was taking place on neutral ground in full view of the humans milling about on their lunch hour. Unless these guys were a special kind of eejit, there wouldn't be any violence here today. He was only sweating because it was unbelievably hot in Austin, even this late in the summer. He didn't know how anyone could live here, be they human or otherwise, and especially not a pack of werewolves. Like him, their body temperature ran a little hotter than what was normal, and they were definitely better suited for a cooler climate. Why in all that was holy would these fools choose to live here?

He eyeballed their ridiculous ensembles once more and sighed.

Well, at least they seem tae have adapted well tae the local urban cowboy culture.

A slight breeze blew through the scrub brush Texans called trees and Marc squinted against the dust. Even the bloody wind was hot here. He squinted up at the scorching sun. He was beginning to see why everyone moved at a snail's pace here. Scratching the back of his neck, he contemplated sitting down again as it seemed he was going to be waiting a while. It was bad etiquette as he'd already stood to greet them, but fuck it. If they couldn't get their arses over to him in a proper amount of time, then he saw no need to act any differently.

The wind changed course, blowing in from the opposite direction, and he stopped mid-sit. Marc shot upright again, inhaling deeply. His entire body went rigid, straining in the direction of a new, intriguing scent. Digging his utility boots into the grass, he fought the urge to charge off after it with his nose lifted in the air like a hound.

What the hell is that?

It seemed vaguely familiar to him, but wasn't anything he could immediately place his finger on. Yet it called to him with such a force that he was having a bloody hard time resisting.

What the fook is that?

After racking his brain for a full minute, it finally came to him, the place he'd smelled it before. It was Northern

Ireland. Or rather, a brief moment of time he'd spent in Ireland a long, long time ago.

Many moons before, his pack had crossed the North Channel from their homeland of Scotland after rumors of Faerie problems had made it to their ears. He'd been in his wolf form, standing alone in an open field and trying to catch his breath after he'd just run full-out for many miles. Panting heavily, he'd lifted his snout to the sky and breathed in the strong smells of the grass and the wild-flowers, made musky from the recent rain. But there'd been one scent that had seemed to overpower all of the others: the heady fragrance of what he'd later discovered had come from the creamy-white meadowsweet flowers.

Those flowers were native to Ireland, however, so how was it that he was smelling them here? All the way across the ocean? In the desert landscape of Texas, of all places?

His narrowed gaze swept across the manicured lawn of the capitol building. He searched the flowerbeds, the bushes, the trees...but saw nothing that even slightly resembled the dense white clusters he was accustomed to seeing. And then, just as quickly as it had appeared, the smell was gone. Immediately, his muscles relaxed, his heart slowed, and his attention once again turned to the approaching pack of werewolves who were suddenly uncomfortably close to him.

Shaking off the strange occurrence, he kept his gaze steady but passive on the leader of the pack, careful to emit neither dominance nor submissiveness. He wasn't here to have a pissing contest, but rather to warn them of the war that was coming and to propose an alliance between their two packs. There was only one other pack that had taken up residence in the land between them on this side of the North American continent, for werewolf territory ranged far and wide. And if Marc could get these Texas wolves to agree to the truce, it would be easier to talk the middle pack into falling in with them.

The male in front came to a stop a respectable distance away and touched the brim of his buckskin-colored hat. Clear green eyes shone from tanned skin at a level with Marc's own. "Afternoon," he drawled. "Marc Kincaid, I take it?"

Marc gave him a nod of deference as befitted the leader of a rival pack. "Aye. Thank ye for agreeing tae meet me on such short notice, and under these circumstances. Cedric sends his apologies that he could no' make it himself. He had an urgent matter tae attend tae." Marc had no idea exactly what the "urgent matter" was. And when he'd asked, Cedric had danced around the subject until he'd given up.

The alpha nodded once, accepting the apology. "I'm Keegan. Alpha of the McRae pack here." He nodded to the pale-skinned blond on his right. "This is Jace, my second-in-command."

Jace crossed his arms over his muscular chest and gave Marc an arrogant stare, his blue eyes narrowed with mistrust. His cocky attitude reminded Marc of Lucian, and he struggled not to snarl back at him. He didn't like this one. Not one bit.

"And this," Keegan indicated the male to his left, "is Stone."

Marc didn't even bother to try to hide his surprise as Stone stuck out his hand with a wide smile of welcome.

"I'm a bit of a surprise to new people, I know. But here I am," he told Marc amiably. "Welcome to Texas."

"Uh, thank ye," Marc mumbled automatically as he took the proffered hand and gave it a firm shake. He briefly studied the warm umber skin, dark eyes, and broad features before his gaze came to rest on the fangs that were glaringly obvious by that friendly grin. "I apologize for starin'," he said after a long moment. "It's just a wee bit o' a surprise tae meet a male such as yerself."

Although Stone's scent was overpoweringly wolf, there was a tinge of something "other" there as well. If Marc wasn't mistaken, he was staring at the first werewolf half-breed he'd ever met. Or had ever even heard of, for that matter. But it wasn't vampire. He knew the scent of vampires. As a matter of fact, some of his very good friends back home in Seattle were vamps. No. This was something else. These American wolves were just full of surprises.

But Stone just gave a deep chuckle and clapped him on the shoulder. "I understand, man. No worries. No worries. I get that a lot."

Marc waited for him to say more, but it seemed there was to be no further explanation forthcoming. He didn't know what else had sired this male, but whatever it was, it was powerful. That much he could sense.

"Stone is relatively new to our pack, but as you can well imagine, he's turned out to be quite an asset," Keegan told him.

Marc glanced uneasily one more time at those ominous fangs that were such a contrast to the carefree grin that encased them, and then turned his attention back to the pack leader. "However do ye manage to keep him under yer thumb?"

Keegan laughed and gave a small shrug with one powerful shoulder. "My charming personality?" Stone busted up laughing.

Cracking a smile, Marc decided that he liked this particular Texan, in spite of his silly clothes and accent.

"How about we wander over to The Chili Parlor and have us a sit-down?" Keegan said. "Then you can tell us what's so damn important that it brings you all the way down here from Seattle."

Marc didn't know what a "chili parlor" was, but if it involved food, he was all for it. He was starving. So he agreed without hesitation. "Sounds like a fine plan."

There was little talking as they made their way over to The Chili Parlor, which turned out to be a little restaurant that served what was reputed to be some of the best chili in Texas. Making their way over to an empty booth, Marc observed Jace elbowing Stone out of the way to take his place by Keegan's side. Stone rolled his eyes and slid in the other side, leaving Marc the spot on the end. Granting him an easy escape if need be.

His trust in this pack grew a little bit more.

They ordered lunch and as they waited for their food, Keegan put his elbows on the table and laced his fingers together. He was suddenly all business.

Taking his cue, Marc mimicked his pose.

"So now, why don't you tell me what this visit is all about," Keegan said. "It's not often we receive a request for a sit-down from a rival pack. If this were a normal challenge for territory or females, we would just fight it out in the traditional way. And the fact that we're not tells me that this has nothing to do with either of those. Am I right?"

"Aye," Marc agreed. "Ye are correct. This is much more serious than either o' those." Three pairs of eyes were on him now.

Keegan sat back as the food arrived. Smiling at the waitress, he waited for her to leave before he picked up the conversation again. It took her a while, but when she could think of nothing else to offer them without being so blatantly obvious that it would get her fired, she finally gave them another pile of napkins and went to check her other tables.

Picking up his spoon, Keegan said, "Well, might as well lay it on me." Then he dug into his chili with such relish Marc wondered what it was exactly that was in this chili.

"Aye." Marc paused, running his well-rehearsed words through his mind. But in the end, he decided there was no sense in beating around the bush. "They're comin'."

"Who?" Jace asked with an impatient tone.

"The soul suckers." Marc took a big bite of his chili and moaned with approval. He took another bite, and another. They were right. This was some bloody good chili. With his fourth spoonful halfway to his mouth, he realized the rest of the table wasn't eating anymore.

They were staring at him in horror.

CHAPTER 2

Bronaugh watched the four werewolves eat their chili from her perch on the small retaining wall across the street. A sudden sharp pain on her finger distracted her from her vigil, and she looked down at her hand to see a fire ant chomping away on her knuckle.

She flicked it off with a curse. Gods, she hated Texas. Everything here either bit you or stung you. And you didn't have to be visible for them to find you either; the damn things sniffed you out from a mile away. Ignoring the sweat trickling down her spine, she went back to spying on the werewolves.

Uh oh. Something big was going down. She could tell by the look on the alpha's face as he spoke to the blond. And by the harsh lines twisting his handsome features, it wasn't good.

Leaning forward, she tucked her hair behind one slightly pointed ear and strained to hear what was happening. But it was no use. Between the traffic, the glass window, and the chattering humans as they bustled around on their lunch hour, she couldn't hear a word of what the wolves were saying. But she didn't dare try to get closer again. That damn new wolf had nearly sniffed her out back at the capitol the last time she'd tried that. With an impatient sigh, she leaned back on her hands again and continued to watch and observe. After all, that was what she did best.

What she really wanted to know was: who was the new guy? And what was he doing with these dickwads? She'd been trailing this pack for months now, and this was the first time she'd seen *that* particular tower of hunkiness. She was sure of it. A male like that she would've remembered. There was no doubt about it. Even now, her eyes continued to be drawn back to him again and again, instead of concentrating on trying to read the pack leader's lips.

When she'd first seen the new guy waiting on the others in front of the capitol, her stomach had given a lurch and chills had shot down her arms—and not in a bad way. That canine was one manly hunk of wolf. And she would've bet anyone a shitload of money that he smelled great too. With her blood roaring through her veins loud enough to drown out the warning her brain had been trying to tell her, she'd been unable to resist. She had to see him up close and personal. Stepping heel to toe so as not to make the slightest sound, she'd walked right up to him while praying to any gods that happened to be listening that he wouldn't hear the pounding of her heart. She'd snuck so close, in fact, that she'd been able to see the depths of color in his eyes—such a deep brown they were nearly black, but with little tiny gold flecks in them. Darker than her own orbs. Darker than his hair that fell in short layers just to the bottom of his strong, tanned neck. She'd hoped to get near enough to be able to hear his voice. But then he'd suddenly straightened to his imposing height, and his powerful body had tensed as those sharp eyes studied his surroundings with new interest. Knowing she'd been sensed, she'd panicked and quickly retreated to a safe distance and then some.

Bronaugh sighed. She supposed it would all be revealed in time.

Maybe he was here hoping to get into their pack, although he didn't seem to act like a young pup who was trying to win over the alpha. He appeared respectful to the pack leader, yes, but not overly so. He certainly wasn't groveling. Was he an alpha from a different pack? But that didn't make sense either. Rival pack leaders didn't sit around and talk through their differences over lunch. They settled things the way wolves always did. Physically. And may the more dominant and powerful male or female win.

The blond said something to the new guy, but the way his head was turned, she couldn't quite make out what he was saying. Whatever it was blondie was saying, he wasn't happy about it. Then again, that dude didn't seem to like it when anyone took the spotlight away from him. The alpha spoke to him, and Bronaugh could practically hear the patronizing tone in his voice from all the way across the street. But then he threw his hands up in the air and let the blond out of the booth. With one last parting shot she lip-read to be something like "Y'all are a bunch of morons," he stomped out of the restaurant and took off down the street.

And the plot thickened.

She debated whether or not to follow him, but decided to stay where she was. For although she was pretty sure the blond was the key to finding what she was looking for, she couldn't seem to force herself away from the stranger who even now was staring right at her through the window.

Wait. He was staring right at her!

Bronaugh froze, unsure what to do. Even with the street and sidewalks of people between them, his eyes bore right through to shake her very core. Without taking his eyes from her, he said something to the others at the table. The alpha and the dark-skinned one both started searching the people lingering outside the restaurant. Then the alpha shrugged. He said something to the new guy, who blinked and turned to glance at him. As soon as he took his eyes away from her, she made herself scarce.

Running as fast as she could, she headed toward the UT campus. She needed people to hide among. It was summer, so it wouldn't be as crowded as normal there, but she didn't know where else to go. She could only hope he didn't take her disappearing act as a challenge and give chase.

CHAPTER 3

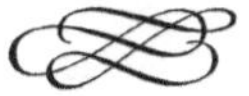

Marc busted out of the restaurant and searched the area. Careful not to knock down any pedestrians, he made his way to the outer edge of the sidewalk and looked up and down the street.

He could've sworn he'd seen something, or someone, watching them from the wall on the other side.

"Don't worry, lunch is on me," Keegan joked as he and Stone joined him outside.

Marc shook himself for the second time that day. "Did ye see something? Across the road there?" He pointed at the stone wall that bordered the small slope of lawn.

"Something like what, exactly?" Stone asked.

"I thought I saw a lass…" Looking around again, Marc shook his head. "Never mind. It was nothin'. I think the heat is making me daft."

Keegan glanced around. "I didn't see anything, man. But maybe you should drink some water. Sounds like you're dehydrated."

"It's verra possible."

Glancing around one more time, Keegan took off his hat and scratched his head before covering his short dark hair again. "I'm sure it was nothing. Humans stare at us a lot."

"And who can blame them? Especially the females," Stone added with another grin, careful to keep his fangs under wraps around the humans who were milling about waiting for their tables.

"Ach. Aye. You're right. It was probably nothin'," Marc acceded. Yet he still had the strangest feeling it wasn't nothing. That it was actually a very big something.

"Tell you what," Keegan told him. "We have to head out. I've got another appointment I need to get to and I need Stone with me for this one." He took off his hat and wiped the sweat from his brow, then looked up rather sheepishly. "Honestly, I didn't expect this 'meeting' to happen. I was half expecting to get jumped. But why don't you come by the house tomorrow afternoon and we can talk some more? If what you were saying is true, we have some more things to discuss. Do you have a cell on you? I'll give you the address."

Marc pulled out his phone and saved the address Keegan gave him.

"If Jace was still here, I'd have him show you around a bit..."

"That's quite okay," Marc assured him. "I have a map." He pulled one out of his pocket that he'd picked up when he'd hit Austin. "I can find my way."

They shook hands and the cowboys took off, leaving Marc alone on the street. He watched them until they turned the corner, then he looked both ways before dodging four lanes of traffic to the other side of the street.

It wasn't "nothing." He'd seen someone watching them. He was sure of it. Listening to his instincts, he headed in the opposite direction, toward the college. He'd only gone about three blocks when he caught his first whiff.

Meadowsweet flowers after a heavy rain.

As the scent hit his nostrils for the second time that day, his entire body shot awake almost violently, and he allowed himself to do what he'd wanted to do back at the capitol. Letting his nose guide him, he hung a sharp left and then a right onto Guadalupe, dodging humans and moving as casually as he could. He followed the scent a few more blocks before coming to an abrupt stop in the middle of the sidewalk.

Dammit. He'd lost it.

Glancing around, he saw he was in front of the University Co-op. He pulled open the door and was immediately assaulted with racks and racks of burnt orange—T-shirts, sweatshirts, hats, backpacks—anything a burgeoning UT college student could ever need to support his or her school team.

And meadowsweet after the rain.

"Can I help you find anything?" The question came out a bit breathless.

Marc barely glanced at the young female who apparently worked there. "Nae. I'm good, thank ye." She blinked hard a few times at what he could only assume was the accent, smiled a strange smile, opened her mouth to say something, but then turned abruptly and went back to the clothes she was in the process of hanging on the wall display. Every few seconds, she would glance at him out of the corner of her eye and smile as a blush reddened her cheeks.

Marc cocked an eyebrow. The cowboys may have had a point about the females flirting with them here. In Seattle, they weren't quite so transparent about it, if they swooned over him at all. Of course, it rained a lot there. And most everyone went about their business under the cover of raincoats, with their noses in their coffees.

Turning his back to her, he surveyed the store, searching for…he didn't know who, or what. He followed the scent to a back clothing rack with a big "Clearance" sign on it and pretended to look for something in his size as he made his way around the circle of clothing. The musky smell got stronger as he got closer to the rear corner of the store. It flooded his senses until he could barely think, but try as he might, he couldn't pinpoint where it was coming from. And he even checked inside the clothing racks.

With a frown he pulled his head out of the clothes to see the salesgirl watching him from a few racks away, and she wasn't smiling this time. Rather she looked like she was wondering if she needed to call for backup.

"Are you sure I can't help you find something?" she asked warily.

With a start, he realized he'd been looking through the women's section. Marc forced himself to smile at her. "Cannae find a shirt large enough to fit me."

"The *men's* big and tall section is over there," she told him, indicating the other side of the store.

"Ach. Aye. Thank ye." Not knowing what else to do

without making himself look even more suspicious, he headed over that way and proceeded to look for something in his size. The intriguing scent of the flowers faded as he walked away. But he didn't know what else he could do without raising more suspicion, and that he could not do. Staying under the radar of the humans was fundamental to their survival.

* * *

Bronaugh held her breath as she watched the werewolf move away from her and head to the other side of the store. As soon as he was far enough away, she blew out a relieved breath. Then as quietly as she could, she made her way back toward the front doors and waited until another customer came in. A young guy flung open the door after just a few seconds and blew inside, and Bronaugh ducked under his arm and rushed past him and out of the store before it closed again.

Running full-out, she put as much distance as she could between herself and that male. She didn't bother cloaking her form anymore—she was moving too fast for the human eye to track now anyway. No one would see her until she stopped, and she wasn't stopping until she got to her room at the Holiday Inn.

When she got to First Street, she hit the hike-and-bike trail that hugged the edge of Lady Bird Lake and dropped down into the water, disguising her trail with the smell of fish and algae. She wasn't taking any chances that the wolf would follow her to her only safe place here. Back up on the trail, she blasted past the joggers, not slowing until she got to her hotel near I-35. Dodging a group of runners, she took the path that connected the trail and the hotel and walked into the foyer. The hot Texas sun had nearly dried her clothes already, so she didn't attract any undue attention as she got into the elevator. Letting herself into her room, she locked the door and leaned back against it.

Breathe, Bronaugh. Just breathe.

That had been entirely too close. How could she have been so stupid? She'd almost let herself be seen by the creatures that had been hunting her and her kind for hundreds of years. Getting herself captured now was not going to help her family. And now that she'd tracked them to this city, she needed to keep her wits about her so they didn't slip out of her grasp again.

She knew those wolves had something to do with her family's disappearance. Tomorrow, she was going to follow the new guy and find out for herself.

And when she showed herself, it would be on her terms. Not his.

Marc pulled his rental car to the side of the dirt road and checked Keegan's directions again. He'd been driving for over an hour, half of which had been spent sitting in traffic not going anywhere fast. He hated the fucking traffic here, but at least he had air conditioning inside the vehicle.

Comparing the address to the map on the GPS, he figured he was getting close. Close to what, he had no idea, because he was in the middle of fucking nowhere just outside Driftwood, Texas. And the GPS had only gotten him so far before he'd gone off grid.

Maybe this wasn't such a good idea. For all Marc knew he could be driving right into a trap. *Eh, fook it.* He'd already come all the way out here, and his instincts were telling him Keegan was a male who could be trusted.

Throwing the car back into drive, he continued on until he saw a rusted-out metal sign with the name of an old gas station nailed to a tree. Just past it was another dirt road, and Marc turned onto it. According to his directions, the den of the Texas pack should only be about three more miles down that road.

When he finally reached their home, he thought for sure he had the wrong place. Stopping the car, Marc stared out the front windshield at the impressive ranch house. Built entirely of stone with wood accents, the one-story home sprawled across at least a half-acre of land, with separate buildings, at least one of which was for the kitchen, he assumed, due to the heat. A gravel driveway formed a semi-circle, and wooden steps led up to a front porch that wrapped around the front and sides of the house as far as he could see. A long line of Harleys was parked right out front, blocking the curve of the drive.

Small rocks pinged the underside of the rental car as he made his way up to the house and threw it into park behind the bikes. Killing the engine, he'd just gotten out and locked it up when he saw the cowboys come out onto the porch to greet him. Apparently, Jace had returned, and he'd been joined by a few others. That made a total of eight werewolves waiting to greet him.

Not very good odds if things turned sour. But then he shrugged to himself. He'd actually had worse odds before and managed to survive. And Cedric was depending on him to lock down this alliance.

Keegan descended the steps to greet him. "You found us!" Slapping Marc on the shoulder, he ushered him over to the others. "Come on over here and meet the rest of the pack."

Marc greeted Stone and Jace with a nod, then stuck

out his hand as Keegan introduced the rest of them left to right.

"Marc Kincaid of the Seattle Kincaid pack, meet Tony, Alex, Zach, Lorrent, and this here," he pulled a statuesque brunette female toward him, "this here is Corrina. She's the only thing here that keeps us from turning into complete animals."

She looked Marc over from head to foot with eyes that were nearly as icy blue as Cedric's before she ran her tongue over her bottom lip and gave him a pretty smile. "Hey there, handsome. Welcome to Texas. Keegan has told us…absolutely *nothing* about you."

Marc laughed. "There isnae much tae tell, I'm afraid."

A new flicker of interest lit her eyes when she heard his Scottish brogue. "We'll just see about that." She gave him a wink and then headed back toward the house, saying over her shoulder, "You're just in time for the show."

"Cor runs this place with a firm hand," Keegan said. "Pick up after yourself and don't be late for grub and you'll be just fine."

"And whatever you do," Stone chimed in, "do not, I repeat, do NOT make any negative remarks whatsoever about her cooking. Or you'll be living on ramen and Hot Pockets until you're groveling at her feet, begging her to forgive you."

Marc held the door open for Stone, frowning as Jace pushed his way past them in front of the others. That pup needed to learn some manners. "I do ken how tae cook for myself," he told Stone while scowling at Jace's back.

Stone caught his eye and gave a slight shake of his

head, ignoring Jace's rude manners, just like the day before. "Sure. We all do. But she hides the matches, man. We can't light the stove." Grinning, he disappeared inside the house after Jace.

Keegan went in after him, leaving Marc to follow them on his own. He paused for a moment before going in, an eerie feeling creeping over his skin. The hair rose up on the back of his neck. Looking over his shoulder, he sniffed the air. But all he saw was the empty drive and all he smelled was cedar trees. Then, just as quick as the feeling came upon him, it was gone. He lowered his head, his entire body suddenly feeling heavy and old. He didn't know what he'd been expecting. The musky scent of meadowsweet, perhaps? But he needed to shake off... whatever this was. He had business to take care of for Cedric. And hopefully, he wouldn't get himself killed in the process.

By the time he joined the others around the large wooden table in the state-of-the-art kitchen, drinks were being passed around and conversations were in full swing. He took the only empty seat—a place of honor to Keegan's left between him and Stone. Jace glared at him from across the table where he sat to Keegan's right, but Marc took a cue from Stone and ignored him. He didn't know what the guy's issue was, but he didn't have time to play schoolyard games.

As he sipped the whiskey that was set in front of him, he tried not to appear as distracted as he was. Although it wasn't the company at the table that had him on alert, but rather the persistent feeling he was being watched.

"So, Marc." The table immediately quieted down when

Keegan spoke. The alpha didn't waste any time, getting right down to the crux of the matter. "Tell me again, for the sake of those who weren't with us at lunch, why you've come here." Though the words were casually spoken, his green eyes were sharp.

Marc set down his glass. On him were eight pairs of eyes of all different shades, some friendlier than others. But still, they were his kind. They needed to be warned. "As ye all ken, I'm here from Seattle as a representative of the Kincaid pack. Cedric, our pack leader, sends his regrets he could no' come himself." The others nodded, accepting his apology as Keegan had at lunch. "The reason I came all this way is tae warn ye. Recently, a new member of our pack took a female. She's no' one o' us. She's a Fae."

Gasps were heard around the table, and a few of the others even scraped back their chairs and stood up, their stances hostile. Marc did the same, his hackles rising at the implied threat.

"We don't accept those kind here," Jace growled. "And we don't accept wolves that do."

Keegan held up his hand from where he remained sitting at the head of the table. "Let him finish what he has to say before we go judging him or storming out of the room. Or worse." One by one, he leveled a meaningful look around the table at the wolves who were standing until they sat down again.

Jace was the last to remain standing. But when Keegan reached him, he dropped his eyes and sat back in his chair, reprimand noted. Although from the sardonic twist of his mouth, Marc got the impression it wasn't taken as seriously as it should be.

Once they were all seated again, Marc also took his seat and continued as if nothing had happened. "As I said, she is Fae, but no' one o' the soul suckers. She is different. She's good. There are different tribes, apparently. Heather is one o' *na daoine maithe*, the good people. Her male, Brock—a fine and braw young wolf—had the…opportunity…tae meet the prince o' her people." He paused, waiting for the gasps and mumblings to quiet down again. "This prince, though a bit daft in his old age, told Heather some upsettin' news that she believed tae be true. He told her the soul suckers were comin', and that we need tae be ready for them. And they're comin' soon. I dinna think I need tae tell ye what will happen when they do."

The table was quiet this time as everyone absorbed that information. Although most of them, like Marc, were too young to have fought in the war between the Fae and the Werewolves, they'd all heard the tales from those who had. Tales of wild-eyed creatures running around like meth addicts hyped up on bath salts, taking out everything that breathed in their path—including a number of the werewolves that had fought them—until the wolves had been shown the portal and locked them away.

Now that he thought about it, he'd never thought to ask where the portal had come from, or how the elder wolves had known it was there.

"So, what are you wanting from us?" Jace asked, interrupting his thoughts.

Marc leveled his gaze on the cocky wolf, trying not to let his dislike for him show on his face. "I came here tae warn ye all, and tae talk aboot the possibility of ye helping me get all the packs together tae form an alliance of sorts."

"An alliance?" Keegan repeated.

"Aye. An alliance. For the time being, we put all o' our scrabbles aside. No fighting for territory or females. No fighting for rank in the pack amongst yerselves. We work together tae fight the threat that is coming for us."

"How do you know this isn't all a lie?" Corrina asked from her spot next to Jace. "Whether the female believes it to be true or not, how do you know this Fae 'prince' isn't full of shit?"

"I dinna. But do ye want tae take that chance?"

The group sat lost in their own thoughts, considering what he'd just said, their whiskeys forgotten on the table in front of them.

Finally Jace brought up the question Marc knew was going to cause the biggest problem with Cedric's plan. "And say we agree to this. Who's going to lead this alliance? You can't expect us to bow down before your alpha. Keegan is our pack master. We answer to no one but him. And he answers to no one but himself."

Voices rose again at that point, and Marc lifted his hand to silence them. "The pack leaders will work together as equals."

Jace guffawed and glanced around at the rest of the table. "That's never been done. Not even during the last war. From what I've heard, each pack just took care of their individual territories. Which is how it should be. And that's how we should do it this time."

"Aye. They did. Because by the time our kind started tae fight back, the soul suckers had swarmed the land like locusts. They were everywhere. However, we were hoping that this time, if we got enough packs together, we could cut them off as soon as the portal opens again. Cut them off before they can spread tae a larger area. It would mean everyone would have tae be ready tae travel as soon as we ken that it's aboot to happen, and come join us at the portal."

Keegan had sat quietly during their exchange, listening. But now he said, "And how will we keep them in there this time if the portal doesn't want to close?"

"We cannae. We will need tae kill them if that happens."

One of the younger wolves, Tony, asked, "How many are there?"

"Too many for my pack tae handle alone. Maybe too many for all o' us. But we have tae try. I dinna see that there is any other choice. We are the only ones that can see them, and that's only when we're in our wolf form. Brock found that out the hard way during his adventures." Brock had told quite the wild tale about his run-in with the Fae when he'd shown up again with his female in tow.

Jace looked around at all of the serious faces that surrounded the table. "Ah, come on, y'all. They're not that bad. We can handle a few Faeries."

"I don't think ye understand…" Marc began.

Jace's blue eyes shot back to him, narrowing with dislike. "Oh, I understand. We all understand. A lot more than you know."

"Jace," Keegan warned.

But Jace didn't heed the warning, as usual. "What? We do." Throwing himself back in his chair, he crossed his muscular arms over his wide chest. "Maybe we should just show him. If he's gonna be staying here, he's going to find out what we have here eventually anyway."

Stone spoke up. "Believe it or not, I agree with Jace. And we could use another rider on our side next time."

The rest of the table started tossing in their opinions of whether Marc should be allowed to "ride" or not. He listened to them going back and forth for a few minutes, trying to glean what the bloody hell they were arguing about. But when a few of them stood and started snarling at each other, he slammed his hands on the table, effectively getting their attention along with a growl from the pack leader. With a quick apology to Keegan for overstepping, he asked, "What the fook are ye all arguing aboot?"

Tempers ran hot in wolf packs, and there were times you just had to rise up to the heat level, much as Marc hated rolling around in the dirt. He'd much rather talk things out logically.

Keegan sat as he had during much of the argument, elbows on the table with his fingers steepled beneath his chin. His whiskey sat untouched. In the ensuing silence, his eyes went to each of his wolves, starting with Jace. As his gaze hit each one in his pack, they either nodded or looked away.

Ah, they were taking a vote, then.

Marc sat back and waited for the results. There really wasn't much other choice.

Corrina was the last one to give her vote. "All right, Seattle," Keegan said with a smile. "Come with us." It was finished.

Everyone stood up and began to file out of the kitchen, talking excitedly. Marc shot down the rest of his drink and then rose to follow them out of the house. But as soon as the screen door slammed shut behind him, he pulled up short and took a deep breath.

Meadowsweet.

He hadn't been imagining it.

CHAPTER 5

From her spot on the front porch of the lion's den, or rather the wolf's, Bronaugh peered through the window and saw the group of werewolves get up from the table and head to the back of the house. She didn't worry about them seeing her, for she'd gone completely incognito again. The mangy mutts had no idea she was there. Still, she tried to be quiet as she crept down the steps and ran around the side of the house. They might not be able to see her, but they could hear better than any other supernatural creature she knew of.

By the time she got around the big house, the entire pack was already out the back door. A few of the wolves, including the female, ran on ahead toward an oversized, weathered barn-like structure set back quite a ways from the house. Other than its size, it wasn't much to look at. She doubted she'd even have noticed it if she'd been a casual visitor, partially hidden as it was by scrub brush and cedar trees.

A loud motor revved not far in the distance and Bronaugh stopped and listened. It was a pickup truck if she wasn't mistaken. No sooner had she identified the source of the noise than a lifted red truck came barreling down a hidden dirt road off to the side of the barn. The truck skidded to a halt in the clearing behind the house a mere three feet from the she-wolf. The female yelled and shook her fist at the driver as dirt and rocks kicked up to splatter her fancy jeans, then scooted out of the way when he laughed and revved the engine again.

More vehicles rolled onto the property and parked in the clearing behind the house. A whole line of them that just kept coming and coming. Bronaugh had never seen so many werewolves gathered in one spot before. A drop of sweat that had nothing at all to do with the heat rolled down her back.

The new guy was the last to come out of the house, and her blood warmed as she caught a whiff of his clean, masculine scent. As the screen door slammed shut behind him, he stopped to scent the air. Bronaugh's heart began to race, and not just from the fear of being caught. Though gods, he was huge.

And hot. He was definitely hot. For a werewolf.

He stilled and looked around slowly, his sharp eyes not missing a thing. She dared not move as they passed slowly over her and back again, even though she knew he couldn't see her. He breathed in deep, holding the air in his lungs for a few moments before exhaling in frustration. Then he noticed the crowd of newcomers gathering, seemingly for the first time, and his muscular shoulders tensed up under his retro T-shirt. He narrowed his eyes and tightened his hands into fists, cracking his knuckles before rubbing his palms on his hard thighs. Shaking his head slightly at all the commotion, he trailed after the others down the steps and toward the large barn.

Bronaugh froze, unsure of whether to follow or not. That damn wolf knew she was here. But how? He couldn't see her; her cloaking was on point, always. Besides, his eyes had gone right through and past her when he'd looked her way. It was impossible for him to know she was there.

Yet somehow, he did. There was no doubt in her mind.

She transferred her weight from one foot to the other, debating what to do for a few more seconds, but in the end she followed him. She hadn't come this far to back down now just because this guy might or might not sense she was near. He could twitch from his spidey senses all he wanted to—he couldn't actually see her. And he never would, unless she wanted him to.

Or unless he turned.

Bronaugh had tracked her family to Texas six months ago, and then promptly lost their trail. But what she *had* found was a pack of werewolves sitting outside a bistro in downtown Austin talking about some feisty Faerie chicks they'd just acquired for their "show." She'd followed them on foot to the edge of town, but once under the cover of some trees, they'd immediately stripped down and began to transform into the animals they were. Bronaugh had run as fast as she could in the opposite direction at the first sound of a cracking bone. She was desperate, but she wasn't stupid. If she'd hung around, they'd have seen her for sure once in their true form.

After that day, she'd haunted the city searching for those males. She didn't dare try hunting them in the back country again. It was safer when they were in their human form. Weeks went by without seeing so much as a hairball. Until one day, by some quirk of fate, she'd practically walked right into the alpha wolf mere blocks from her hotel. As she'd mumbled an apology and went to make a quick escape, she'd noticed something—an unusual tree pendant that belonged to her cousin hanging from the thick silver chain around his muscular neck. A cold sweat broke out all over her body at what the sight of that pendant implied. Stiff with shock and dread, she'd stood there stupidly as he'd ambled around her, shooting her a strange look. She'd stumbled after him before he could disappear, but she was so shaken he'd lost her by the next block.

Since that day, she'd been tracking this pack. Watching…waiting. She worried that her family was all dead, but then she'd remember the "show" they'd mentioned. And she figured a dead Faerie couldn't entertain anyone. So over time, she'd convinced herself that just because he had her cousin's necklace, it didn't mean they'd killed them. And whenever doubts crept up to crack holes in her conviction of this, she swiftly and firmly stomped them back down again.

But this was the first time she'd actually made it to their den, and she'd only been able to do so because the new guy had been stuck in traffic and then, once he'd gotten off the highway, he'd driven so slow trying to find the place that she'd easily been able to keep up. Running along behind his car, she'd followed him straight to their home.

And now she knew she was right. Her people were here. And they were alive. She could feel them. That wolf wasn't the only one with spidey senses.

As she approached the building, she was struck by the sheer size of it. Nearly as large as the house, it was built in the shape of a barn, but she made a startling discovery when her arm accidentally bumped the door as she rushed inside behind the new guy—this barn wasn't made from normal wood. The wood was reinforced somehow with bits of iron. Upon closer inspection, it appeared to be ground right into the wood grain. How had they done that? And why had they done that? Unless they knew when they'd built it who they were going to be holding here.

The rumbling voices of an excited crowd and the smell of sawdust greeted her as she walked inside. The first thing she noticed was the dirt arena that took up the entire center of the space in a large oval. It wasn't flat like a normal rodeo arena, but had dirt ramps and shallow ravines, just deep enough for a calf or other small farm animal to hide in. Bleachers surrounded it, broken up only by the entrance, and the entrance to some type of long tunnel. But instead of the usual metal fencing that separated the crowd from the entertainment, there was a large iron cage completely enclosing the arena and protecting the spectators. From what, she didn't know yet. And honestly, she was a little bit afraid to find out.

The second thing she noticed was that those bleachers were filling up fast—with werewolves. Bronaugh's heart pounded in her chest so hard she was sure they would hear it in spite of all the racket. She started feeling dizzy from the blood rush. Where were they all coming from? In her experience, packs normally weren't this large. They had to be neighboring packs, coming in to see the show. But that didn't make sense either. Werewolves were notorious for how territorial they were. Other packs were seen as rivals, not buddies to invite over to the barbecue.

Bronaugh stayed as close as she dared to the new guy. He stood just inside the large barn doors, and seemed as reluctant as she was to enter any farther. His expressive eyes were narrowed with apprehension as he took stock of the commotion going on inside, while hers were so wide she felt like they were about to pop out of her skull.

She had a really bad feeling about this.

What the hell was she thinking even coming in here? If any of these other dogs got even the slightest inkling that a Faerie like her was anywhere near them, she'd be ripped to pieces before she could take two steps. She glanced up at the towering male by her side and inched a bit closer to him. It made no sense, but she felt safer being near him. Which was stupid, really. He'd probably be the first one to take a bite out of her.

Bronaugh scowled and stepped away again. She didn't need him to protect her. She could protect herself. She could slink in and out of here and none of these idiots would even know she was there. Werewolves were all brawn and no brains.

Just then, a couple of males pulled the tall doors closed and dropped a large wooden beam across the front of them, locking them from the inside. It was reinforced with iron clasps that they snapped around it at intervals.

Bronaugh's bravado faltered a bit. There was no escape for her now. Strong as she was, the iron would still affect her. But then she threw back her shoulders and lifted her chin. The only way to find out what was going on here was to be inside. So that's where she would be. Her family was depending on her.

The new guy glanced over his shoulder uneasily at the locked doors, then went and sat down in the front row next to the female from the pack. Bronaugh sidled closer to him without thinking about it. She didn't want to delve into the reasons for her attraction at the moment.

There was nothing to do now but watch and wait and see what happened.

The alpha who wore her cousin's pendant strode into the center of the arena and climbed to the top of one of the rises, his boots slipping in the dirt. The crowd whooped and hollered with enthusiasm when he made it without falling. Some of them even blew air horns and banged on cowbells, adding to the noise. He turned in a slow circle and waved as the crowd cheered and stomped their feet, then gestured for them to quiet down.

"Welcome to our rodeo!" His voice boomed loud and clear. He waited while another round of cheering went through the crowd. "I'm Keegan, alpha of this pack and ringmaster of this here circus. Now as some of you know, this is not your normal rodeo. It's better!" The crowd whooped and clapped. "Some of you have been here before." He smiled as a good two-thirds of the people cheered. "If we have any brave souls out there who think you have what it takes, go see Jace over there and sign up for the event you'd like to compete in." He pointed to the bucking chute where the blond werewolf stood with a clipboard in his hands.

Jace walked a few steps out into the arena and raised his arm so everyone could see him. A few younger males immediately jumped up from their seats and headed his way.

Keegan called for the crowd's attention again. "All right, y'all! We're gonna go ahead and get this party started. Our first event is gonna be Tie-Down Roping! If you don't know what that is—and I don't know how anyone who lives in this fine state of Texas wouldn't know, but just in case you don't—Tie-Down Roping is a timed event where the cowboy on horseback catches a calf by throwing a loop of rope from his lariat. The goal is to toss the rope around its neck, then dismount and restrain it by tying its legs together. Of course, we've had to make a few adjustments," he added, gesturing to the uneven ground around him. "Stone is our first cowboy up!"

A loud rumble sounded from the left, and the crowd went wild. Bronaugh strained to see around the people who had gotten out of their seats and were now pressed up against the iron cage. An engine revved, and the crowd went wild. Her attention was drawn back to the bucking chute where she could just see the top half of a small female with dark spiky hair and bedraggled clothes. She was standing patiently, waiting for the gates to open. Bronaugh strained to get a better look through the metal bars of the bucking chute, but she didn't really need to. A harsh, angry sob rose from her chest as her body flashed hot and cold, and rage such as she had never experienced before rose up to flood her veins. Lucky for her, the sound was drowned out by the all of the noise.

Bronaugh knew who the "calf" was.

Marc watched, his mouth twisted with disgust, as the female was released from the bucking chute and coerced into the arena with the help of a cattle prod. Stone, wearing a number on his shirt and straddling a KTM dirt bike, let her get to the center before he tore across the packed-down dirt after her. When the female saw him coming, she stopped where she was, turned, and watched him come. He admired the lass's gumption. She could've easily played the mouse, or calf, and jumped down behind one of the dirt mounds. But instead, she was refusing to play the game.

Corrina cheered next to him and he turned to her, attempting to sound less affected than he really was. "Are there no' supposed tae be cattle in a rodeo? Horses? Sheep? A bunch o' humans too afeart to move doesn't seem like much of a challenge tae me."

Corrina laughed, casually putting her hand high on his thigh. "They're not humans, hon. They're Faeries."

Marc frowned at her. "Wha'?"

"They're Faeries," she repeated, louder this time.

"Where did they come from? How did you get them here?"

"We have our ways." She winked and turned back to the show, her expression giving nothing away.

"But—" Marc was at a loss at what to say...what to do. "No' all Fae deserve something like this, Corrina." He waved his hand at the spectacle in front of him. Stone had just lassoed the female, but instead of jumping off the bike and tying her up, he kept going, dragging the girl around the ring while she clawed at the noose around her neck and tried to keep her head from bouncing off the hard-packed earth. "They are no' all bad. I just told ye all that at dinner."

Corrina, never taking her eyes from the "sport" in front of her, patted his leg where her hand still rested. "It's all good, handsome. These aren't the good ones. They're soul suckers. We found them a few months ago, terrorizing the humans in town."

Not knowing what else to say but unable to stay, Marc stood up to leave. Corrina looked up at him quizzically, her hand falling back into her lap, but he'd be damned if he was going to sit here with her and watch this horrific stuff. He stomped off toward the doors.

"Hey, where are you going?" Corrina called after him, but he pretended not to hear her.

Tony and Lorrent, two of the younger wolves of the pack, were standing guard at the exit. They closed ranks as he approached. Arms crossed over their massive chests, they both stared at him steadily. Marc gestured for them to move aside, but Tony shook his head.

"Ain't no one allowed to leave during rodeo," he said, raising his voice to be heard above the crowd. Marc didn't even want to know what sadistic act they were cheering this time.

"Let me pass," he growled. "I willnae stay here and be a witness tae this."

"No. One. Leaves," Lorrent spit out, two inches from Marc's face.

Marc could feel his muscles twitching, itching to explode out of his human form so he could take these eejits out. He stretched his jaw, trying to ease the ache there and keep it under control. Unclenching his fists, he tried to talk reasonably to them. "I need tae leave, and I need tae leave now. I'm no' here tae make trouble. I dinna care what ye do here. I just dinna want tae watch it."

They exchanged amused glances, and then Tony barked out a laugh. "Wait till I tell Keegan and Jace that our *friend* from Seattle is nothing but a goddamned pussy."

"Maybe Keegan should consider taking over that pack too," Lorrent said. "Bring them here. It's obvious their leader doesn't have the balls to teach them what real Weres are. Seems to me, the only reason he still has a pack at all is because he's the alpha of a bunch of pussy-assed lap dogs." He eyed Marc up and down. "You probably suck his dick for him. Maybe you could do the same for me." He smirked, and his hand dropped down to play with the fastening of his jeans.

Marc clenched his teeth and swiped at the sweat from

his brow, fighting the change with everything in him. Insulting him like that was one thing. Insulting one's alpha was an unforgivable offense. "Yer overstepping yer bounds, ye fools." Or perchance they knew exactly what they were doing. "Ye dinna want tae challenge me, young ones," he growled.

Lorrent got right back up in his face. "Yeah? Well, maybe I do. What the hell are you gonna do about it, pussy?" He swept his arm in front of him, taking in the arena and the throngs of werewolves in the stands from neighboring packs. "You can't win here, Seattle. So why don't you just sit your ass down and enjoy the show." It wasn't a request. It was an order.

Marc didn't take well to orders, unless they came from his alpha. And especially not from a couple of hyped-up, teenage, wannabe cowboys. "Dinna say I didnae warn ye," he gritted out. Then he stopped fighting his feelings and let the anger and frustration overtake him. He was much older and more in control of the change. Maybe he could take them by surprise, incapacitate them and get outside before any of the others noticed what was happening. He needed to get the bloody hell out of this place.

Pain ripped through his jaw, his muscles, his very bones as his body swelled and morphed. His arms and legs broke and reformed. Muscles tore and healed into their new shape. His teeth broke and re-grew as his jaw stretched forward. The change was hard and fast, and he kept silent through it all, knowing if he drew the others' attention from the show it would mean the death of him.

Tony and Lorrent were still only half turned when he attacked. He leapt forward, slashing out to the side at

Tony with his long claws, and left him lying on the ground with a trail of bloody tracks across his face and chest. He landed with his jaws clamped around Lorrent's throat. Biting down hard, he tore out a large chunk of flesh and jugular and tossed him aside. Whipping back around to Tony, he swiped him again with one large paw, hard enough that he went flying underneath the back of the bleachers closest to the door and landed with a thud against the metal legs. The crowd was too engrossed in the rodeo to notice anything amiss, what with all the engine revving, screaming, stomping, and cheering going on.

Marc lowered his head, preparing another attack, but neither of them got up again. Chomping down on Lorrent's still human arm, he pulled him underneath the bleachers on the opposite side of Tony. He needed to get the hell out of there before someone found these guys. They would heal; he had no worries about that. But Keegan was not going to be happy with him.

He came out from under the seats, noticing for the first time someone standing by the doors. The sight stopped him short. It was a wee female with chin-length, choppy blonde locks and devilish curves that belied the innocence in her sweet face. Her eyes, when she glanced back at the arena, were angry and full of tears. But what made him pause were the colors. All of the colors of the rainbow shone from those eyes. They swirled in and out like a kaleidoscope, a child's toy he used to have. The crowd roared and she covered her face, breaking the spell.

Scenting the air around them, he growled low in his throat.

Meadowsweet after the rain.

He knew then why he'd kept smelling that scent. It was this lass. And he also knew why she smelled like she did to him.

She was Fae. And being that he was only seeing her now, while in his wolf form, she was *an olc*—a soul sucker. Or she would be eventually.

He briefly wondered if she'd been captured with the other female and had escaped the iron cage somehow. But upon another quick inspection, he didn't see how that could be, as her clothes—though simple—were in much better condition. Unless she hadn't been here as long.

She dropped her hands and looked his way, and his heart turned over in his furry chest at the sight of the tears running down her bonnie face. Then those strange eyes widened until they seemed to take up the majority of her face, and he knew that *she* knew he could see her. With a last glance around to make sure the others were still too preoccupied to notice, he padded closer to her, slowly and carefully so as not to frighten her. She swiped at the moisture on her face and spun around frantically, searching for a place to run. But when she realized there was nowhere else to go, she stilled, and he could practically see the cloud of calm acceptance wash over her. Raising her chin, she turned to face him again. The expression on her face was resolved and accepting of her fate.

Ach. For as wee as she was, she was a fine, brave lass.

Padding over to the doors, he raised the beam out of its iron shackle with his nose, standing on his rear legs to push it all the way up. Dropping down onto all fours, he pushed open one of the doors just wide enough for him to squeeze through. Looking back at the Fae lass, he tossed his head and pointed with his snout out the open door. With his eyes, he attempted to impress upon her how strongly he felt that she should leave with him, while letting her know that she would be a lot safer out there with him than she would inside. Then he swiftly left the building.

Once outside, he positioned himself behind the open door and waited. A few seconds later, she dashed through the opening, pulling up short when she saw he was still there waiting for her.

Nudging the door all the way closed again, he gave her a nod and trotted off toward the house.

CHAPTER 7

Cedric checked his phone for any missed messages from Marc and shoved his cell into the back pocket of his jeans when he saw none. He tilted his head from side to side, stretching the muscles there to ease the tension in his shoulders and then took a deep breath to calm his nerves. It didn't help.

Well, there was nothing for it. Better to get this over with. Steeling himself as best he could, he rapped on the door with his knuckles and waited.

"Maybe he's not here," Brock said hopefully from behind him.

"He's here." Heather, Brock's Fae mate, didn't sound overly happy about it.

"Dinna fash yerself," Cedric told them. "I'll handle the prince." He glanced back at Heather. "Ye're both only here because he requested yer presence, Heather, and this one" —he indicated Brock with a lift of his chin—"would no' let ye come without him."

"I go where Heather goes," Brock said. Worry lines creased his forehead and he brushed his long hair out of his eyes, agitated. "What if this nut job gets another wild hair and whooshes her away to play one of his games again?" He shook his head, answering his own question. "Oh no. With all due respect to you, Cedric, but I'll be going with her if he does."

Heather leaned into his side to give him a hug. When she went to let go, Brock held her there against him. She glanced up at the worried look on his bearded face and settled in against him.

They quieted down, and Cedric faced the door again to listen for any indication that someone was on their way to answer it. He fussed with his own hair, slicking it back from his face and checking it was neatly tied back in its ponytail. But there was really nothing he could do to prepare himself for this meeting with the Fae prince.

At least this time, the daft bastard had let him drive here instead of just "whooshing" him through time and space to land in his kitchen. It wouldn't have been so bad if he hadn't been right in the middle of a "Sons of Anarchy" Netflix binge watch.

He lifted his hand to knock again when the door was suddenly flung open and the prince of the Fae people himself stood there to greet them. He looked exactly the same as the last time Cedric had seen him. The prince was a very distinguished-looking gentleman, with his long silver hair and fancy suit. He even walked with a cane. But it was obviously more for show than anything.

"Finally! You're here." He grinned like a loon at Cedric. Though the prince was a tall male, he still had to tilt his head way back on his neck to look up into the six foot seven inch alpha's face.

"Aye, we're here." Cedric glanced at his cell phone and scowled. "And we're no' late. We're fifteen minutes early."

Prince Nada, as he was called, reached around the large werewolf to grab Heather's hand and pull her away from Brock and inside the house. "Come, come my dear. We have so much to talk about."

She stumbled as she tried to squeeze past Cedric, and Brock jumped forward to catch her, knocking him to the side. He followed his mate inside with a firm hand on her elbow and an apologetic look back at his new alpha.

Shaking his head, Cedric entered the small house where the prince and his court had taken up residence, pulling the door shut behind him. The three of them kept pace behind the elder through the sparsely decorated living area, down a drab hallway, past the kitchen, and into the prince's private sitting room.

"Where is everyone?" Heather asked.

"Who would that be, my dear?" the prince responded.

"Who?" She glanced back at Brock and Cedric with a frown before answering the prince. "Like, Frank. The dude who grabbed me from the bus stop and brought me here. And all of the other males who were here when I got here."

The prince stopped and turned to her with a look of utter confusion on his distinguished features. "I'm not sure I know whom you're talking about."

"They were in suits? Lots of arguing about your plan to play nice with the werewolves this time?" After a brief pause, Heather said, "Nothing?" Then she smiled. "Never mind. It doesn't matter. It was a stupid question."

Nodding in agreement, the prince resumed walking. He ducked inside an open door to the left, pulling her in behind him.

Heather looked back at Brock just before entering the room, her expressive face letting him know she was flabbergasted that this was the leader of her people. He grinned and winked in typical carefree Brock fashion. She resisted the prince's pull, an alluring scent rising in the air as her eyes roved over Brock's face: the scent of her mounting desire for her mate.

Cedric rolled his eyes and noisily cleared his throat. She quickly faced front again as she turned an attractive shade of pink, and disappeared through the doorway. He noticed Brock's eyes drop to her rounded arse as she walked away. He couldn't really blame him. It was a very nice arse.

Cedric clapped him hard on the shoulder to jog him out of the lustful thoughts he was sure were sending all the blood to the wrong head, and back into the reason they were here. With a look in his blue eyes that held not one ounce of shame at getting caught ogling his mate, Brock followed her into the room with Cedric bringing up the rear.

Prince Nada sat in the center of the small room on a golden throne that was so large the only thing Cedric could think about was to wonder how the bloody hell they got the monstrosity into the house, never mind the room.

So distracted was he by the sight of the ridiculous

thing that it took him a moment to realize there was another sitting beside the prince on a much less obnoxious seat, though still a throne. When the female noticed his attention on her she smiled, and Cedric stopped breathing completely as the entire room lit up with a dazzling light. Or at least it seemed that way. He could feel the heat lighting his eyes and knew they would be glowing so bright they would appear white, but he couldn't help it.

She was bloody exquisite.

And if he were to judge by the kaleidoscope of colors lighting up her wide-set eyes, the attraction was mutual.

"Ah, you're here!" The prince clapped his hands with delight. "May I introduce my frenemy, Duana. Leader of *an olc*, the Dark Fae."

The female nodded regally in greeting, but her eyes were locked on Cedric. "The pleasure is all mine." Her voice was soft and smoky, the greeting spoken with a slight lilt that Cedric found pleasing.

Aye, very pleasing indeed. Maybe this meeting wouldn't be so bad after all.

It took a full minute for the words used in the prince's introduction to sink in.

"Did you say leader of…the Dark Fae?" Brock was the first one to find his voice. Out of the corner of his eye, Cedric saw Heather reach out and clasp Brock's hand like it was a lifeline to the sane world.

The rainbow of colors in her…in Duana's…eyes flashed bright and then dimmed to the color of a rich brandy as she tore her gaze away from Cedric.

Duana. An exquisite name for an exquisite lass. Dark Fae or no'.

She answered Brock's question. "I am now. My brother, the prince, was killed during the war."

"I'm verra sorry," Cedric told her. He was surprised to find that he meant it. And by the look she gave him, so was she. He was rewarded for his sympathy with a sad but beautiful smile.

Prince Nada spoke. "Shortly after the war, Princess Duana appeared on my doorstep, so to speak. She and I came to a mutual understanding. As long as she stayed out of the sight and mind of those of us still here of *na daoine maithe...*"

"Nadoo...what?" Brock asked.

"It means The Good Fae," Heather whispered.

"As long as she stayed out of sight," the prince continued with a reprimanding look at the two of them. "I wouldn't take her head," he finished. A broad smile lit his features. "As you can see, the princess has been good enough to stick with our deal."

"Then why are ye here?" Cedric asked her. Her regal gaze landed on him once again, and he automatically pushed his shoulders back and straightened his stance. "I mean no disrespect, yer highness," he told her. "Just curious as tae what would make ye come out of hiding now, when if the prince is tae be believed, war will be upon us once again in the verra near future. Wouldn't it be safer for ye tae stay in hiding?"

She nodded in acquiescence of his concern, her dark hair falling forward over her shoulders. "Safer for me, yes. But I want to help." Rising from her seat, she began to pace back and forth in front of him.

Cedric couldn't keep himself from admiring her

bonnie curves as she passed in front of him and beyond. Her long, wavy hair perfectly framed the delicate features of her face. She wore a tight, short-sleeved modern dress of emerald green that clung to her full hips and fell just below her knees. Her heels clacked on the wooden floor as she walked with the natural grace that befitted a female of her station. She was all woman, not the type of thin waif that was considered attractive these days.

She even had a little pooch of a belly, and he hardened at the thought of all that womanly softness lying naked beneath him. He was so lost in the fantasy of her that he neglected to notice she had asked him a question. Forcing down his rising libido, he had to clear his throat twice before asking, "Could ye repeat the question?"

Narrowing her eyes, she stepped closer. So close, he could see a light dusting of freckles across her wee nose. He smiled at the sight of them.

"Is this amusing to you?" she gritted out from between clenched teeth.

Cedric schooled his features into something more serious. She barely came up to his chest, yet she stood there glaring up at him like an angry kitten. Only she was more like a wee panther kitten, not a harmless little house kitten. "There isna any need for attitude, lass, just because I didnae hear yer question the first time."

"Maybe you should pay better attention the first time," she retorted. "Unless, of course, you don't think a mere female has anything worthwhile to say?"

Prince Nada, who'd been watching them banter back and forth with an amused twinkle in his eyes, spoke up from his seat on the giant throne. "Would you both please refrain from all of this flirting until after we discuss what it is we brought you here to discuss? Duana, please repeat your question to the wolf daddy."

Cedric turned his scowl onto the prince. "I'm no' flirting," he snapped. "And I'm no' anyone's daddy. I'm the pack leader, ye eejit. And my pack are all quite manly in their own right. They dinna need a daddy tae take care of them." He turned back to Duana. "Now, what did ye want tae ken?"

She narrowed her eyes at him, but refrained from baiting him further. She resumed her pacing. "How much do you know about the war between my people and yours?"

"More than I want tae," he admitted in low tones.

"Were you there?"

"Aye. I was."

Duana gave the prince a look. "You neglected to tell me this."

He tapped a finger to his chin and stared off into the distance. "Did I? I could've sworn I'd told you." Then he looked past her and smiled at his daughter by tribe. "Heather! Come sit by me, my dear."

"Oh, I'm good where I am," she told him above Brock's growl of displeasure.

The prince rolled his eyes. "Oh, for goodness' sake. Your pet can come with you."

She glanced up at Brock and then back at the prince, uncertainty written all over her face.

"I promise not to send you off into another dimension," the prince said. "I just want to enjoy your company after missing so much of your life." He hung his head and gave her his best pout, his long silver hair falling forward to hide the twinkle in his eyes. She sighed and went over to stand next to him, Brock close on her heels with one hand wrapped tightly around her wrist. Once they had relocated, Prince Nada beamed happily. "Continue on without me, Duana. I trust you can handle this conversation. I'd like to catch up with my daughter."

During this entire exchange, Cedric had not taken his eyes off his bonnie princess, nor she from him. He cocked one eyebrow. The ball was in her court.

She gave his attitude right back to him with a lifted eyebrow of her own. "I don't need to tell you everything that happened then, with the first war."

"Nae, ye do no'. I was there. I witnessed what happened with my own eyes. I was young, but I remember it all. But what I want tae ken is how ye came tae still be here in the outside world? I was under the impression that yer entire family had gone the way of the soul eaters."

She studied him for so long that he began to think she wasn't going to answer. "When things began to get…out of control…with my people, my brother brought me to Prince Nada and talked him into hiding me. I was right there under your noses the entire time, in plain sight of everyone. You all ran right past me in your fervor to attack my people."

"We did no' 'attack' yer people, Duana. No' without cause, and ye ken that. Yer people were killing humans! And no' only humans, but anyone they came across. Including us. They were out of control. Through no fault of their own, aye, I ken that. But they were annihilating the population of this planet. What exactly did ye expect us tae do?" He stopped, taking a calming breath. "I'm sorry for what happened. Truly, I am. But it was something that needed tae be done, ye ken."

"You didn't even give us a chance…" she began.

"A chance for what, exactly? A chance tae let the soul eaters run amok in the world? Tae destroy us all?"

"A chance for us to help them!" she cried.

Cedric began to laugh. "Help them?" he asked with a snort. "Help them? Duana, I'm sorry, lass. But there is no helping them."

They stood at an impasse, neither wanting to back down, but Cedric knew the wolves were right to do what they did. Behind Duana, the prince chatted it up with Heather while Brock growled every time he touched her. Cedric allowed them to momentarily distract him from the infuriating female in front of him. What she was saying was naught but wishful thinking. There was no other option for the ones who were turned. They had to be removed. The wolves did them a kindness by sending them away. They could have just killed them all.

In retrospect, it probably would've been the better choice.

Amused by Brock acting like the overprotective, mated wolf that he was, Cedric grinned before turning his attention back to the princess. She stared at him with wide eyes that suddenly glimmered with colors as they traveled over his features. Fascinated by the multi-faceted hues, the smile fell from his face, and her eyes gradually went back to their normal color.

Duana looked away and took a faltering step back. An intriguing scent filled the air between them, and Cedric breathed it in with a low growl. Her head snapped up again at the sound. Quickly, she turned and resumed her pacing.

Cedric tracked her every graceful movement, his body suddenly racked with a hunger that had nothing to do with food.

"As I was saying before," she said, "I think I've found a way to help those of my people who have gone over the deep end."

Her voice had a husky quality to it that was new, and it was all he could do to stay standing immobile in front of her. "There is no help for them," he insisted distractedly. "They have an addiction, lass, an incurable addiction. There isnae anything ye can do tae save them."

She stopped within arm's length of him. When she looked up, her features were twisted with the passion and pain she was feeling at his words. "I think you're wrong! They're not a lost cause. I think there is a way."

Okay. He would bite. "What makes ye think this? Have ye discovered some magical cure?"

Her hand came up to rest on his chest. The innocent touch burned through his thin flannel shirt. "I think they can be freed of their addiction. Put through rehab, so to speak. Just like any other addiction."

"And what makes ye so certain?" he asked. "Has this been done?"

She dropped her hand. "No. But I have to believe it can be done. We have things that can help. Mixtures of herbs and other medicinal plants that can ease their withdrawals and help them gain back control of themselves."

Cedric wanted to believe her, he truly did. He hated

seeing this look of desperation on her face. But he shook his head. "I dinna think there is a cure for an addiction tae souls, lass…"

"But there is," she insisted, raising her chin. "I have to believe that. The only other choice is to accept the extinction of my people. And that I will not do."

CHAPTER 8

As she stood looking out the open barn door, Bronaugh was torn between sobbing with relief that her people were still alive, and biding her time to come up with a smart rescue plan, or diving into the arena after the wolves with all the fury that was throbbing through her and killing as many as she was able before they took her down.

Only two things had stopped her: she couldn't get through the iron bars, and if she couldn't kill enough of them before they killed her, she would be of no help to her family. So in the end, although her heart had screamed in denial, she'd followed the new guy out of that horrid place and jogged behind him as he loped back toward the ranch house. Her cousin, the female in the arena, would live through this day. She knew that. Faeries were very hard to kill. But it still hurt to see her being abused like that. Although knowing Bitsy the way she did, she'd shake it off like the dust they'd stirred up. She was tough like that.

Flashes of what she'd just witnessed popped in and out of her head, and not just what had occurred inside the cage. She'd never seen a werewolf change that fast, or show that much control once he had. He could have easily killed the two assholes that had challenged him, and in her opinion, he should have. Those two were almost bigger dickwads than that Jace guy. But he hadn't. He'd injured them just enough to keep them from raising the alarm or following, but in a way they would easily heal from. And he'd done it quickly and efficiently.

She watched him as he trotted along in front of her, looking back over his shoulder every few seconds to see if she was still with him. He was just as impressive in this form as he was in his human one, if not more so. His sparse fur was a dark brown, like his hair. And he was large—way larger than a normal wolf—with more muscle mass. He was something in between a human and a wolf, yet he moved with the dangerous grace of a top predator. But those deep, dark eyes were intelligent, aware, and almost kind. It was strange for an animal to have eyes such as those.

They skirted around the side of the house and he went directly for his car. Bronaugh came to a skidding halt, not sure where to go from here. Should she just leave? Or should she stay and thank him? Did he expect her to drive? After all, a wolf driving down the road would cause quite a bit of suspicion…

Oh.

The werewolf had gone around to the far side of the

car and she heard him grunt, then a loud popping sound was followed by a wet sucking gurgle. He dropped down out of sight then while she stood, unsure of what to do while she listened to the sound of him changing back. All she could think was, *that has to be fucking painful.* But to his credit, other than a few grunts at the beginning, he didn't make a sound throughout the entire thing.

When the gruesome sounds stopped, and all she could hear were the cicadas in the trees, she tiptoed around the back of the car. He was there, breathing hard, on his hands and knees in the gravel, in all of his glorious nakedness. And what a sight he was to see. He was over six feet of lean, strong muscle, without an inch of fat on him. Even his flaccid manhood was impressive where it hung between his powerful haunches. The muscles deep inside her clenched with desire as she imagined the size he must be when fully erect.

He started to rise then, and she backed away, a thread of fear shooting through her. But he only opened the car door and popped the trunk. Shamelessly, he strode around to the back of the car stark naked, opened the trunk, and pulled out a pair of jeans.

Bronaugh tried to swallow, but her throat was suddenly dry. Crossing her arms in front of her to hide her hardened nipples, she watched him as he got dressed. She was almost sad to see him cover up all that fine maleness. The male was seriously beautiful. That wasn't a word she would normally use when talking about the opposite sex, but it was the only thing she could think of to describe him.

Putting one foot up on the bumper, he laced up his boot. "I ken that yer still here. I can smell yer scent."

With a start, she remembered he could no longer see her now that he'd changed back. Not unless she wanted him to. She breathed a sigh of relief.

"I willnae hurt ye, I promise ye that." Switching feet, he said, "If ye would like a ride back tae the city, just get in the car. If no', I willnae tell anyone that I saw ye." Then he walked around and opened the car door. But instead of getting right in, he stood there and held it open while he waited for her to decide.

Bronaugh again found herself in a quandary. A ride would be nice. She was shaken up by what she'd seen and could use the time to regroup. Supernatural creature though she was, she'd run all the way here in the heat, and wasn't looking forward to running all the way back to her hotel. And the sooner she got back there, the sooner she could start planning a way to break her family out of this sick place.

But could she really trust him? *Yes.* Her instincts told her that she could. And he hadn't done anything to prove otherwise. Not yet. And he *had* seemed pretty upset by what was going on with her people, even arguing with the female in the pack about it and fighting his way out of there.

"I dinna have all day, lass."

Bracing herself, she walked past him and climbed into the car.

MARC TOOK A DEEP BREATH, inhaling the Fae lass's scent as she passed by him, and he knew she'd taken him up on his offer. Getting in the car after her, he pulled the door shut and started the engine.

He didn't speak until he was out on the main road. And then he waited a few more minutes after that. He didn't know where he was taking her, so he just headed back to the city. "Ye may as well show yourself. I ken that ye're there." No one answered him. He tried again. "I meant what I said. I willnae harm ye, lass. I swear it." The silence was so absolute that part of him was beginning to wonder if he'd only imagined her.

But no, he'd *seen* her. He wasn't going mad.

Keeping his eyes on the road, he waited. He thought he heard an intake of breath in the seat next to him, but then doubted himself almost immediately after. Maybe he *was* daft. "I sensed ye back in the city. Ye were watching us." He paused again. Still nothing. "I'm no' mad aboot it. I ken ye must have yer reasons."

"I do have reasons, and you were just looking at one of them."

Even though he'd been expecting it, even though he'd been talking to her this entire time, he still jumped a little when the lass appeared in the seat next to him. "I was feart that was the reason," he told her. He glanced over at her. She was looking straight at him, and he was struck anew by her eyes, brown now like his. Haloed as they were by her shaggy blonde locks, she looked like an angel. And those eyes...*ach*, those eyes...they seemed to stare straight into his deepest parts. "Ye ken who they are?"

She looked away to stare out the windshield.

"Ye can talk to me, lass. I will nae hurt ye."

"You would if you knew what I am." She smiled sadly.

But Marc had already figured that out. "I ken what ye are. Yer a wee Fae lass."

She didn't really seem surprised that he knew, in spite of what she'd just said. "How did you know?"

"I caught yer scent easily enough, but I didn't place it at first. It didnae take me long tae figure it out though. Only Fae folk can make themselves disappear like ye did, as far as I ken."

She neither confirmed nor denied what he'd said.

"So, are ye following me or them?" he asked, meaning the Texas pack.

"Both," she said after a moment.

Marc nodded and glanced at her again. *Ach,* she was a bonnie lass. And her scent made him want to bury his face in her graceful neck, and maybe take a bite. He discreetly adjusted himself in his seat as images of all the parts of her he'd like to bite ran through his mind. This was not the time or the place. And besides, the lass was obviously upset.

In an effort to distract himself from his own thoughts, he asked, "What's yer name, lass?"

"Bronaugh." No pause this time. "Bronaugh Lane."

"Bronaugh. Tis a fine Irish name." A flush warmed her cheeks, and he wondered what was causing it.

"And you?" she asked. "What's your name?"

"Marc Kincaid. I'm here visiting from Seattle," he added.

"I know," she stated. "I heard. You came here to warn these idiots."

He laughed. "Aye."

"Don't werewolves normally go about these things differently?"

He frowned. "What do ye mean?"

"I mean don't you all normally just fight things out? As in, 'let the stronger wolf win' and all that?"

"Aye. Usually that's how it is. But I'm no' here for the normal reasons."

"You're here to align your packs. I know that too. I was listening when you all were at the table earlier."

"Something like that."

They were both quiet as he pulled onto the highway that would take them into Austin. It seemed neither of them wanted to bring up the reason he was hoping to form the alliance.

After a few minutes of silence, Marc cleared his throat. "I don't have anywhere tae stay yet. I dinna ken where I'm going. I just wanted tae get ye away from that ranch—"

She interrupted him. "I'm staying at the Holiday Inn downtown. If you could drop me there, I'd appreciate it. Um, just get off at the next exit."

Marc gave a nod and followed her directions to the hotel. As they pulled up out front, he mused aloud, "I wonder if they have another room?" Bronaugh stiffened beside him and he was quick to clarify. "I dinna mean tae intrude on ye, lass. I swear it. I just need a room. And as I don't know the city well, I thought I would just try here." *Where I can keep an eye on ye.* "And maybe we could grab a bite and try tae put our heads together aboot what tae do with the situation at the ranch."

She wrinkled up her nose at him. "You want to eat? Really?"

He laughed. "Ach. Aye. We wolves have good appetites. Come on, ye must be famished. Ye didnae have any dinner yet either if ye were spending all yer time outside listening in on us."

No sooner had he said the words then her stomach let out an obnoxious rumble, and he smiled.

"Come on, lass. I wouldnae want ye tae starve on my watch. My treat." Getting out of the car, he hurried around to her side and opened the door for her. "Just let me see if they have a room, and we can get tae that dinner."

CHAPTER 9

Bronaugh allowed him to help her out of the car, not quite sure how she'd managed to get herself into this situation. She was supposed to be spying on the werewolves, not sitting down to dinner with them. She should have stayed back at the ranch, figuring out how to rescue her people. But she'd found herself following this male away from them instead.

In retrospect though, he was right to leave. And she'd been right to come with him. It would have been suicide if she'd gone off half-cocked and made herself known with so many werewolves there. She would need help even just to get them out of the building. Iron was like poison to the Fae, and her family was surrounded by it in there.

"Bronaugh? Are ye coming?"

Chills ran down her spine at the sound of him saying her name with his Scottish brogue. Nodding, she went with Marc—the *werewolf*—into the lobby.

I've completely lost my mind. That's the only explanation.

Eyeing the muscular back, tight ass, and long legs that were strutting into the hotel just in front of her, she had to admit that maybe there was an upside to fraternizing with the enemy. The male didn't seem to realize how good-looking he was, but she and every other female certainly did. Even that female wolf had been feeling him up. With everything else that had been going on, Bronaugh was a little surprised that she'd noticed, but it had been kind of hard to miss the sight of the female's long, white hand creeping up his thigh.

But it was more than that. He carried himself with a confidence that was strong and attractive, but wasn't cocky. He was obviously intelligent. He was kind enough to help her. And he had an accent. He offered to buy her dinner, spoke to her politely, and even opened doors for her. She might be Fae, but she was still a girl. And a male with all of those qualifications would be hard to resist for any female in her right mind.

Her stomach growled again.

Plus, she was hungry. And maybe he could help her figure out a way to get her family free from these Texas wolves. The two packs obviously weren't all buddy-buddy. Having someone on the inside could be helpful.

Immediately, she rolled her eyes at the thought. Why would he help her? Nice as he seemed to be, he was still a werewolf, and she'd do well to remember that. Werewolves and Fae did not become friends. They did not hang out together. They shouldn't even be eating dinner together. What if another one of their kind came in and saw them? It would be disastrous.

Marc turned from the counter with a room key in

hand and a happy grin splitting his handsome face. "My lucky day. They happened tae have a room."

Bronaugh blinked a few times. It was all she could manage to do, blinded as she was by that smile. She raised a hand to her chest and tried to calm her racing heart. His smile fell and a look of concern took its place, and she was suddenly reminded that she needed to stay away from him. Clearing her throat, she said, "You know, I don't think this is a good idea. Um, thank you for the ride and the dinner offer. But I'm just gonna go up to my room now."

The concern on his face deepened. "Did I dae something, lass? I swore tae ye that I would no' harm ye. And I meant it. I just thought we could..." He shrugged his heavy shoulders. "Talk."

She didn't think he would harm her. It wasn't that at all. She didn't know why, but she instinctively knew that she could trust this male. Picking her words carefully as the desk clerk was still there pretending not to be listening, she said, "No. It's not that. I just don't think it would be very, um, safe."

"I dinna understand..."

"To be in public, I mean," she whispered.

The clouds cleared from his face and that heart-stopping smile flashed down at her again. "Ach. Aye. Room service it is."

As he turned around to inquire about room service, Bronaugh stared at his broad back with her mouth hanging open. Somehow she didn't think that being alone in a hotel room with Marc was going to be any safer for her than being in public.

She watched as he thanked the clerk, and then he took her by the hand as he said, "Come on, then. It's a wee bit late for room service, but the lad is going tae order some food in for us. I hope pizza is okay?"

Digging in her heels and refusing to go along where he was headed, which was to the elevator that would lead to his room, she tried again to extract herself politely from the situation. "Really, it's okay. I should just go to my room."

The dark eyes that gazed down at her were full of hurt. "I promised ye dinner, lass. I would no' feel right just sending ye off without feeding ye first. Yer wee enough as it is. And besides, I already ordered the pizza. I could no' eat it all myself."

Now how was she supposed to say no to that? Heaving a sigh, she finally caved. "All right. Fine. Just dinner." She gave him her sternest look.

He grinned at her again, amusement lighting his eyes. "Aye. Just dinner."

She was lost in thought on the ride up to his room, her mind and her heart back in that building with her family. She was sure they were all there if Bitsy was there. Her Aunt Nancy and Uncle Ken would not have separated from their only daughter.

As though he knew what she was thinking, he brushed a stray lock of hair off her forehead. "Ye never did tell me who they are."

"Who?" she asked, pretending she didn't know what he was talking about.

"The people back on the ranch. The female in the rodeo. I gather that ye ken who she is?"

She stared down at her Converse sneakers. She might as well tell him. Maybe he *would* help her. It wouldn't hurt to try.

"That was my one of my family in there. And if she's there, I think they're all there."

The bell chimed that they were at his floor, and he casually took her hand again as he led her to his room, like he'd been doing it for years. He didn't release it to open the door, or when they got inside and it closed again behind them.

"Who was it that was in th' arena?"

"My cousin," she whispered. "Bitsy. Though she's more like a sister to me. And my aunt and uncle must be there somewhere too."

"Look, lass. I ken that there are those o' your kind that deserve that kind o' treatment—the Dark Fae, the soul suckers—but I also ken that most of ye do not."

"But I am one of those kind." *Oh shit.* Why did she just say that?

He released her hand. "What did ye just say?"

She stared up at him. She knew he'd heard her the first time. No sense trying to backpedal now. "I am of *an olc,* the dark ones." Guess she would see how trustworthy he really was.

He took a step back before he caught himself. He immediately stepped forward again, but it was too late. She'd seen his reaction.

"I should just go."

"Nae. I dinna want ye tae go." Then he frowned. Like he wasn't sure why he'd just said that. A look of resolution crossed his strong features. "Nae. I ken what ye were when I first saw ye. I was just hoping that I was wrong. Ye seem so…sane." He ran a hand through his hair. "It does no' matter. Ye should stay. Eat. And ye and I can talk more. I'd still like tae try tae help ye."

Hope flared within her, but she quickly quashed it down. "Why would you help me? Your kind kills my kind. I'm just a soul sucker. You said it yourself."

He smiled down at her. "I dinna see ye sucking any souls at the moment. So I would guess that I am safe. At least for now."

She stared into those soulful eyes, looking for any signs that he was tricking her or something, but she saw nothing there but honesty and kindness.

A swift knock on the door behind her had her nearly jumping out of her skin and she went ghost again without thinking.

"Dinna leave," Marc ordered in her general direction as he went to answer the door.

She scooted out of the way so he didn't hit her with it, her heart continuing to pound until she saw it was just the pizza he'd ordered.

Grabbing some money from his suitcase on the bed, he paid the delivery guy and shut and locked the door. "You can come out now, lass. He's gone." Setting the pizza boxes on the small table next to the bed, he bent down and opened the small fridge. Taking out two sodas, he set one can on the table for her and popped open the other one, taking a large swig before he rubbed his hands together with anticipation and opened up the first box.

The smell of cheese and onions assaulted her and her

stomach growled loudly. Feeling a bit like a fool, she solidified again so he could see her.

"Ach. There ye are! Help yourself, Bronaugh. There's plenty tae feed us both." He sat down on the bed and shoved half a slice into his mouth, his eyes nearly rolling back in his head as he moaned with pleasure.

That was enough to convince her. Pulling off a slice, she took a bite. He was right. It tasted amazing.

They ate in silence, stealing glances at each other until there were only a few slices left. Wiping his mouth neatly with a napkin, he leveled his narrowed gaze on her.

Uh, oh. It appeared it was time to talk. Taking a drink of her soda and following it with a deep breath, Bronaugh swallowed her trepidation. She could trust him. Her instincts told her so, and her instincts were never wrong.

MARC DIDN'T KNOW what had stopped him from killing her as soon as she'd confirmed to him what she was. But his blood had iced over in his veins and he'd had to force himself to remember to breathe at the mere thought of harming her in any way. Unlike his physical reaction, his mind spun as he'd checked her out more closely. There were no crazy eyes, no erratic behavior…just the opposite, in fact. She'd stood there poised and calm, stating loud and clear what she was and daring him to do something about it.

"So Corrina was no' lying. They're all Dark Fae, then… yer family."

"No," she said. "Not all of them. Just me. The girl at

the…rodeo—" The word seemed to stick in her throat. "She's not of my tribe. She's *na daoine maithe*…Good Fae. Her mother and father found me after the wars and took me in. We've been together ever since. I call them 'aunt' and 'uncle' and Bitsy is my cousin. We've gotten very close over the years."

"Are they the only ones there?"

"I don't know."

He studied her, his mind continuing to spin as he tried to figure out what he could do to help her without hurting his own cause. His heart ached for her, for what she must be going through. Much as they argued, he loved his own pack family. Even Lucian, in spite of the fact that he'd gotten Marc thrown in a cell for weeks because of one of his rash decisions. All had ended well and no harm was done. But he was still a royal pain in the arse.

She must've read the intense emotions he was feeling as being aimed toward her, for she said, "I'm not going to attack you and suck out your soul. Please stop looking at me like that."

Immediately, he dropped his eyes and tried to clear his head. But he couldn't seem to keep himself from staring at her. Of their own accord, his eyes crept back up—over her Converse sneakers. Her tight jeans that hugged every ample curve. The simple peach cotton shirt that made her skin glow with the kiss of the sun. The swell of her rounded breasts where a tree-shaped pendant hung from a thin silver chain. The graceful arc of her collarbone. Her elegant neck and sharp jawline…right up to her kissable lips, wee nose, messy hair and those chestnut brown eyes.

A low growl rumbled up from his chest as he let his

gaze roam over her once more. *Och. Aye.* She was the most perfect thing he'd ever seen—wee and curvy and thick and bonnie. Plenty of woman to handle a male like himself. His jeans grew uncomfortably tight, his cock swelling fast and hard at the new visions in his head.

But while his body had one idea of what he should do with her, his mind was arguing a few valid points of its own. She was Fae. And not only that, she was one of the soul suckers. The fact that she hadn't turned yet didn't mean anything. She would. They all did. It was only a matter of time.

But she wasn't one of them yet...

She scowled up at him. "Now you're looking at me like you want to eat me."

Her soft-spoken words crashed into his head, scattering any logical arguments that were trying to take hold there only to be replaced by images of her naked and spread out on the bed with his face buried between her soft thighs and his mouth tasting her sweetness.

He took a step toward her, and then another, until he was close enough to touch her.

"Marc?" Her voice was a bit shaky, but she held her ground.

His eyes were drawn to that pendant nestled in her cleavage. It rose and fell with her rapid breaths, and he realized he was looming over her with his hands fisted at his sides. He forced himself to relax. He was frightening her. Unclenching his hands, he stopped fighting what his wolf was telling him to do and gave in to the impulse to touch her.

Slow and careful so she didn't think he meant to harm

her, he ran one palm up her bare arm. Her skin was soft and supple and warm, and goose bumps broke out where he touched her. *Interesting.* He didn't pause to analyze what he was doing anymore, he just let his instincts guide him, something he rarely gave himself the luxury of doing. With just the tips of his fingers, he traced the bottom edge of her sleeve around to the side of her breast, then lightly scraped his thumb over the hard bud of one nipple.

Bronaugh inhaled sharply, but didn't move to stop him. And when he found the courage to let his gaze wander up to her face, her expression had him taking a ragged breath of his own. Her lips were parted and wet for his kiss, her expressive eyes full of such heat he nearly tossed her to the bed and ripped her clothes from her body right then. But somehow he resisted the urge. Cupping her face in his shaking hand, he tried to make sense of what was happening, tried to form his thoughts into some type of coherency. But her scent was all around him, and her warm skin was under his hands, and her hungry eyes were staring up at him with an intensity that drove all thoughts away except the one that was telling him to kiss her.

So, he did.

Her lips were as soft as they looked when he brushed them with his own. Once. Twice. And again. Pulling back slightly, he took in her reaction, half expecting a slap in the face or at least a rebuke of some sort. But she surprised him yet again.

Smiling a vixen's smile that heated his blood, she gripped her wee fists in his shirt and pulled him back down to her. Taking control, she pressed her mouth to his, moaning softly when contact was made. Her tongue ran along his bottom lip, tasting him, and then she rose up on her toes and increased the pressure on his mouth until he gave her full access. She kissed him until he was mindless for her—her little tongue teasing him, her soft curves pressing against him, her arms now wrapped around his neck and pulling him closer still.

Giving in to her passionate attack, he dropped his hands and gripped her full hips, pulling her into him until he couldn't get her any closer. His cock surged against her as it came into contact with her soft belly, and his hands slid down to her plump bottom to lift her up and impossibly closer. The scent of her arousal drifted in the air around him, fogging his brain, and his fingers dug into her arse as another growl left his throat.

Marc had never felt this loss of control with a female before. And being that he was hundreds of years old, it was quite disconcerting. But she had him so twisted up inside he couldn't bring himself to worry about it. And she'd accomplished that with only a kiss.

He was hers to do with as she pleased. She was giving him no other choice.

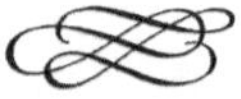

CHAPTER 10

Bronaugh felt the long, hard length of him pressing against her stomach and her body responded with a sudden rush of moisture between her legs. Her head swam and her blood pulsed with a lustful intensity she hadn't felt before with a male. She wasn't quite sure how she'd gone from being semi-afraid of him to wanting to jump his bones like nobody's business, but as soon as he'd touched her arm, she'd gone completely pliant. His hand was hot on her skin, and when his lips had touched hers, she'd wanted nothing more than to throw him onto the bed and love him until he gave up the careful self-control he held onto so tightly.

She wanted to hear him groaning in her ear, wanted to feel all of that hard muscle against her body, wanted to make him come so hard his eyes would roll back in his head and he'd never have sex again without thinking of her.

If she were completely honest with herself, she'd admit

that she'd been intrigued by him the moment she'd first seen him. He exuded a sexy confidence that had drawn her to him like a moth to a flame, for lack of a better comparison. His aura had called to her even back at the capitol. It's what had made her want to get closer to him, in spite of the danger to herself. Or maybe that's exactly what called to her—the danger of being so close to a werewolf. Whatever it was, it had brought her to this moment in time. And she was going to enjoy taming her wolf.

Letting her hands roam over hard shoulders and hard pecs, she worked her way down rippled abs until she found the bottom of his shirt. She slid her hands underneath it and back up to his chest, pushing the material up as she went and exposing bare skin. His skin felt hot, almost feverish. She wondered if all wolves had that body chemistry. Unable to resist, she nipped his bottom lip and ended the kiss so she could fill her vision with the sculpted mass of muscles now revealed in front of her. She leaned in and dropped kisses on his diaphragm, and he gripped the back of her head with both hands to hold her to him. His head fell back and he groaned as she worked her way over to one flat nipple and took it between her teeth, teasing it with her tongue.

Oh yeah, that's the sound she wanted to hear.

Her nails dug into his sides, and by the sounds he was making, she got the feeling he didn't mind her being a little rough. Testing her theory, she nipped him hard as she kissed her way down his stomach. In response, his hips rolled toward her and his hands tightened in her hair. Smiling, she slid her hands under the waistband of his jeans and around to the button and zipper that were barely containing what she wanted. She could see the outline of him, and she had to admit it was even better than she'd imagined. Just the thought of all of that thick hardness inside her had her clenching in anticipation.

She'd just gotten the button undone and gripped the zipper to pull it down when one of his hands covered hers and stopped her.

"Nae, Bronaugh. We cannae be doing this." His voice was rough, like it was taking him a great effort to say the words.

Ah...gods. Don't back out on me now.

She ignored him and renewed her efforts. She managed to get the zipper down about halfway in spite of his hand still being there to stop her. The broad head of his cock was exposed to her view, the tip glistening with a drop of milky moisture. She licked her lips, wondering how he would taste. Dipping her head, she lapped at him with her tongue and moaned with delight.

Something between a growl and a shout sounded above her, and she went in for another taste. But he gripped her by the upper arms and physically moved her away from him and then held her there. They stared at each other for long moments, breathing hard, while he blocked every effort she made to get close to him again. Her eyes dropped to his open jeans, where his exposed cock pulsed against his tight abs, and she made a frustrated noise.

He growled low in his throat. "Dinna look at me like that, Bronaugh. We have tae stop."

"Why?" she moaned.

When he finally answered her, the only lame excuse he could come up with was, "Because it's no' right."

Gods, that accent and that gravelly voice were going to send her over the edge.

"Marc…" She leaned in close to him, until she could again smell the clean scent of soap and male coming off his heated skin.

"Nae, Bronaugh. I'm sorry." And with that he set her firmly away from him, turned and walked across the room, doing up his pants as he went. He didn't turn back around until the entire length of the hotel room was between them. "I just cannae do this with ye."

Because she was a dirty Fae from the wrong tribe. Yeah, she got it. Loud and clear.

Without a word, she ghosted out, turned on her heel and walked purposely to the door. Yanking it open, she strode out of his room without bothering to close it behind her and hurried to the elevator. The doors opened right away, and she walked inside and pressed the button to her floor.

"Bronaugh! Dinna run, lass. Let me explain!"

The last thing she saw was Marc rushing toward the doors right before they closed in his face.

MARC BALLED up his fist and pulled back his arm to release his frustration on the wall in front of him, but caught himself before he caused any serious damage. Taking a deep, calming breath, he spun around and went back to his room.

What the bloody hell had just happened?

He paced the floor of his room, ignoring the discomfort of his suddenly too tight jeans, and tried to figure out what would be the best plan of action here. He'd just walked out on the Texas pack and their "rodeo" after severely injuring two of their members. Then he'd brought a Dark Fae lass back to his room and nearly ravished her without thinking twice about it. The only thing that had stopped him was the sound of a loud horn coming from the nearby highway. It had startled him, shaking him loose from his lustful thoughts just long enough for some logical thought to take over.

His cell phone rang from where he'd laid it next to the television. He rushed over to it, hoping it was Bronaugh, and picked it up and hit the answer button before remembering that she didn't have his number. He looked at the number again before putting the phone to his ear.

"Cedric," he greeted.

"Marc! I was beginning tae wonder aboot ye." His alpha's strong Scottish brogue came across the line. "Good tae hear yer voice. How are things going there in Austin? Have ye met the pack there yet?"

"Aye, I have," he answered, trying to keep his tone neutral.

He must have failed miserably, because Cedric's next words were "What happened?"

Sitting down heavily on the bed, Marc proceeded to relay everything that had occurred since his arrival. The only part he left out was Bronaugh. He wasn't sure why he didn't tell Cedric about her—if anyone would withhold judgment about her, it would be him. The leader of a bunch of hotheaded werewolves had to be a fair and just male if he wanted to keep that position of authority in the pack. And Cedric more than fit the bill. But Marc just couldn't bring himself to do it. She wasn't a Good Fae like Heather, Brock's lass. She was one that should be locked away with the rest of her tribe, and somehow Marc didn't think that even levelheaded Cedric would be okay with him getting turned inside out over one such as her.

"Ach. Ye've gotten yerself intae a fine mess." Cedric sighed heavily. "We really need these alliances, Marc. We cannae handle what's coming all on our own."

In the long pause that followed, Marc didn't know what to say. He had no excuse for his rash behavior.

"I'm sorry I'm no' there in yer place," Cedric finally said. "It should be me there, no' ye. It isna fair of me tae ask so much o' ye."

Marc hated hearing the defeat in his alpha's voice. Straightening his shoulders, he strove to reassure him. "I willnae let ye down, Cedric. I will fix things. All is no' lost just yet."

"Just do yer best, Marc. But dinna get yerself in a situation. If things become too touchy down there, ye hightail it back up here tae Seattle. Ye ken? We'll figure something else out."

"Aye, I will."

"Good luck, my friend."

They said their goodbyes and Marc hung up. Falling back onto the bed, he set his mind to figuring out how to make things right with the Texas pack.

And more importantly, with Bronaugh.

CHAPTER 11

Bronaugh spent most of the night curled up on her bed fully dressed and watching bad porn. You'd think for what she was paying for the room, they'd have some better options.

She sighed and flicked off the TV with the remote. It didn't really matter what was on the screen. She wasn't paying attention to it anyway. The room fell into darkness and she rolled onto her side to stare out the window at the lights across the lake.

She wasn't doing what she should be doing, which was coming up with a plan to get her family away from that horrid place they were in. She wasn't worried about their lives. At least, not yet. Because if the wolves killed her family, they'd have no one to participate in their rodeo, and it was obvious that the damn dogs were enjoying themselves too much to give it up. The females might get banged up a bit, as she saw firsthand watching her cousin get dragged around the arena with a rope around her neck, but they'd be all right. Fae people healed much faster than humans. Almost as quickly as vamps and wolves.

No, what she was thinking about was completely inappropriate. But no more inappropriate than her behavior had been a few hours ago. Granted, she was *an olc*, and her passions ran hot and intense when something—or someone—brought them to the surface. And that yummilicious hunk of a werewolf had certainly done that. The question that plagued her was why him?

She'd been around plenty of males, both human and otherwise, throughout her long years of life. But none had affected her like this one, and she'd never dared to get this close to a werewolf. With one hesitant touch, he'd crumbled her walls and flung her caution to the wind. Like a switch had been flicked on inside, her body had responded with a burst of sexual hunger she'd never experienced before.

Bronaugh sat up and swung her legs off the side of the bed. This was dangerous, for both of them. She should stay away from him. Besides, he'd already shut her down once because of what she was. He had no interest in taking up anything with her. She would respect that choice. Deep down, she knew it was the right choice. They probably had nothing in common anyway. He'd been right to stop things before they'd gone any further.

There was only one problem. She *wanted* him. And she wanted him badly.

A soft knock sounded on her door.

Bronaugh's heart picked up until it was beating double time. It was Marc. It had to be. No one else would be knocking on her door this time of the morning, before the sun was even up. And no one else knew she was here. The only others that might have found out sure as hell wouldn't be knocking.

The knock sounded again, a little louder this time, and she realized she was still sitting on the bed staring in the direction of the door. Jumping to her feet, she ran over and unlocked the safety latch before she flung it open.

The air left her lungs in a rush. *Ah, gods.* He was even more handsome than he was the last time she'd seen him just a few short hours ago. She ran her eyes from the tousled hair on his head to his deep brown eyes that stared at her with such intensity it made her uncomfortable. She dropped her eyes down over his broad shoulders, strong arms, wide chest, flat stomach, narrow hips, and all the way down his long, muscular legs to his thick-soled boots.

She would bet money he even had sexy feet. How the hell was she supposed to resist all of that?

Sighing in defeat, she stepped aside and indicated that he should come in.

Shoving his hands in his pockets, he stayed right where he was. "Actually, I was wondering if ye would like tae go get some breakfast with me."

Bronaugh raised one eyebrow. "Food again?"

He looked past her into her room, his eyes landing on her rumpled bed. "Aye. Food," he said with tone of finality. "I thought we could put our heads together and try tae figure out a way tae help yer family."

"Why?" It was a nice offer, but she knew as well as he did that going up against the local pack would be suicidal for him. She couldn't ask him to do that. Especially now that she thought she kind of liked him.

He scowled down at her. "What do ye mean 'why'? Did ye no' see yer cousin getting dragged around by the neck behind a dirt bike?"

Bronaugh crossed her arms in front of her, and his eyes immediately dropped to her cleavage before he seemed to remember himself and forced them back up to her face.

"Yeah, I saw her. It didn't look fun."

"Nae. It didnae. Dinna ye want tae go save her?"

"I still do. And I will. But why do you want to get involved? Aren't you supposed to be playing nice with the cowboys? Making a pact and all that?"

"Aye. I can do both."

She raised the other eyebrow this time.

"Stop looking at me like that. I cannae stand by and let them do that tae innocent creatures. I ken what I'm getting myself into. I can handle it. It will be fine."

She shrugged. It was his funeral. "Let me get my shoes." She let the door close in his face and went back to the bed where she'd left her sneakers. As she laced them up, she tried to tell herself that this was a really bad idea. She should really try to convince him that although she greatly appreciated his offer of help, she could handle things on her own. If he was to get involved and they got caught, it would mess up his entire reason for being here at the very least. More likely, it would cost him his life. Wolves didn't mess around with things like trust and honor. Gathering up her cash and her fake ID, she shoved both in her front pocket and looked around to make sure she wasn't forgetting anything she might need before she left her room. She never left anything of value in her room, just in case she didn't come back for one reason or another.

She found him leaning up against the wall by the elevator with his fingers laced in front of him, staring out the window at the end of the hall. He straightened to his full height as she approached and dropped his hands to his sides, clenching them into fists, his eyes roaming over her the way they did every time he saw her. And by the way those eyes lit up, he liked what he saw. It almost made her blush, the hunger with which he looked at her.

If only he wasn't so damned moral.

He waited for her to join him and then reached out and pushed the button, ushering her inside without touching her when the doors opened. She noticed he stayed as far away from her as possible after the doors closed, cracking his knuckles as he watched the numbers change. When the doors opened on the lobby floor, he breathed a sigh of relief and indicated for her to precede him. *Ever the gentleman.*

They left the hotel and found his car. Unlocking the passenger side door for her, he waited for her to get in before shutting her door and walking around the front of the car to the driver's side. He made her buckle up before he started the car and carefully pulled out of the parking lot.

"So, um. It's four in the morning. Where are we going to find breakfast?"

He shot her a smile. "There's an IHOP no' far from here. Just a few blocks. Open twenty-four hours."

Nothing more was said until they arrived at the restaurant and got settled into a booth. After the waitress took their orders, Marc sipped his coffee while studying her face. Lines of concern creased his wide brow.

"Ye look tired, lass."

"It's four in the morning," she repeated. "And I was just kidnapped out of my hotel room to come and eat breakfast with my adversary instead of sleeping like I should be." She smiled at him over the rim of her cup to let him know she was teasing, but he still scowled.

"I didnae kidnap ye, I asked ye nicely."

She laughed. "It's okay, I'll survive. So, tell me what it was that made you feel compelled to bang on my hotel door at this hour, since it obviously wasn't anything fun. Some brilliant, foolproof plan to get my family away from your friends, perhaps?"

He didn't laugh with her. "They're no' my friends. But, aye. I do have tae play nice with them. For now."

"So what's the plan, then?"

"I dinna ken. I was hoping between the two o' us we could come up with something that would help your people and no' get me killed in the process."

She became somber at his words. "Marc, you don't have to involve yourself. Seriously. I can figure something out on my own."

The waitress showed up with their food, and they were quiet for a few minutes while she set down their plates and they dug into their food.

"But I think ye do…need my help," he clarified when he came up for air.

She picked up her coffee to wash down her eggs,

shaking her head. "No, I don't. I can sneak in and get them out myself."

"How are ye going tae get through the iron bars?"

She paused mid-drink. *Dammit.* She'd forgotten about the iron cage.

"Correct me if I'm mistaken, but ye can't even touch the things tae let them out. Is that no' right? How would ye unlock them? How would ye even get into the building, reinforced as it is with iron shards right in the wood?"

"All right, all right. You've made your point." Pushing her plate aside, she rested her chin in her hand and scowled at her coffee.

"Ye should finish yer breakfast, lass. I have a feeling yer going tae need the nourishment."

Now he was just teasing her. "I'm not hungry anymore." She sighed and sat back in her seat to watch him eat. "So, you got any better ideas?"

"Aye. I was thinking I could go back over there today. Apologize for being a wee bit crabbit yesterday."

She quirked an eyebrow at his blasé description of what he did to the two wolves guarding the door.

He ignored her look. "Tell them I didnae expect what I saw, that it took me by surprise, and when Tony and Lorrent would no' let me leave, my emotions got the best o' me." He shrugged one powerful shoulder. "It happens a lot with us. We lose our tempers often. I may have tae do a bit o' groveling, let them get even with me for what I did, but they willnae hold a grudge. Once I'm in good with them again, I can eventually find a way tae get inside the building and free your people. It will be up tae ye tae run with them. As far away as ye can before anyone is the wiser."

A picture of Lorrent with his throat torn out popped into her head. "What do you mean by 'get even'? I don't want you going back there if it means you possibly getting hurt."

His eyes were warm as he smiled at her. "I have tae go back. And it has nothing tae do with you. Cedric, my pack leader, is counting on me tae form this alliance between our packs. Without them, and the other packs near us, we willnae be able tae stop the soul suckers..." His words dwindled off, and he looked down and stuffed a forkful of pancakes in his mouth.

But it was too late. She'd heard what he said.

"Why are you helping me?" When he opened his mouth to answer her, she waved her hand back and forth, cutting him off before he could say anything. "I know, I know. You're a softie who doesn't like innocent creatures being used for entertainment. But you also made it perfectly clear that you don't want anything to do with me."

His fork clanked down on his plate. "Bronaugh. I didnae say..."

"And for all you know," she continued, "I could be totally lying about them being good. They might be dark ones that just haven't turned yet, like me. I could be tricking you into helping me. Evil forest creature that I am, and all."

His dark eyes locked onto hers. "Is that what yer doing? Tricking me?"

She considered telling him yes, that was exactly what

she was doing. Maybe he'd get pissed off and tell her to go to hell. Her heart gave a lurch at the thought, but if it would keep him safe, she'd happily lie to him.

However, when she looked into his face and those forthright brown eyes, she found herself shaking her head. "No. I'm not tricking you. Everything I've told you is the truth."

Reaching across the table, he laid his hand on her arm where it rested next to her coffee. "Ach. Aye. I ken yer not lying tae me. I just wanted tae hear ye say it." He rubbed her arm. "It'll be all right, lass. We'll get them out."

"I won't let you put yourself in danger, Marc. If things get too hairy in there, so to speak, I want you to forget about this plan. My family will be okay until I can figure something else out. But I want you to know that I totally appreciate what you're doing and the risk you're taking."

Flagging down the waitress, he paid the bill. "Let's go get our things together. The cowboys mentioned something aboot me staying there at the ranch. I'm hoping they'll extend the invite again. Will ye be all right staying outdoors? Maybe somewhere nearby, but no' too close," he ordered.

"I'm a Fae. Nature and I are like this." Raising her hand in front of her, she crossed her fingers.

"All right, then. Let's go, lass."

CHAPTER 12

Marc wondered for the sixtieth time in as many minutes what the bloody hell was wrong with him. He'd gone to Bronaugh's room with the full intention of apologizing for his behavior and to try to convince her to leave the city before she was caught too. Instead, here she was sitting right next to him in his rental car...way too close for his comfort...and they were on their way out to the den of the Texas pack.

They were still a couple of miles from the turnoff when Marc wrenched the wheel to the side and skidded to a sudden halt on the shoulder of the road. He stared blindly out the front windshield.

He shouldn't have agreed to this.

"Marc? What are you doing?" she asked, adjusting her seat belt that had tightened around her neck. "And next time, please warn me before you swerve off the road for absolutely no reason at all that I could see." Her attempt at humor didn't hide the slight tremor of nervousness in her voice as she eyed his white-knuckled grip on the wheel.

He twisted around in his seat and cupped her small face in his large hands. In his chest, his heart thundered with fear for her. A fear he didn't understand, for he barely knew the lass, and she was more than capable of taking care of herself. Yet still, he needed some reassurance that she wouldn't put herself in any unnecessary danger.

Catching her eyes with his own and refusing to let her look away, he said, "Bronaugh. I want ye tae swear tae me that ye will no' do anything tae risk yourself. Swear it!" he insisted when she just looked at him with a quizzical expression.

Instead of making the promise he needed to hear, she wrinkled her nose at him. "What's gotten into you? I'll be fine. It's you who needs to worry. You're the one who wolfed out on two members of their pack."

Marc pulled her in until their noses were nearly touching. "Swear it tae me, lass. Or I'm no' letting ye anywhere near the place." A heavy silence filled the car. He could well imagine the rebellious thoughts shooting through her blonde head. "I mean it, Bronaugh."

She wrapped her fingers around his wrists, but didn't try to pull his hands away. With a sigh, she told him what he needed to hear. "Fine. I promise I won't knowingly put myself into any unnecessary danger." And then she smiled sweetly at him.

An overwhelming feeling of possessiveness filled him at that smile, though he didn't trust it for a minute. He knew she was just trying to distract him, and it was fookin' working. His eyes dropped down to her sweet lips. An animalistic growl filled the small space, and he realized with a start that it was coming from him. She inhaled sharply. The sweet musk of her answering desire rose in the air, and Marc was lost.

He took her mouth almost violently, pouring all of the fear and protectiveness he was feeling into the kiss. Bronaugh groaned as her hands slid down his arms to grip his shoulders. She kissed him back, hard, and her tongue dueled with his in a fight for dominance. Marc moaned, her sweet taste making his blood rush through his veins.

After a long time, he broke it off and touched his forehead to hers. He fought to catch his breath as he silently cursed the seat belts for keeping her lush body so far away from him. Without another word, he kissed her nose and released her, then pulled back out onto the road.

"Dinna forget tae make yourself scarce," he reminded her. "We're aboot tae turn onto their drive." She didn't move or respond, and he glanced over to find her staring at him, a strange expression on her face.

"What? Oh. Yeah." As they pulled on to the dirt road that led up to the house, her form flickered and disappeared.

Chills ran across his skin, and he gripped the steering wheel tighter. He'd never admit it, but her ghosting out like that gave him the heebie-jeebies. He didn't like her being there but not being there. What if he forgot and said something aloud not meant for a lass's ears? Or accidentally touched something he shouldn't be touching without her permission?

Although that was actually a moot point after last

night, for he'd touched plenty of things he shouldn't have been touching. Of course, that did not give him the right to keep on touching if she was opposed to him doing so.

Taking a deep inhale, he breathed in her scent of meadowsweet and woman's musk, trying to commit it to his memory. For he didn't know when, or if, he would see the lass again. She would be in hiding, and once he got her family out of that building he didn't imagine they'd be hanging around to thank him. Not if they were smart.

As he pulled up to the house and threw the car into park, Jace came out onto the porch, letting the screen door slam behind him. Squinting against the hot morning sun, he hooked his thumbs in his front pockets and waited for Marc to get out.

Pretending to reach down to get something out of the cup holder, Marc whispered to Bronaugh, "Be careful, lass. And dinna go too far away, but just far enough."

She squeezed his arm and he flinched away, startled at being grabbed by a ghost. He quickly recovered himself. But not quick enough it seemed, for he heard a sound that sounded an awful lot like a wince, like he'd hurt her feelings. *Ach.* Dammit.

He didn't have time to set things straight right now. Frustrated, but unable to do anything about it, he straightened up again and found the rest of the pack had joined Jace on the porch, including Keegan. Opening his door and getting out, he pretended to drop something on the ground to give Bronaugh a few seconds to get out. When her scent blew past him and faded, he shut the door and walked toward the house. He stopped at the bottom of the stairs and bowed his head.

"Well, well," Jace drawled. "You're pretty ballsy there, buddy. Showing up here after attacking Tony and Lorrent out of the blue like you did yesterday. You nearly killed them."

"Ach. I dinna even come close tae killing them," Marc scoffed. "And none o' that would have happened if they had stepped aside and let me leave as I asked them tae, instead o' blocking the doors like a couple o' rabid curs."

"What do you mean they were blocking the door?" Keegan asked.

"Just what I said. They would no' let me leave."

Keegan crossed his arms and glanced over at Jace for confirmation.

"Sorry if you Seattle boys are nothing but a bunch of candy-ass bitches who can't handle how we do things down here," Jace sneered.

Keegan lowered his arms to his sides and gave him a quelling look. Clenching his jaw, Jace lowered his eyes to his alpha and took a step back.

Marc approached the pack leader and took up a submissive posture. "My sincere apologies tae ye, Keegan. I would no' have done such a thing tae any of yours if I had been given any other choice. What ye do here…it all just took me a bit by surprise is all, and I felt the strong urge tae make myself scarce before my emotions got the best of me. With my pack mate just recently taking up with one o' their kind and all, I had a bit o' a time swallowing how that Fae lass was being treated." He lifted his head. "But I thought on it, and I ken that I overreacted. Heather, our Brock's female, though Fae by birth, grew up as a human. She's no' like them. She was no' involved with her people and all of their games and trickery. And she's one of *na maithe*, not *an olc*." He shrugged one shoulder. "These others are no' so innocent, I ken."

Keegan thought on it for a minute and then walked down the steps to meet him and extended a hand. "I accept your apology. Our rough way of life here in the South can be a bit much for those who aren't used to it."

Marc thought about some of the creatures he'd had to kill recently up where he was from and had a hard time keeping a straight face while he accepted the handshake. "Thank ye for understanding," he said in a solemn tone. "I ken there will be some retribution for my actions. Whatever ye think is fair is fine with me."

"Tony and Lorrent should be up and around in a few hours. You'll need to let them get a few good shots in on you, so they can feel avenged and not hold any grudges."

"Aye. That's fair enough."

"And to make it up to me, you can hang out here with us for a few days. We can get to know each other better and you can see more about us and how we run things. Maybe it'll help you feel better about what you saw yesterday."

It was exactly what he'd been hoping the alpha would say, but he didn't want to appear too eager. "I'm no' sure I should stay that long. I really need tae be getting back home…"

Corrina hopped down the stairs and smiled brightly at him. She really was quite bonnie, he supposed, though in his mind, she didn't hold a candle to his Bronaugh.

"Stay!" she said. "It'll be a good time. I'll cook you some homemade southern meals that'll stick to your ribs for a week. And we have lots of land to run on. I'll bet you've never felt as free as you will being here."

Marc thought of the miles and miles of forest-covered mountains he had back home. He longed to feel the mist clinging to his fur as he and his pack mates roamed through the quiet of the hemlock trees and fished for salmon in the many streams and rivers. "Aye, tis quite crowded in Seattle. Though we do have a bit o' land just outside the city."

She took his arm and started walking with him up the stairs to the front porch. As they reached the front door, she pressed her small breast into his arm as she reached across him to open the door. "As a matter of fact, I'll bet you'll never want to leave by the time I get through with you."

Marc glanced up at Jace as they passed. He was staring at Corrina's hands on Marc, his blue eyes green with jealousy. He wondered if Corrina was aware that she had a suitor. She certainly didn't seem to be. Unless she was hoping to play them against each other, in which case she was about to be sorely disappointed.

He fought the urge to look over his shoulder for Bronaugh as Corrina ushered him into the house.

"Corrina," Keegan called after her. "Why don't you show Marc up to the guest room and I'll have one of the pups bring in his stuff."

"Sure thing, boss." She smiled at Marc and led the way up the stairs and along the landing that overlooked the grand main room. As they walked, she showed him where the others slept. "But my room is in this wing, by yours. I can't stand sharing a bathroom with so many males. Here we are." She stood aside and indicated for him to go in first.

The room was large, but not extravagant. It contained simple wooden furniture and a bed that was of a size to sleep a large male comfortably. But what caught his eye was the bay window directly across from the door. White curtains hung to either side, and when he walked over he could see across the backyard all the way to the barn.

"Will this be okay?" Corrina asked from just inside the door.

"Aye," he told her, turning around with a smile. "Thank ye, Corrina. I'm sure I'll feel right at home."

She took a few steps farther into the room. "Well, if you need anything at all, you know where I'll be. Just two doors down." She tilted her head to the side in the direction of her room. "You can come knock on my door anytime, day or night."

Her innuendo was more than obvious, but Marc pretended not to notice. "Thank ye. I'm sure I'll be fine."

Just then one of the younger wolves showed up with Marc's duffel bag and set it on the bed. Marc took the opportunity to ask him some questions about the ranch, and with a promise to catch up with him later, Corrina took her leave.

Marc watched her go as he only half listened to the young male. He was going to have to do some fancy footwork if that one decided to take a real shine to him.

CHAPTER 13

Prince Nada handed Duana an old-fashioned goblet filled with a rich red liquid. She took a sip and smiled in appreciation. "This is good," she told him.

"It's been in my basement for a few centuries," he bragged.

She walked over to the dining table to hide the fact that she was rolling her eyes at his misguided sense of self-importance. She'd been with the prince for long enough to know that it was better to just let him live in his own little world, for he was very old, and he preferred it there.

Honestly though, he was getting a bit bizarre these days, even for him. But she needed his protection. Setting her goblet on the smooth oak surface, she tucked her skirt underneath her legs and sat down before picking up her drink again.

The prince came over to join her. "How did your

conversation go with the alpha wolf? Is he going to give you a chance to save your people?"

She gave a delicate shrug. "I honestly don't know. He said he would, but I don't trust him." After some more pleading on her part, the alpha had crossed his muscular arms over his wide chest, narrowed his beautifully eerie icy-blue eyes at her, and gave a single nod of his dark head. Instead of the feeling of victory that would normally overcome her at a moment like that, all she'd been able to think about was reaching out to touch the ponytail that had fallen over one broad shoulder, just to see if his wavy black hair was as soft as it looked.

The tip of her tongue wet her bottom lip as she wished she could see the mass of it falling free around his striking face. The thought of the combination of all that softness against such strong features had her clenching her thighs together. His hair would fall like a curtain around them as he braced himself over her, the primal strength of him dominating her smaller size...

The prince interrupted her vivid daydream. "Well, I can't say that I blame him."

She blinked hard, then took a large gulp of her drink.

"I mean," he continued on, oblivious to her discomfort, "have you ever actually seen any of those who are lost to the addiction? It's like they're possessed."

"They are," she said. "They're possessed by the high of what they're doing. I imagine it's a thousand times worse than any drug the humans indulge in. And yes, I have seen them."

The prince paused with his drink halfway to his mouth. He lowered it back down to the table. "Of course, you were there. My apologies, princess. I forget things sometimes." He tapped the side of his head with one finger. "There's a lot to remember in here after all these years, you know." Then he gave her a broad smile and saluted her with his goblet before taking a healthy swig.

Duana shook her head and smiled. She was fond of the prince, crazy as he was. She'd only been a child when she'd been brought to him, but he'd done what he told her brother he would do and had kept her protected until she matured. He did more than protect her; he included her in the business of ruling his people. In secret, of course. As a result, she'd grown up as one of the members of the royal family should. She was knowledgeable about both tribes of the Fae, her people and his. She was capable and strong. And she would be an excellent leader for her people.

If she could only save them from themselves.

CHAPTER 14

The next morning, Marc held a bag of frozen peas to the side of his face as he followed Keegan out to the "barn." True to his word, the alpha had given Tony and Lorrent the chance to redeem themselves after the beating Marc had given them, and Marc had let them get the best of him so they could save face within their pack. As a result, he was now sporting a busted lip, a sore jaw, a pretty good shiner that he was attempting to reduce the swelling of—hence the peas—multiple scrapes and bites, and a few broken ribs.

Afterward, they'd all sat down and had a fine breakfast, any and all offenses forgiven and forgotten. It was the way with wolves. Simple and easy. He'd be all healed within a few hours anyway.

Corrina had made it a point to sit down next to him at the table, jumping up to offer him seconds when he'd scarfed down her amazing grits and eggs. She'd laughed when he'd apologized for his lack of manners, and more than once he'd felt her breast graze his arm when she'd reached across him to get the syrup. She didn't bother hiding her flirting from the others either, and Marc noticed Keegan staring at him throughout the meal, a thoughtful expression on his face.

Now, as the rest of them went about their daily routines, Keegan invited Marc out to get a firsthand look at the workings of the rodeo and the creatures that played in their games.

As they approached the tall doors, he got an intense whiff of meadowsweet in the rain. Squinting up at the sun beating down on their heads even this early in the day, he knew it could only mean that Bronaugh was near—very near—and he cast about frantically for something to distract Keegan from taking him inside. Damn the lass! She was supposed to be concealed nearby, not hiding in plain sight. What if something happened that caused the pack to feel the need to defend themselves? All they had to do was change into their wolves, and she would be exposed for all to see.

He didn't want her going into this place again, but he didn't see how he could stop her without being the one to give away her presence. But it was too late. Keegan was already at the doors. Any backpedaling he did now would just seem suspicious.

Marc pulled the large double doors shut behind them, hoping she hadn't had time to sneak in. But a second later he knew that she had. Swallowing his fear for her, he figured that if she insisted on following them, he could at least try to get some information for her. "So, tell me again, if ye dinna mind, how it was that ye caught these Fae. I ken they're no' easy tae keep in one place."

"Nope. They sure as hell aren't," Keegan agreed. "It took us a couple of tries, to be honest with you, until we found the one thing that they couldn't break out of. Their ultimate weakness—iron. And even then, you have to have that shit everywhere. I mean, *everywhere*. We had to grind it up and mix it in with the wood, making composite planks to build this structure with. Their cell bars are all iron. All of the windows have iron bars. They can't get anywhere near it."

"What happens if they do?"

"It saps them dry. They practically start smoking like a vamp out in the sunshine. I've even seen them pass out cold, not to recover for days on end." He smiled brightly. "It's awesome."

"Do they have tae touch it? Or…?"

"They have to touch it to get the full effects. We haven't seen any side effects from them just being near it. It weakens them some, but not enough to take all the fight out of them."

"But it isnae fatal tae them…"

"Not that we've ever seen." He took off his hat and scratched his head before plopping it back onto his head. "I suppose if they were exposed enough, it may be possible."

"So, the Fae ye have here could be slowly dying from exposure tae all o' the iron they're surrounded by." It wasn't a question.

Keegan smiled without a speck of remorse. "It's quite possible."

Marc said nothing else as Keegan led him inside the cage. The smell of sawdust and oil was so strong now, it overpowered everything else, including Bronaugh's delicious scent. Keegan showed him the dirt bikes they rode in lieu of horses, told him about all of the different competitions they held and how they were different using Fae rather than animals, and explained to him how they'd reinforced the cage and the building to prevent any escapes.

As they wandered over to the bucking chute, Marc could see a tunnel that went right through the center of the stands on the other side of it. "Is that where they're held?" he asked.

"Yeah. Wanna see them?"

Hiding his anticipation, Marc shrugged casually. "Aye. Might as well." As they started down the hall, he asked, "How many do ye have?"

"Four total. But two of them we only use for very special events."

"Why is that?"

"You'll see." Keegan was practically rubbing his hands together with glee. Reaching the end of the hall, he unlocked the padlock on the door and swung it open.

Marc followed him inside and looked around. They were standing in a large, bare room with a dirt-packed floor. Support posts held hooks with loops of rope and chains hanging off them. A bench along the far wall held what looked to be numerous cattle prods. Cells with iron bars lined the far back wall. And inside the cells, contained by the iron, were Bronaugh's family.

Marc studied the two females behind the bars. One

was young, maybe Bronaugh's age, with spiky dark hair. She was the one he'd seen in the arena. Next to her was another female with similar coloring, only older— Bronaugh's aunt and cousin. The uncle appeared to be missing.

He tried to contain the disgust rising swiftly inside him. They were filthy, wearing nothing but strips of cloth wrapped around their emaciated bodies. They stood up when the males approached and backed as far away from the cell door as they could without touching any of the bars. Marc's chest tightened when he saw the young female with the spiky dark hair being careful to keep her weight off one leg. He searched her for other injuries, but she appeared to have otherwise healed from being dragged around the arena. At least physically.

He also noticed that although she was practically spitting venom at him, Keegan didn't so much as glance at her at all the entire time they were there.

The cell next to them was empty, but Marc felt heat flood his body when he saw what was in the third cell. Two males were pacing back and forth inside, muttering to themselves in angry tones. They paid no heed to their visitors. They were completely taken over by the malignancy of the Dark Fae.

Bronaugh hadn't mentioned these two. Perhaps she didn't know them? As he approached the bars, one of them finally deigned to notice him and immediately rushed the bars with a roar. Marc didn't even flinch as its face slammed against the iron, its clawed hands mere inches from Marc's shirt. Leaning in closer, he noticed a marking underneath the flop of red hair that fell on the male's forehead. It looked like a "V" tattoo.

They were definitely Dark Fae.

Backing away, he never took his eyes from the creature as he said, "I take it these two are yer special attraction?" Bile rose in his throat as he thought of his lovely Bronaugh turning into one of these things. He swallowed it down with great effort.

Keegan came up next to him and clapped him on the shoulder. "Wolves come from miles around to try to kill these things before they suck their souls."

"I see no one has succeeded yet."

"Not yet. Care to give it a try?"

"No' today," he said. "I'm still a mite sore from this morning." He watched the thing for a few minutes before saying with a touch of sadness, "It's like a drug addict that cannae die from their withdrawals. Instead it just drives them mad."

Keegan shook him from his musings, his tone unusually somber. "The fact that no one has managed to kill them yet doesn't bode well for our kind, does it? If these two are this bad while getting an occasional fix here, imagine what's going to be coming out of that fucking portal. If what you're saying is, indeed, fact."

Marc took out his cell phone, put the camera on video, and pushed record. Cedric was going to need to see this.

* * *

WITHOUT THINKING, Bronaugh rushed toward the nearest cell as soon as she spotted the two females inside.

Catching herself just in time, she stopped before she hit the iron bars. Her aunt and cousin stood just on the other side, facing away from her. She looked at the kind female who had taken her in when she'd needed help most and treated her as if she were one of her own. Her adoptive aunt was dirty, wrapped in rags, and had lost a bunch of weight, but was still a beautiful woman.

Bronaugh knew Aunt Nancy would sense her presence, and silently willed her to turn her head and see her. When she finally did, Bronaugh quickly raised her finger to her lips and urged her to keep quiet. Though her aunt could now see a ghostly image of her, the others were still unaware of her presence, and she wanted to keep it that way.

At the sight of her, her aunt shook her head slightly and looked toward the open door with frantic eyes.

No. I'm not leaving you.

"Well, maybe you can try one of our other competitions." Keegan picked up the conversation between the two males, startling her. She turned to look at them, knowing what Marc would say, but wanting to see how Keegan would react when he turned him down.

At least she thought she knew what he was going to say.

"Aye. Sounds fun. I haven't been on a dirt bike in a long time. I would need tae practice, or I might verra well end up on the wrong end o' the rope."

Keegan laughed heartily. "We can arrange that. Come on." Looking toward the females in the cell for the first time since they entered, he touched his fingers to the brim of his hat. "Ladies."

Bronaugh noticed with interest that his eyes clung to her cousin for just a little bit longer than necessary, and her head whipped around to look at Bitsy. But she needn't have worried on that account, for if looks could kill, that male would be flat on his back, writhing on the floor and in some serious damn pain.

Blowing her aunt a kiss and mouthing, "I'll be back," she hurried after the wolves, barely managing to slip through the doorway before Keegan closed it.

She wanted nothing more than to be far away from Marc—aka the traitorous asshole—and his new best friend, but she couldn't leave until someone opened the double doors for her, so she found herself sitting on the bleachers all afternoon watching them kick up dirt on those stupid motorcycles as they practiced their roping techniques. She didn't know whether to be proud or horrified at how good Marc was with only a little bit of practice. But she had to admit that seeing him effortlessly handle all of that power between his strong thighs did plenty to keep her entertained. And those bare arms had not an ounce of fat on them. They were a thing of beauty, is what they were.

Every werewolf male Bronaugh had ever seen was a fine specimen of masculinity, but there was something about Marc that was just...more. He had a quiet dignity about him that was unusual for a species that thrived on raw emotion and frequent displays of penis measuring.

After what seemed like eons but was probably only an hour or two, the guys did one final race down the length of the arena while swinging their ropes at a practice post, skidded to a halt, and called it a day.

"Let's go back to the house and get washed up," Keegan called from his end. "Corrina will have some grub ready soon."

Marc killed the engine and swung one leg over the back tire, then rolled the bike into its stand. Stripping off his borrowed riding gloves, he glanced around the arena, then said, "If ye dinna mind, I thought I'd go for a bit o' a run first before I get cleaned up for dinner. Get a taste o' the nature ye have around here and clear my head. Think on what I need tae say tae Cedric when I check in with him tonight," he added, indicating he wanted to be alone.

Smart.

Keegan only paused for a second before saying, "Sure. Just stay on the trails. Lots of rattlers around here. They won't kill us, but it still sure as hell ain't pleasant if they bite you. The food should be ready in about an hour."

They started to head out of the cage and toward the doors and Bronaugh hurried to catch up to them so she didn't get stuck inside. That would be bad with so much iron around. She could already feel it sapping her energy, and she needed all of her strength so she would be ready when the chance came to help her family. Once outside, Keegan headed to the house to get his shower. Marc watched him for a few moments, then took a deep breath. A low growl rumbled in his throat.

"Come with me," he whispered. Heading toward the trail Keegan had pointed out to him, he rolled his head on his shoulders and stretched his arms across his chest while he walked. Once he reached the trailhead, he broke out into a casual jog until they reached a small stream and were far enough away that no one would be able to hear them.

Bronaugh stayed camouflaged until Marc walked the area in a wide arc, sniffing out any unwanted visitors they might have. When he was assured that they were alone, he said, "All right, lass. No one's here but us."

"How do you always know I'm here?" she asked, letting him see her again.

His eyes roved over her. They were hungry...or angry...or maybe a little bit of both, but he kept his distance. "I told ye. I can smell ye. Ye smell like the wild-flowers in Ireland after the rain."

No shit. Huh.

He paced back and forth a few times, cracking his knuckles. He must know he was being irrational; that it was too much to ask, expecting her to sit idly by while her kin suffered.

Apparently not.

He let loose on her with a roar. "What the bloody hell do ye think yer doing? I told ye tae stay away from this place! Tae keep yer distance! What are ye doing following us in tae the barn? Are ye *trying* tae get caught? Do ye *want* tae be a part o' their fookin' show?"

She crossed her arms and rolled her eyes, unmoved by his show of anger. "He didn't even know I was there."

"Nae, he didn't. But I did. And what if something happened and I gave ye away somehow? I can only hold a door open for so long before it looks suspicious. I even tried not tae kick dirt up in yer direction with my bike!"

She *did* notice that. She'd thought it was sweet. It almost made her forgive him for taking the side of the hick werewolves over hers. Almost, but not quite. "You're overreacting, wolfman. I'm fine. Besides, if anyone should be angry, it should be me!"

"Ye should be angry?" he repeated in disbelief. "Angry at what, exactly?"

She stomped up to him until she was so close she could punch him in the face if she wanted to. And when she caught the smell of sawdust and bike oil…and another female…on his clothes, she realized that she did want to, so she hauled back her fist and landed a solid uppercut right under his chin.

"What the hell was that for?" he bellowed, rubbing his jaw.

"You lied to me," she gritted out.

"Wha'? I did no'!"

"Yes, you did! You said you were going to help me! Not join them in their sick little games!" And then she punched him again. "You even smell like that female! Have you been having fun with her while I've been hunkered down out here in the brush and nettles?"

"Ach. Stop it, lass! Is it no' enough that I had tae let those two eejits pound on me this morning? They dinna exactly take it easy on me."

"Whatever," she scoffed. "You're probably completely healed by now."

"That's beside the point."

"Did that she-bitch kiss your boo-boos? You must have had a lot of them, because you reek of her cheap perfume."

He stared down at her, completely baffled. "Corrina helped me after, aye. But she did no'…I did no'…"

Bronaugh waved her hands in front of her face. "Just stop. I don't want to know."

Furious with him, and even more so with herself for ever thinking she could trust a wolf, no matter how good he kissed, she turned and stomped over to the stream. Squatting down on her haunches, she splashed some water on her face, wishing it was colder. Wishing it was so cold it would freeze the memory of the taste of him from her mouth. She stayed like that, watching the water trickle by over the rocks.

It was fine. She didn't need him. She would get them out herself.

Her back suddenly warmed like the trees had somehow disappeared and the Texas sun was shining directly on her skin, then a pair of strong arms encircled her, engulfing her in his heat. His deep brogue rumbled softly in her ear. "I didnae lie tae ye, Bronaugh. I gave ye my word that I would help ye get yer family out o' that horrible place, and I will. I promise ye."

She noticed that he said nothing about her accusation of him being with the female of the pack. But then she sighed and pushed her feelings of jealousy aside. She had no claim on this male, much as she was starting to think she'd like to. "Then why did you tell him you'd be a part of it?"

"I had tae, lass. It will keep them from suspecting anything is amiss. And it will give me a reason tae be in there so I can figure out a way tae get them out without anyone becoming suspicious."

She sniffed. It made sense, she guessed.

He touched the side of his head to hers briefly, and

then stood up, and she suddenly felt cold in spite of the temperature. "But I need ye tae stay out here where it's safe and let me do what I need tae do."

"I can help you." She stood up and turned around to face him, trying not to let the hurt show when he took a step back. If she had any sense at all, she'd let that she-bitch have him.

His features settled into a stubborn mien. "I will get yer family out, and I will send them here, tae this bend in the stream. Once they find ye, run. Run so far away no one will ever find ye."

"Including you?"

He stared at her a moment, and then dropped his eyes and cracked his knuckles again. When he raised them again, they were steely with resolution. "Including me."

Bronaugh swore she'd just felt her heart crack open. "You don't mean that."

"I dae."

Blood rushed from the crack in her heart. She took a step closer. "But why?"

"Ye ken why, lass."

"No, I don't." She took another step forward.

He stepped back. "Yer one of *them*, Bronaugh. The crazed ones in the cells with yer family."

"But I'm not like them."

"Aye. No' now. But ye will be. And I dinna want tae be the one tae have tae kill ye when ye are."

Ah, so that's what this is all about.

Bronaugh paused, unsure what she could say that would ease his mind. Because there really weren't any words. He was absolutely right. She might very well end up a soul sucker one day, and she might not. There was nothing she could tell him to prove that she wouldn't. Only time would tell. And nothing she said now would convince him to take that chance with her. Words were only words.

But there was one thing she did know. She wanted him. And she wasn't a girl who gave up without a fight.

Bronaugh made her decision. That she-bitch could not have him. Gripping the bottom of her cotton tee, she pulled it up and over her head and tossed it on the ground. A rush of desire and a hint of satisfaction went through her when his mouth went slack as she reached behind her back and unhooked her bra, slid it down her arms, and dropped it on top of her shirt.

CHAPTER 15

Bronaugh's jeans were halfway off before Marc found his voice. "Lass, what are ye doing?"

"Getting naked," she responded with a "duh" tone in her voice.

"I can see that." When she kicked her Converse from her feet and slid off her jeans, he had to clear his throat before he could speak again. Even so, his voice still sounded hoarse. "But why are ye getting naked?" Her perfect breasts jiggled as she straightened again, entrancing him, and he had to close his hands into fists to resist the urge to reach out and heft their heavy weight in his palms.

She had just slid her thumbs under the tiny pieces of material that made up the sides of her panties, but at his question she paused. "Because I want to have sex with you," she said.

Marc's mouth went dry at her blunt answer, and then it began to water as she wiggled out of her panties and left them on top of her pile of clothes. He scrubbed his face with his hands.

She was still wearing her socks.

And it was fookin' sexy as hell.

He tried to speak, cleared his throat, and tried again. "We cannae do this, lass." Had he said that already? He felt like he'd already said that. Why wasn't she listening?

She strutted toward him, slowly, giving him time to look his fill. His eyes shot down to her perfect breasts, over her rounded belly and full hips, and to the blonde thatch of soft curls between her thighs. "Why not?" she asked innocently.

She stopped so close to him he could feel her heat and smell the flowery fragrance of her skin mixed with the musk of her arousal. Her eyes glowed with that strange kaleidoscope of colors. He couldn't look away. It took him a moment to realize she was waiting for him to answer her question. What was it that he'd been saying? Oh, aye. "We cannae dae this because o' what I just said."

She leaned into him and her hands slid around his waist. He could feel her hard nipples rubbing his stomach through his shirt. "Because I'm a bad girl?" she teased.

"Aye," he breathed, then scowled down at the top of her pale head. "Nae!" he said. "Yer no' bad. Yer just..."

"A soul sucker." She pressed her lips against his sternum.

It was like he wasn't even wearing a shirt. His cock, already at high alert and pressing painfully into his zipper, swelled with a fresh surge of blood. "Aye."

One small hand had somehow made its way between their bodies. She ran her palm down the hard length of him, then cupped his balls and gently squeezed. "But I'm not a soul sucker yet."

Marc's head fell back and he closed his eyes, asking the gods for the strength to push her away. They didn't seem to be listening.

Her other hand joined the first and began to work at the fastening of his jeans as her lips began to make their way down his stomach. He knew exactly where she was going, and he wanted her to go there. *Verra* badly. He'd never wanted to feel a lass's mouth on him like he did this one, but he'd meant what he said. If he let things go on as they were, he wouldn't want to give her up. And the day would come when she would turn, as all the Dark Fae did, and it would be up to him to stop her.

His heart shattered just thinking about it.

Gripping her upper arms, he pulled her up against him. She must have felt the change inside him, for her colorful eyes flew up to his and the smile slipped from her face. "Nae, Bronaugh," he growled.

Tears filled her eyes right before she closed them tight. Probably hoping he wouldn't see, but it was too late. He'd already seen the tears, and how her eyes started fading back to their normal brown. "Let me go," she ordered.

He didn't want to let her go; he liked the feel of her against him. And all he wanted to do was shift his hands from her arms to her arse and pull her up his body, wrap her legs around his waist, and thrust inside her until he was buried up to his balls in her wet heat. But somehow he found the strength to do what he needed to do.

He let her go.

She kept her gaze averted from him as she turned away

and went back over to her clothes where they lay on the ground. Shaking out the dust and anything else that may have found them, she began to get dressed again without a word.

Gritting his teeth, Marc turned away from the mind-altering sight of her voluptuous behind, shoved his insubordinate cock back into his pants and refastened the button with a wince. He walked over to the stream to give her some privacy. Falling to his knees, he splashed some of the tepid water on his face and arms. A small breeze blew through the cedars, helping the water cool his skin a bit along with the setting sun. But it did nothing to cool his ardor.

He needed to tell her how he felt. He didn't want her to believe he didn't think she was bonnie, or that he was repulsed by what she was. He wasn't. If anything, her Dark Fae nature turned him on. She was like nothing he'd ever met before—independent, smart, and she took what she wanted without fear. Including him. He discreetly rubbed his palm over his engorged cock, trying to ease the ache there a bit.

When the rustling of clothes stopped behind him, he gathered up his courage and stood up to apologize to her. Turning away from the water, he said, "Bronaugh, lass, please allow me tae explain…"

But she was gone.

BRONAUGH HAD NEVER BEEN ashamed of who or what she was. She'd never felt the urge to go after humans, never worried that someday she wouldn't be "her" anymore. Never felt like she was wrong for being up front and honest about what she wanted. She'd always been happy being by herself, even before she met her adoptive family. Never felt lonely. She lived her life free and without regret. But with two words, Marc had succeeded in doing what no one else ever had.

Nae, Bronaugh.

Those two words were stuck on replay in her head as she tromped back toward the barn where her family was. With only those two little words he'd made her feel unwanted, unclean, and like a silly girl—instead of the strong, independent female she prided herself on being.

"Well, well, well. Lookit what we have here!"

Too late, Bronaugh realized that she'd gotten too close. She'd forgotten to go ghostlike. Her head whipped up and she saw Jace and two of the others not six feet away from her.

"Looks like we got ourselves a new challenge, fellas! And a pretty one too. With those tits and ass, I bet she'll be mighty fun to wrestle down."

Bronaugh spun on her heel to run, but they moved lightning fast and had her surrounded before she could get away from them. An iron cuff with an attached chain was clamped around her wrist before she knew what was happening. She twisted her arm while pulling the cuff with her other hand, trying to yank it loose. But Jace was waiting for her to be distracted and snapped a collar around her throat. The properties of the iron seeped into her skin. She could feel it sapping her dry, but she kept fighting.

"Let me go!" she screamed. She pulled on the collar with one hand while she stuck her other hand under her arm and tried to rip it out of the cuff. It was pointless, she knew, but that didn't stop her from trying. She'd be damned if she was going to go meekly to a cell like an animal.

"I like 'em feisty," one of the others said. "This one is gonna make the crowd go wild."

"Yeah, she will." Jace laughed. Bending over in front of her, he caught her around the thighs and tossed her over his shoulder while she kicked and tried to throw herself off him. "Somebody get the door for me," he ordered.

Her head slammed into the side of the building when he swung around to take her inside, and she literally saw stars. Her stomach rolled and she stopped struggling so she could concentrate on not vomiting. By the time everything stopped spinning, he was in front of the empty cell next to her aunt and cousin. The door was already unlocked and he pulled it open and tossed her inside. She landed hard on her hip and right arm, and as she did so, she felt something snap just above her elbow.

The door was slammed shut with a clank, and Jace turned the lock and left the room, laughing with the others.

Something yanked her hair and Bronaugh screeched and tried to pull away, but her one arm wouldn't work. So she twisted her body around and pushed against the bars with her feet as she gripped the Dark Fae's wrist and tried to pull his hand from her hair. She still had the iron cuffs on, but somehow she found the strength and managed to remove his hand, though he took a good hunk of her hair with him.

Scooting back to the other side of the cell, she collapsed on her back onto the dirt floor, exhausted.

"Bronaugh? Oh, no…" Her aunt's voice was little more than a whisper.

Twisting her head to the side, she said, "Hey, Bits. Hey, Aunt Nancy. I told you I'd be back."

"Hey, Bro." Her cousin greeted her just as casually.

Her adoptive aunt shook her head at the two of them and reached through the bars to touch Bronaugh's arm. Her voice was full of tears as she said, "Honey, I think this arm is broken."

Propping herself up on her good arm, she looked down at the unnatural bend between her shoulder and elbow. Although she felt no pain at the moment, she knew it would hit her hard as soon as the shock wore off. "Yeah, I'd say it is. We're going to have to fix that." A cold sweat broke out on her forehead just at the thought of the pain she was about to have to endure.

"We can wait," Bitsy said. "Those iron shackles they left you in will keep it from healing."

"These fucking shackles are the reason it broke in the first place," Bronaugh grumbled.

"Watch your mouth, Bronaugh," her aunt reprimanded.

Bronaugh's lips twitched. "Sorry, Aunt Nancy." She found it endlessly amusing that her aunt insisted that they act like "ladies" in spite of all the quite *un*ladylike things they did sometimes to survive.

Aunt Nancy gave her a reproving look. "Can you scoot

over a bit this way? And we'll see what we can do about that arm. Bitsy, I'll need you to hold her down."

Bronaugh got into position against the bars, and her aunt used the chain that was hanging from her cuff to carefully pull her broken arm through to her side where she could reach it.

"Okay. Hold her, Bitsy."

Bitsy reached through and put one hand on her shoulder and one on her hip. Putting her slight weight into it, she held her down.

Aunt Nancy gripped the chain in her hands and braced her feet against the bars on either side of Bronaugh's arm. "On three. One..." She pulled hard and fast on the chain, pulling the broken bone apart.

Bronaugh screamed, unable to help herself. At the sound, the soul suckers in the next cell threw themselves into the bars in their excitement to get to her.

After too many long, excruciating seconds, her aunt got the broken ends lined up together again and released the chain. "We need something to stabilize it with."

Bronaugh lay panting, and wiped from her cheeks the tears she hadn't realized she had shed. "It's okay. I'll just hold it really still."

"No. Here," Bitsy said. She ripped a swath of material from the bottom of her already tattered shirt. "We might need some of yours too, Bronaugh."

"Okay," she agreed weakly, but her cousin was already tearing a piece off her tee before she could get up the energy to move.

Between the three of them, they managed to gather enough material together to make a half-decent wrap and sling. When they finished, Bronaugh moved away from the bars and sat up. She teetered there for a minute, taking deep breaths to fight the nausea and get her bearings.

"Where's Uncle Ken?" she asked.

"We don't know," her aunt answered. "He wasn't with us when we were caught."

"Where the hell was he?"

"Bronaugh. Language."

Bitsy said, "He'd gone to try to find you."

"What?" She looked to her aunt for confirmation, and she nodded.

A wave of guilt flooded through her. Dammit. What the hell had he done that for?

"I'm sorry," she told them after a moment. "I'm sorry I took off the way I did. I just thought…"

"You were wrong," Aunt Nancy said. "You were wrong, Bronaugh. We love you, all of us. We don't care what you are. You should know that by now."

"I was just trying to protect you," she told them.

When she and her family had come through Austin on their way to the East Coast, Bronaugh had heard rumors about a couple of humans who had gone on a killing spree in the city. And then they'd suddenly disappeared, never to be heard from again. The different details of the stories —some that sounded completely crazy—had her suspicious, and so she'd gone out one night to do a little digging around. And what she'd found was the scent of werewolves, a large pack of them, and she knew what had happened to the two who had disappeared. They were *an olc*, soul suckers like her, who had managed to be in the right place at the right time during the war and so had avoided being sent back to their world. Only unlike her, these two must have turned, and the werewolves had hunted them down.

She looked over at the two idiots slobbering all over their cell. Looked like she'd found the missing males.

Worried that the wolves would be on her trail next, she'd left her adopted family a note and set off on her own. If she was being hunted, she didn't want them caught in the crossfire. She honestly didn't think any of them would be stupid enough to try to come after her.

"It's okay, hon," her aunt said. "Maybe he's okay. We haven't seen or heard any indication that he was ever brought here."

"Or that any of these dogs had found him at all," Bitsy added.

Bronaugh nodded and tried to smile.

After a long while, Aunt Nancy said, "Well, I guess this is our life now. At least until they get bored and decide to kill us."

"That won't happen," Bronaugh assured her. "I won't let it."

"Honey, I don't think there's much you can do about it."

She snorted at the lack of faith. "Just watch me. I'll think of something and I'll get us out of here. I just need to convince them somehow to take these damn cuffs off me."

"Oh, don't you worry," Bitsy said. "They'll take them off you just in time to shock you with one of those cattle prods over there. And by the way," she leaned closer, "you do realize that the iron sickness takes a while to wear off, right? You're not gonna be superwoman as soon as the cuffs are gone. Why the hell do you think we're still in here?"

Her aunt agreed. "If we're going to escape, we're going to need outside help."

But they were wrong. They didn't need help. Especially not from anyone here.

Nope. Not even him.

While Bitsy and her mom talked quietly in the next cell, Bronaugh came up with her own plan to get them all out of there. "Do they ever take you both out together?" she asked them.

"Yeah," Bitsy answered. "Not every time. But once in a while they take us for their 'barrel racing' competition. All of us," she emphasized, glancing at the two gone males. "Except we're the barrels, and instead of weaving their bikes in and out of our line, they try to run us down. So not only do we have to avoid being attacked by these freaks, we have to do so while not getting run over and while trying to maneuver a rider between us and them so they get attacked and not us."

Bronaugh nodded. She just needed to wait until they had another barrel racing competition again. In the meantime, whenever she was part of the show by herself, she could use that time to work out how to get out of the cage around the arena. That would be the hard part. But she hadn't survived this long without having a few tricks up her sleeve.

It would be risky, but it would work. She would save her family. And she would do it all on her own.

CHAPTER 16

Marc made his way across the dirt parking area and back lawn and into the house. He'd followed Bronaugh's scent back to the barn, but there'd been no sign of her anywhere. She'd just up and disappeared. Frustrated with himself and with her, he'd finally given up.

Jace, Alex, and Zach were coming out of the barn as he passed. They were talking excitedly and slapping each other on the back. "Hey, Seattle!" Jace greeted him.

"Jace," Marc nodded in greeting at the others.

"Where've you been?" Jace asked him.

The hackles went up on the back of Marc's neck. Jace was being entirely too congenial for his comfort. "Just went for a run. What's all the commotion aboot?"

Jace eyeballed him for a moment, then told the others, "Go on back to the house, fellas. We'll catch up with you. I want to show our new toy to Seattle here."

Unease crawled up Marc's spine as he watched Alex and Zach walk away. But by the time he turned back to

Jace, he had his emotions under control. He raised one eyebrow in silent question, cool as could be.

"Come on, city boy." Jace waved him forward. "I'll show you what we just caught."

Marc purposely made his mind blank as he followed the tall blond through the arena and back toward the cells. As soon as they went through the first door, he smelled it—meadowsweet. His heart began to pound and he nearly stumbled over a discarded piece of old tack on the floor.

Jace glanced back over his shoulder with a smirk. "You all right there, Seattle?"

"Aye." Willing his heart to slow with sheer force of will, he indicated for Jace to carry on.

With another knowing look, Jace started walking again.

Get it under control, man. The bastard is on tae ye.

By the time they arrived at the door that would take them into the cells, Marc knew what he would see. And he was prepared for it.

Or so he thought.

But when the door opened and he actually saw Bronaugh shackled on the dirt floor of the previously empty cell, one of her arms in a homemade sling, he had to fight the urge to punch Jace's smirking face and break her out of there. Outwardly however, he showed nothing but a vague interest, or so he hoped, as he glanced over Bronaugh and looked over the others. "What was it that ye wanted tae show me?" he asked.

Opening the door to Bronaugh's cell, Jace grabbed the loose chain hanging from her neck and dragged her to her feet. "Look what I found right outside the barn just a few minutes before you came waltzing down the trail yourself!" Though she fought his hold, Jace pulled her back up against him with ease. Wrapping his arms around her and resting his chin on the top of her blonde head, Jace gave her an over-exaggerated squeeze. "Mmm, mmm! Love me a female that has a little something to her to hang on to."

Quick as a whip, Bronaugh threw her head forward and back. She was aiming for his jaw, but Jace lifted his chin just in time. He smiled over the top of her head at Marc as she continued to struggle. The pleasant look was in direct contrast to the glare of hate Bronaugh was giving him. Her eyes danced with colors in her anger.

"She's a feisty one too," Jace added. "I sure can't wait to ride her." His double entendre was more than obvious.

Marc thought seeing Bronaugh trussed up inside the cell was the hardest thing he had encountered so far. He'd been so very, very wrong. Seeing her in the arms of this eejit was so much worse.

"I found her right outside. Did I tell you that already? Yeah, it looked to me like she'd just come from a run on our land too. Strange coincidence there. Don't ya think?"

The fire in her eyes was scorching him from the inside out, and Marc had to forcibly tear his eyes away from her. "Aye, that it is."

"You didn't see her while you were out there? Didn't see this bright blonde hair?" One of his hands wandered up to finger a lock of her hair before lowering back down to squeeze her breast. Bronaugh struggled against him, the chains clanking together as he lifted her feet right off the floor and jiggled her up and down in his arms. Jace laughed out loud. "Seems a damn shame that you missed out on all of this."

"What exactly are ye trying tae say, Jace?" Marc snarled before he could help himself. Try as he might to keep his emotions in check, his muscles kept twitching and his blood was practically boiling in his veins. The violent urge to turn and rip out Jace's jugular was nearly unbearable.

"Don't go gettin' your hackles all up now. She's just a Faerie, man."

The bastard was goading him. He needed to calm down.

Besides, he was right. She was a Fae. A Dark Fae. And no matter how bonnie and sweet she appeared now, at some point it would all turn. If he stuck around, the only thing he would succeed at doing was being her first victim. "I just dinna like seeing a female of any kind handled like that."

"Oh, that's right. That's why you freaked out at the rodeo then, right? Is that it?"

"Aye. Where I'm from, we treat females with a wee bit more respect."

"And that's all it is?"

"What more would it be?" He kept his gaze steady on Jace's, refusing to look at Bronaugh.

"You don't know her? Haven't met her before?"

Marc shook his head.

"No? You sure about that?"

"Aye. I think I would ken if I'd met a bonnie lass like that."

With a smirk, Jace opened his arms and let Bronaugh drop to the floor. She automatically threw out her hands to catch herself, letting out a yelp as she landed on her wounded arm. Before she had time to get to her feet, Jace gripped her by the hair and started dragging her back to her cell.

Marc had taken two steps after him before remembering himself and stopping where he was. Turning his back to them, he clenched and unclenched his fists, resisting the urge to crack his knuckles although he was grinding his jaw together. Turning away, he began to casually observe the cattle prods lying on the shelf. His conscience, or maybe his inner wolf, screamed at him to help her. He felt all tight and itchy, the muscles quivering underneath his skin, wanting to burst through and contort into his other self. His gums burned where his canines fought to drop down and tear into Jace's throat.

He took a few deep breaths, his body flashing hot and cold as he struggled against the change.

He felt powerless. He wanted to help his lass, but he couldn't. If he showed any compassion toward her at all, they would see right through him. They wouldn't leave it alone, eventually exposing his interest in her, and they would all know he cared about her. He'd be reported to his alpha, and Cedric would know he'd failed him. With this pack, he'd be considered a traitor. And if they couldn't shame him enough to satisfy them, they would use her to break him. Neither of them would get out of Texas alive.

Bronaugh cried out in pain, and Marc started talking to distract himself. "So, ye use these things tae get them intae the arena? How do they work?" Picking up one of the cattle prods, the urge to use it on Jace became so overwhelmingly strong he had to set it back down again. Marc heard a thud and a wince and then the clank of the cell door being closed and locked. He forced himself to turn around, keeping his eyes averted from Bronaugh as he grinned at Jace. "Do they jump when ye prod them? Or do they just glare at ye like that one?" He pointed toward Bronaugh's cell with his chin.

Jace tilted his head to the side, and he didn't answer for so long that Marc cocked an eyebrow at him in question. He must have passed Jace's inspection, for he smiled and smacked Marc on the shoulder.

"Sometimes they glare, and they always jump." Laughing, he led Marc from the room.

Marc chuckled alongside him, fighting the urge to look back one last time when they reached the door. "I'd like tae see that next time. When's the next show?"

Jace locked up the door behind him and turned to him with a scowl. "It's called rodeo, Seattle. And you'd better not let anyone else hear you call it a show. That's a major offense here in this part of the country." Then he smiled again. "C'mon. Let's go talk to Keegan about getting you into the next round."

Marc followed him back to the house, his mind spinning. He shouldn't be getting involved in this freak show, but what the hell else was he supposed to do? And he wouldn't be able to protect her from outside the cage, so he would figure out a way to get himself on the inside. Besides, he'd told Cedric he had this pack handled, and he was being counted on to do just that. He would not let his alpha down.

Even if it cost him the first female he'd felt any attraction to in a long, long time.

CHAPTER 17

Brock knocked a few times and then let himself into Cedric's apartment.

After they'd all gotten back from the meeting with the Fae royalty, he and Heather had gone straight back to their new apartment to finish unpacking the boxes her parents had sent her from her home in China. Brock had thought they were full of keepsakes, perhaps, or dishes, or other things one would need for a brand-new unfurnished apartment. But no. There wasn't a useful item in the bunch.

What was in the boxes? Clothes. Clothes for any possible season or occasion she could ever think of, as he'd discovered when she'd shown them all to him. Every. Single. Piece. Piles and piles of clothes. And then they'd spent a good two hours trying to figure out where they were going to put them all.

In the end, he'd left her to mourn the loss of the ones she was going to have to give away.

A large smile creased his rugged face as he thought of her forlorn expression. She had the most adorable pout, but he much preferred her smile. It lit up his entire world. She was the sunshine of his life, and he counted himself a damn lucky son of a bitch that she'd agreed to stay with him. He'd never do anything to risk losing her.

Which was why he'd had her best friend, Grace, put protection wards around not just the apartment, but around the entire complex. At least it was one place where her Faerie godfather couldn't get to her. Prince Nada had told them both numerous times he wouldn't pull anything, but after that first meeting, Brock didn't trust him. The prince might get bored again one day, and he didn't want himself or his female anywhere near him when that happened. Because the last time the prince had needed entertainment, he'd sent them off to play a game of survival, and they'd barely managed to make it home again in one piece. The only good thing that had come out of it was that it had bonded Heather to him.

It suddenly occurred to him that maybe the prince wasn't so crazy after all.

"Cedric! Hello?" Brock walked around the corner and into the main room of the apartment. A male with a shock of rust-colored hair stood up from the couch to face him. Brock stuttered mid-step at the sight of the unexpected guest, but caught himself and continued into the room. With a determined stride, he walked over into the sitting area and faced the male who used to be like a brother to him.

"Lucian. I didn't know you were going to be here."

Lucian spread his arms wide, his bicep muscles

stretching the thin cotton of the solid green long-sleeved shirt he was wearing. "When my alpha tells me tae be here, I show up. Why are ye here?" The cocky smirk on his face belied the deference in his words.

Brock sat down in the chair catty-corner to the couch, and after a brief pause, Lucian sat again as well. "I wanted to ask Cedric something about the meeting we went to earlier," Brock told him.

Lucian rolled his eyes. "Aye. The daft Fae prince. He calls, and Cedric goes running."

Brock studied the male in front of him, trying to see some remnant that was left of the friend he'd grown up with. Anything. But there was nothing there that resembled the male he'd called "brother." "What happened to you, Lu?" he burst out. "Where's the guy who used to raid the food stores and fish all day with me? The guy who was like my own brother." He scooted forward to the edge of his seat. "We used to hide out in that fort by the loch so we wouldn't have to do our chores. We spent so much time there it was like our home away from home. Even stayed there on our own after our families were killed." A thread of desperation entered his voice. "We fought for our places in the new pack together! Do you remember?"

Cold, stormy gray eyes nailed Brock to his chair. "Of course I remember. I'm no' an eejit, Brock. I remember everything. Like yer Scottish accent. If we're playing the game of twenty questions...what happened tae that?"

"I haven't lived in Scotland for a long time," Brock answered.

"Me either," Lucian shot back. "But I still speak with the brogue of my homeland. As should ye."

Brock scrubbed his face with his hands. This was going nowhere fast. He was done making pleasant conversation. Things needed to be said while they were alone together, and he was going to say them. Ever since he'd joined the pack just a few weeks before, Lucian had always found one reason or another not to be caught alone with him. "I was *banned* from our homeland, Lucian. Because I was stupid enough to cover for your ungrateful ass and took the fall for you when you broke an unforgivable rule of the pack."

Lucian pressed his lips together and looked away.

Brock barked out a disdainful laugh. He couldn't help it. Lucian was acting like a child...still. Even after all these years. Back then, they'd been the equivalent of human teenagers, and this type of behavior was to be expected. But now?

Unable to sit still any longer, Brock pushed himself up off the chair and paced over to the large window to stare out at the view. A forest of towering evergreen trees that were common to the Pacific Northwest greeted him on the other side of the glass. He had to admit, the Seattle pack had chosen a good location for their den. Close to their friends in the city, yet at the edge of town near open land where they could run free under the light of the full moon whenever the urge struck them.

"What do you want me to say, Brock?" Lucian spoke from the couch behind him.

Brock spun around so fast he had to push his long hair back off his face. "What do I want you tae say? How aboot 'Thank you, Brock. Thank you for destroying your life tae save mine.' How aboot something like that, ye arsehole!"

Lucian smiled. "Ah. There it is, my friend. I ken ye didn't lose yer roots completely, no matter how ye try tae act like it."

Brock barreled across the room and grabbed Lucian by the front of his shirt. He hauled him to his feet and a few inches higher so he could look him in the eye. "The way I talk should really be the least of yer worries right now. *Friend.*"

Gray eyes stared coldly into his own for long moments, but he didn't try to get away. Instead, Lucian's upper lip lifted on a sneer. "The way I see it, yer life isnae verra bad at the moment. I think I did ye a favor by letting ye take the blame."

Un-fucking-believable.

Brock opened his hand and released Lucian, adding a little shove in there for good measure. He had no words. He could think of nothing to say that would break through the icy exterior that now surrounded his oldest friend. He turned away. He couldn't even look at him anymore.

Lucian exhaled heavily behind him. "I'm sorry. I'm being fair crabbit, and ye dinna deserve that from me. I do appreciate what ye did, Brock. Of course I do," he gritted out. "How could ye ever think otherwise? Ye probably saved my sorry arse from a verra unpleasant death. I'm no' as strong as ye are. I ken that. I had no doubt that ye would survive the banning ritual. I would no' have. So...thank ye."

Turning back to face him, Brock was greeted with the first sincere expression he'd seen on Lucian since he'd found out all those weeks ago that he was here. He took a deep breath, releasing the tension in his muscles. "You're welcome," he said simply.

Clearing his throat, Lucian sat back down and Brock resumed his seat in the armchair. "So, what have ye been up tae all of this time?" Lucian asked a bit awkwardly. "Other than rescuing damsels in distress, of course," he said, referring to Brock's well-known adventures with his now mate.

Brock gave a shrug. "I moved around a lot. Stayed under the radar."

"That's no' exactly what I heard," Lucian said. "I heard ye were a great hunter of demons when they found ye, or some such nonsense. Is that true?"

"Yes and no," Brock answered vaguely. To be exact, he'd been hunting demon-possessed vampires when he'd run across this pack. That was also how he'd met Heather. Her best friend, Grace, had a run-in with the things he'd been following. She'd managed to escape them, and he'd followed her to Heather's apartment and graciously offered his help to the ladies. It was a good thing too. He'd gotten them out of there in the nick of time.

He vividly remembered the first time he'd ever seen Heather. She'd opened the door in yoga pants and a tank top, all curves and soft woman, and smiled up at him with a naughty glint in her eye right before her friend had slammed the door in his face. He'd lost his heart that day, though he hadn't realized it until a few weeks later.

A coaster from the end table hit him in the chest and he realized Lucian had said something. He grinned at the scowl on Lucian's face. "Sorry. Just thinking about something. What did you say?"

"I was waiting for ye tae embellish on yer answer," he said.

"Not much else to tell. I just happened upon some weird shit one day and started following some dudes."

"Vampires."

Brock nodded. "Possessed vampires, it turns out."

"What the bloody hell would a demon want tae possess a vampire for?" Lucian asked.

"Don't know. I didn't stick around long enough to find out. I just got Heather and her friend Grace out of there safely, and then shortly after I got taken in by this pack."

Lucian averted his eyes and started picking invisible lint off his pant leg. "I'm surprised ye accepted their invitation after finding out that I was part of that pack."

Leaning forward in his chair, Brock told him sincerely, "You're my brother, Lucian. My family. You may be a pain in my ass, but no matter what has happened in the past, that fact hasn't changed."

Lucian fell silent for a long time, and Brock could see him struggling with what he was feeling, though he was trying hard not to show it. Finally, he looked up, his gray eyes wet with tears that made them look more like shiny steel. "I have no' been a good friend tae ye, Brock. Nor tae anyone. I dinna deserve yer kindness. I just…" He paused, visibly struggling to find the words. "I lost everyone and everything that ever mattered tae me, and I'm no' just talking about our families. I lost the female I loved. I lost my brother. I left my pack because I could no' handle being around the place where I had found such happiness." He paused. "I lost everything."

Brock was confused. He'd seen Sara and her child—

Lucian's child—at Prince Nada's house when he'd called them there to question what had happened with her and the old pack before giving his blessing for Heather to be with him. "I don't understand. I thought me taking the fall would give you and Sara time to figure out how to release her from her mating so you could be together."

"Aye. It should have. But it didn't. She changed her mind. She didnae want tae be with me."

Brock scrubbed at his face again, completely confused. "But she had your child…"

Lucian scoffed. "That is no' my child," he growled out with such a look of disgust that Brock didn't dare argue with him.

Could he be wrong? He could've sworn the little boy was the spitting image of Lucian as a young pup. "I don't understand."

It was Lucian's turn to get up and pace the floors. "Sara is no' the female I thought she was. After the trial and yer banishment, she came tae me and told me that she didnae want tae be with me, that she was going tae stay with her mate. A short time later, she was with child. It's no' my child. It's his."

Brock wasn't convinced. He'd seen the child with his own eyes. He'd bet anything that there was more going on here than Lucian realized. But he didn't want to argue again. Not when he was just starting to feel like there was a chance of getting his old friend back. So he simply said, "I'm sorry. I wish that had turned out differently for you."

"Aye. Me too," Lucian said. He stopped his pacing and came to sit near Brock. "I am verra happy tae see ye." For a split second, a flash of real pain shone from his stormy eyes. "I've felt so alone after ye left…"

Brock leapt from his seat and grabbed Lucian up in a giant bear hug. "You're not alone, my brother. You'll never be alone as long as I am alive."

A sob escaped Lucian and his arms tightened around Brock. "I've missed ye so verra much. I've been such a bloody arse. I should no' have let ye do what ye did."

"I was protecting ye," Brock told him, his brogue slipping out with all of the emotion coursing through him. "And I would do it again in a heartbeat for ye."

It was quite a while before they released each other and both wiped the moisture from their faces.

Cedric walked in at that moment. He eyeballed the two of them, noting Brock's hand on Lucian's shoulder and the suspicious sniffing that was going on. With a satisfied nod, he said, "So I see ye two have made up. Thank the gods." To Brock he said, "Maybe ye can help me with this one. He has demons, he does."

Brock smiled and slapped Lucian on the shoulder. "Dinna fash yerself," he told Cedric with a smile. "I got this one. He'll be okay."

Cedric raised an eyebrow at Lucian, and Lucian bowed his head. "I'm sorry for being such a bastard. Ye didnae have tae take me in, and ye did. I do appreciate that, and will try tae make ye proud from now on."

"Ach. That ye will," Cedric told him. Then he grabbed a bottle of beer for each of them from the fridge and plopped down on the couch.

The front door crashed open. "Do I smell beer? Ach. And ye didnae invite me?" Duncan strode into the room, not bothering to close the door behind him. Helping himself to a beer, he crowded in next to Lucian and sank down onto the couch. He threw one arm around Lucian's shoulder and grinned at Brock. "He loves me," he told him, indicating Lucian.

Rolling his eyes, Lucian took the drink Cedric offered him and handed one to Brock.

"So!" Cedric said. "Let's talk aboot Faeries." With a toast at Brock, he took a swig of his beer.

CHAPTER 18

One week later, Marc once again found himself amongst a large group of no less than a hundred redneck werewolves. Only this time, he was inside the arena with the others who were waiting to compete.

He'd only caught a few rare glimpses of Bronaugh during all that time, and he'd never gotten close enough to warn her about what was going to happen. He dreaded seeing the look that would surely be on her face when she saw him here, doing what he was about to do. Maybe he'd luck out and they wouldn't pick her for any of that day's events. Then he scoffed to himself. He wouldn't be so lucky. She was new meat. They'd use her until the crowd got tired of her. And if they were as enthusiastic as they were last week, it was going to take a long time for them to be tired of a new female in the game.

Especially one as bonnie and stubborn and brave as his Bronaugh.

His thoughts were interrupted by Stone's grinning face

popping up in front of his own. "Come on, Seattle. We're up first!"

"Aye. I'm coming, I'm coming." Marc stood up and tried to appear enthusiastic as he followed Stone to the end of the arena where the dirt bikes were waiting for their riders. "What event is it going tae be again?"

"Barrel racing, man! Keegan is starting today off with a bang. You know what you gotta do, right?" Stone straddled the bike and sat waiting for Marc to answer before starting it.

Barrel racing? Marc racked his brain for what he'd been told about this one, but his mind had gone completely blank. "Remind me again what this one is aboot?"

Stone kick-started the bike and revved the engine a few times before shouting over the sound of the motor, "You just have to remember two things. First, stay the fuck away from the soul suckers. Always keep one of the others between you and them as you weave in and out."

Marc frowned. "But what aboot them? The lasses?"

"What about them?" The playful smile fell from Stone's face. "They're nothing but Fae, man. Fae chicks aren't good for anything except sucking my cock and using for bait."

Marc was shocked into silence at the vehemence in his voice. But just like that, it was gone and the fun-loving smile was back. It happened so quickly he half wondered if he'd imagined it.

"Second, don't fall off your bike. Or you're completely screwed, man. And not in a good way! But if you do, duck down and try to stay out of sight." With that last parting advice, he eased open the throttle and rode out into the center of the arena to the cheer of the crowd. Standing up as he took the dirt ramps, he waved to the crowd before dropping back down onto the seat and popping the front tire up off the ground a few times.

Marc started his bike and headed to the center of the ring to join him. He put his feet on the ground and let the bike idle while Stone showed off for the crowd.

He tried to recall the two Dark Fae that had been in the cell next to Bronaugh. But honestly, he could remember little about them, or the others in the opposite cell, for that matter. His entire being had been honed in on Bronaugh and how Jace had been humiliating her. *Ach.* He could feel his temper rising just thinking about it. All week long he'd dodged that eejit, afraid of what he'd do to him if he happened to run into him in a darkened hallway.

Stone pulled up alongside him and gave him a thumbs up just as the crowd started stomping their feet in the stands. An air horn sounded, and the door to the bucking chute was thrown wide. Bronaugh's cousin with the spiky black hair came out first, strolling into the arena like she owned the place, no coercion necessary. Completely ignoring the crowd, she leaned her back up against the iron cage, crossed her ankles, and looked at her nails. An older female with long dark hair came out next: the aunt. She joined the other female, but kept a healthy distance from the iron cage. Chin raised high, her eyes shot daggers at the jeering crowd.

There was a commotion inside the bucking chute, and the people nearest it rose to their feet to see what was going on. A few of the males started whistling and catcalling, and Marc caught a whiff of burning flowers.

Meadowsweet after the rain.

Bronaugh was launched out of the chute to the thrill of the onlookers. She landed hard on her hands and knees in the dirt of the arena. Jace sauntered out after her, a cattle prod hanging loosely in his hand. As they all watched, he touched the tip of the prod to the bare skin of her waist where her shirt had ridden up. Bronaugh's body arched forward, her arms and legs flailing out from the shock. She landed flat on her face.

A deep growl ripped through Marc, loud enough that Stone heard him over the sound of the bikes and turned to give him a bemused look. Before he realized what he was doing, Marc opened the throttle wide and his bike caught air as he shot over a ramp to where she was lying. He came to a skidding halt between her and the cattle prod. Not caring if he got shocked or not, he ripped it from Jace's hand and threw it over his head and back into the bucking chute. "Enough," he roared.

Jace just smiled with a knowing look in his eyes, and within the now deafening silence of the crowd, Marc realized he hadn't fooled him at all the day Bronaugh had been caught.

Glancing down at the female in question, he also wasn't surprised at the hatred that spewed from her colored eyes as she looked up at him on the dirt bike, yet it still took him aback. He reached down to help her up, but she slapped his hand away and stumbled to her feet. An aching hole ripped open in his chest when she spat on the ground between them and staggered over to her aunt and cousin.

"Guess the lady doesn't feel the same," Jace mocked from behind him.

Marc turned to tell him where he could shove it, but Jace was already sauntering back to the bucking chute with the fookin' cattle prod over his shoulder. Marc swung one leg over the bike, meaning to go over and check on Bronaugh, but she threw a hand up in front of her and growled, "Don't."

The murmurs of the crowd suddenly rose to a roar. Marc looked just in time to see Jace jump up over the railing and out of the way, barely escaping before the two Dark Fae appeared from the tunnel that led to their cells. He slammed the gate shut to keep them in the chute while Keegan worked up the crowd to an even higher frenzy.

"Fook me," Marc murmured. Starting the bike, he noticed the females were heading to the other side of the arena, Bronaugh being supported in the middle by the other two. Stone buzzed around them on his bike, laughing as they kept changing direction, and catching air right over the top of them.

Marc slowly released the clutch and headed toward the others inside the arena. Maybe if he could distract the soul suckers, he could keep them away from Bronaugh and her family until the wolves got bored with this game and started another one.

An air horn blasted, and Jace leaned over the fence and opened the gate. The males spotted Marc immediately, sitting right there revving his bike as he was, and charged him. He let them get within a few feet of him before he skidded out and rode forward, away from Bronaugh and her family. A quick look over his shoulder showed that they still followed, splitting off to come up on either side of him. In response, Marc slammed on the brakes and spun the bike completely around and rode right back through the middle of them. When he reached the opposite end of the arena, he spun around again.

One of the soul suckers was still on his trail, but the other one had spotted Stone…and the females. As Marc watched that one, the other male suddenly appeared on the opposite side of the arena no more than twenty feet from Bronaugh.

His jaw hit the floor. The fookers could teleport.

A dark haze slid down over his eyes as Bronaugh froze where she was and pushed her family behind her. Then he couldn't see her as Stone skidded to a halt in front of him and screamed in his face, "Move, man! Move!" He took off and Marc just had time to do the same before the other soul sucker was on him. Stone swung around to the left while Marc headed to the right. Gaining speed with every second, he hit the ramp closest to them, flying between the females and the dark one. Landing right next to the soul sucker, he put one foot on the ground and rode in fast tight circles around him, containing him where he was while staying out of reach.

Perhaps he'd been a bit too cocky with that plan of action.

Throwing out an arm, the soul sucker clotheslined him, knocking him right off the back of the bike. In a heartbeat the thing was on top of him with its hands around his throat.

Marc's eyes bugged out of his head as the thing smiled a gruesome smile, and then opened its mouth wide and leaned closer. He struggled to throw it off him, but even with his superior height and weight, he couldn't shake the thing. It was stuck to him like a leech, and felt as heavy as a tombstone on top of him. The world around him began to fade in and out, and he looked about wildly for Bronaugh. He just needed to see her one more time, to make sure she was all right.

A burst of electric energy suddenly shot through Marc, and the thing went flying off him and clear across the arena to slam into the cage on the other side. Struggling to his knees, he saw Stone playing cat and mouse with its friend out of the corner of his eye. He fought to breathe, to get his heart pumping and the buzzing out of his head. A slap on the back seemed to get things working properly again, and he sucked in a grateful gulp of air.

"I had to shock you with a jolt of Faerie juice or that asshole would be the proud owner of your soul right about now. It's the only way to get them off once they're latched on."

He looked up to see Bronaugh leaning over him. She was dirty and angry and the most bonnie thing he'd ever seen in his life. "Thank ye, lass," he told her sincerely.

"Next time you're on your own, asshole." Turning on her heel, she went back to stand guard in front of her family. She'd only just reached them when the soul sucker Stone had been playing with appeared behind her and grabbed her by the hair. Yanking her head to the side, it sank its teeth into the meat between her neck and shoulder.

Bronaugh screamed.

The crowd cheered and stomped their feet at the sight of blood.

And Marc lost all control.

Bones snapping and muscle ripping, his roar joined her voice as he turned. It happened so fast he barely felt the pain as his body contorted and reformed into a new shape. Rearing up in full wolf form, he clamped his jaws down on the thing's head and tore it away from her. Tossing it aside, he barely had time to register that Bronaugh had fallen to her knees as her aunt and cousin crowded around her before all hell broke loose.

Keegan's voice boomed from the speakers as the Texas pack ran out into the arena with chains and cattle prods. Before they could reach him, the soul sucker he had pulled off Bronaugh pounced on him and sank its teeth into his shoulder. Marc threw his head back and howled. Rearing up onto his hind legs, he threw his body backward and landed on the thing, hoping it would let go. It worked, and he rolled away and leaped to his feet.

Stone flew by them on his bike. Swinging a chain like a lasso, he roped the soul sucker and pulled it along behind him, laughing like a maniac. A few of the other males ran over to the females and started corralling them back to the bucking chute, unnecessarily shocking them every few steps as they tried to help Bronaugh keep up. Before Marc could go to her, he was cut off by more of the pack.

Pacing restlessly back and forth, he spotted Keegan watching him from where he stood near the chute with his microphone. The alpha had an unreadable look on his face. Eyes still on Marc, he lifted the microphone to his mouth and tried to quiet the crowd enough to hear him tell them to come back the next day for more fun and games, then he indicated to Marc to follow the others out of the arena.

Still in wolf form, Marc huffed out a frustrated breath through his nose. He wanted to go check on Bronaugh, but disobeying a direct order from the alpha was not an option. Not even one as small as telling him to leave the arena. So he trotted over to the door in the iron cage where Corrina waited to unlock it and let the competitors out. She wouldn't look at him as she took off the padlock and unwound the iron chains. Opening the door just enough for him to get out, she immediately closed it behind him and started to wrap the chains around the bars again.

Pausing for a moment, Marc looked back to make sure all the Fae females were out of the arena before he left and went back to the house to change back and find some clothes. By the time the others returned, he was dressed and sitting at the kitchen table with a glass of whiskey in front of him.

Keegan sent the others about their business, and then fetched himself a glass and sat down across from him. "So, you wanna tell me what that was all about?"

"Which part, exactly, do ye want tae ken?" Marc asked with a sigh.

"How about what the hell is going on between you and the new girl. And how you do know her?"

Marc swished his whiskey around in his glass and then took a swig. "No' a thing," he deadpanned. "I never met her before. I just dinna like seeing females being treated like cattle, or worse."

"You expect me to believe that?" Keegan asked.

"Aye. I do." Marc kept his gaze steady as he stared down the alpha across the width of the table. "Where I come from, the time I come from, that's how it is. There's nothing 'going on' with her. I would no' lie tae ye aboot that." And he wasn't lying. Not now. There had been something going on with them, but not anymore. "I apologize for losing control in there. It caught me by surprise just as much as ye. I'm no' used tae this kind o' thing."

Keegan studied him silently for long, uncomfortable minutes, his face giving absolutely nothing away. Then, still without saying anything, he shot down his whiskey and slammed the glass back down onto the table. Getting up, he refilled it and offered Marc some more before sitting back down again and beginning to speak. "I can understand that this is unusual to you. And I also understand that sometimes our wolf gets the better of us." His tone was a bit strange as he said this, but he didn't give Marc time to question it. "But one of the rules is that we stay in human form when competing. Makes it a bit more challenging. I guess we shouldn't have thrown you in there like we did. I kept telling Jace. But he insisted that you'd get a real kick out of it. I apologize for putting you in that position."

His apology took Marc a bit by surprise, but he gave him a nod. "Your apology is no' needed or necessary. I could have said no, but I didnae."

Keegan grinned as Corrina appeared in the doorway. "Yeah, well. Let's take our drinks and this argument out to the front porch before Corrina has us helping with dinner."

Corrina smiled. "I could always use the help, but I want the meal to actually be edible."

Keegan gave her a wink and Marc went with him out to the porch to finish their drinks and listen to the singing of the cicadas.

CHAPTER 19

This time Bronaugh was thrown into the same cell as Bitsy and Aunt Nancy. She was so angry she didn't even protest the rough treatment they received from the two youngest wolves. The idiots were trying to feel more important than they were.

Damn Marc and his need to be gallant and "protect" her! The two crazies he was trying to save her from were even now smashing their foreheads into the iron bars of their cell like the psychotic addicts they were. She wrinkled her nose, noticing for the first time they stunk like rotten wood. But they were her kind. She could've handled them.

She'd had a plan to get them all out, something those egotistical wolves would never have expected. As soon as she'd gotten to the bucking chute she'd remembered: there was a door leading out of the arena for the wolves to get in and out. She'd seen it when she'd followed Marc inside the week before, but it hadn't really registered at the time, what with her cousin being dragged around by the throat, and all.

And the only thing keeping it closed was a padlock—a padlock that was not made of iron.

All she'd needed to do was maneuver herself and her family near the door and she could've zapped that lock open and gotten them out of there before those stupid dogs realized what had happened. Fae people could move as fast, if not faster, than vampires. So fast in fact, many believed they could teleport.

How she would've gotten out the double doors of the barn? Yeah, that part she hadn't figured out yet. But something would've come to her when she'd gotten there. At least they'd had a chance.

A fresh flood of anger had her cursing under her breath. They'd had a chance until *he* had insisted on protecting her. He'd screwed everything up. Again. Now she'd have to wait until they were all in the arena at the same time again, and from what Bitsy had told her, it didn't happen very often. As her cousin had said, "Only when that asshat alpha wants to liven things up a bit."

"Bro, you're really bleeding." Bitsy knelt behind her and slid Bronaugh's shirt off her shoulder so she could look at the bite there.

"I'm fine, Bits." She tried to pull her shirt back up, but her aunt slapped her hand away and leaned around her daughter to see.

"You're not fine," she said. "It's a bad bite, Bronaugh. And with your arm barely healed enough to be out of the sling…we need to clean that out." She looked around the cell like she hoped medical supplies would suddenly appear out of thin air.

"There's nothing we can do about it, Aunt Nancy. So stop worrying. I'll be fine." She managed to pull her shirt back up this time and shoo their hands away. When she looked up, the two of them were kneeling in front of her with identical looks of worry on their faces. "What?"

Bitsy looked at her mom and then back at Bronaugh. "Is that bite…is it going to turn you?"

"Bitsy!" her aunt scolded.

"Mom, it needs to be asked. I love Bronaugh just as much as you do, but we need to be prepared." She turned back to Bronaugh. "Well? Am I going to have to take you out, cuz?" Her blasé tone belied the horror that was reflected in her eyes at the thought. "Because I will if I have to."

She couldn't lie to them. "I don't know."

Her aunt kind of collapsed over onto her butt to sit on the dirt floor, but her cousin just nodded stoically. "I'll take care of it if I need to, Bro. I won't let you hurt us or anyone else."

Bronaugh felt tears fill her eyes as the last remnants of her anger at Marc dissipated in the face of this new threat. "Thank you."

Her cousin nodded and ripped off another piece of her own shirt. Wadding it up, she exposed Bronaugh's wound again and pressed it there to try to stop the bleeding.

Hours went by as her aunt and cousin talked about nonsensical things, obviously trying to try to keep her mind off what might happen. But her bite wound was the last thing Bronaugh was thinking about. It would do no good to worry anyway. What was done was done. She'd either turn, or she wouldn't. And she honestly didn't know if the…disease, or whatever you wanted to call it, the dark ones suffered from could be transmitted that way or not. She'd been young when it had started to get out of control, and she'd stayed in hiding for so long she hadn't had the chance to know any others of her tribe who had managed to escape the wolves' roundup. And by the time she had, they'd already gone to the wayside, like the two who were here pacing their cell and muttering to themselves.

Occasionally, the one that bit her would zero in on her and rush the cell bars that divided them, lick its lips, and press its face between the bars so hard it left bruises. It really freaked her out. She thought they were soul suckers, not flesh eaters.

Finally, the door to the hall opened and one of the young wolves appeared. Bronaugh thought he was there to bring them their dinner, such as it was. But his hands were empty as he held open the door for someone else.

Bronaugh staggered to her feet. She knew who it was even before he showed himself. She didn't know how, but she did. And she hated that he had to show up now and was seeing her like this, all dirty and bloody and gross. And that made her even more pissed off at him. Her anger returned in a rush. Unless he was finally going to grow a pair and stand up to his friends to get them released from this circus, she wanted nothing to do with him.

"I'll be braw, Zach. Ye can wait for me outside, if ye dinna mind," she heard Marc tell the young wolf. He didn't look at her, but he had a paper bag in each arm. She hoped at least one of them held some kind of food. She was starving.

"Actually," Zach answered. "If you're going to be here for a little while, I could use a break for a minute." His meaning became clear as he bounced from foot to foot.

"Aye. Go on with ye. I'll be fine till ye get back," Marc repeated. He looked over his shoulder then and right at her. "No' much they can do while in there, is there?"

"No. It's perfectly safe. I'll be back in a few minutes." The young wolf took off, leaving Marc alone in the room with them.

He watched Zach leave and then closed and locked the door firmly behind him before he rushed over to her cell and dropped the bags on the ground. "Ach. How are ye, lass?" He went for the bolt on the cell door, but there was no way he could open it without a key. His concerned gaze locked in on her for a moment before he seemed to notice there were two others in the cell with her. "Are ye both all right?" he asked them.

"We're just fine, hot stuff. How about yourself?" Bitsy answered sarcastically.

Aunt Nancy didn't bother to answer.

He gave them both a small smile and turned back to Bronaugh, completely ignoring the two males who were throwing themselves around their cell for his benefit. "Bronaugh, lass. How is yer shoulder?"

She narrowed her eyes at him while she tried to decide whether she should waste her breath by speaking to him or not. Having come to a decision, she walked over to stand in front of him. He scowled as he took in her appearance. *Good.* Let him be disgusted by her. She didn't care. "What do you want, Marc?"

Her acidic tone might as well have been a slap, and he recoiled as if struck. "Bronaugh, lass—"

"Don't 'Bronaugh, lass' me." Her efforts at imitating his brogue were pretty bad, but she was too pissed off to care. "Unless you're here to break us out, you can just take your happy little ass right back to the house and your friends and your food and your nice warm bed. Leave us alone."

"Bronaugh—"

"No!" she spit up at him. "You ruined everything, Marc! I had a plan. I was going to get us out of that cage. But you had to play the frickin' hero…"

"Oh, aye. And then what? Say ye did get ye and yer family out. How were ye going tae get out o' the barn? How would ye get yerselves away from the hundred were-wolves or so that were there?"

"I would've thought of something," she insisted stubbornly. "I always do."

He laughed. "Ye would've thought of something? Of something? When were ye going tae do that? Before or after the wolves had torn ye apart?"

Crossing her arms, she glared at him. "Are you here to get us out, or not?"

Stabbing his hands into his dark hair, he paced away from the cell and back again. He dropped his arms and his shoulders slumped forward. "I cannae do that, lass."

"Because it will ruin your reputation?" she sneered.

He bent down until they were face to face. "Others are depending on me, lass. Ye ken that."

"Yeah, I 'ken' that," she answered sarcastically. Then she took a long look at his handsome face, so close to her own, and turned her back to him to hide her frustrated tears.

She heard his swift inhalation before she felt his hands on her. Reaching through the bars, he held her there by one shoulder while he moved her shirt aside and probed her wound with the other. She tried to pull away, but his large hand had a firm grip on her.

"Stop being a child, and let me see how hurt ye are," he ordered.

She stiffened at the reprimand. Numerous retorts came to mind, all of which would put him firmly in his place and then some, but she couldn't decide on one so she clamped her jaw shut and stood there.

"Let him help you, Bronaugh," Aunt Nancy scolded.

She looked to her cousin, but there was no help there either. With a sigh, she crossed her arms in front of her and planted her feet. She tried not to show that he was hurting her, but she couldn't help it. Every time he wiped or poked at the wound, her shoulder jerked away and she winced.

"I'm sorry, lass."

"Whatever. Just do what you need to do and leave."

Her aunt approached with a good dose of caution. "May I ask why you're helping her? I don't recall seeing you here before. Does Keegan—"

"You mean Asshat," her cousin interjected.

Her mother ignored her. "Does Keegan know you're here?"

Marc's voice was kind as he answered her aunt. "Aye.

He does. Although he does no' ken that we know each other. I'll need ye both tae keep that tae yerselves."

Aunt Nancy nodded. "Of course we will. Thank you. For doing this."

Bronaugh rolled her eyes and Bitsy winked at her with a smirk on her elfin face.

His hands left her and she heard him rummaging around in one of the bags behind her. "Bronaugh, would ye back up a wee bit? Please," he added.

Her aunt gave Bronaugh her best intimidating look, and with another eye roll, Bronaugh did as he asked.

"This might burn a wee bit. I'm sorry, lass. But this bite really needs tae be cleaned." He sounded genuinely filled with remorse for what he was about to do.

"Just do it," she told him, then instantly regretted her words as a trail of fire burned its way down her shoulder. His large hand clamped down on her again to hold her there when she went to flinch away, and she had no choice but to grind her teeth and take it.

"Hang in there, lass. Almost done."

"I'm fine," she squeaked.

His deep, sexy chuckle almost, but not quite, distracted her from the fact that his thumb was rubbing circles on her bare skin as he swabbed at the bite wound. She felt him press a cloth to the wound, then he taped it all around.

"There. That should do it. Try tae keep it clean, if ye can."

As soon as she could, she pulled away and walked all the way over to the other side of the cell before she turned to face him again. She needed to put some distance between them, for her own sanity.

Aunt Nancy looked at her expectantly, obviously waiting for Bronaugh to thank him. But Bronaugh glared back at her until she just shook her head. "Thank you for helping my Bronaugh," her aunt told Marc sincerely.

"O' course," he responded. Then to Bronaugh he asked, "This bite. Will it…is there a chance…"

She stared at him with a stone-cold expression. So that's what he was really worried about? Let him wonder. There was no way she could mollify him anyway. Not about this, because she honestly didn't know.

He opened his mouth like he wanted to say more, but then he just cleared his throat instead. "I have food for ye also…"

"Do you have a key to our cell?" Bronaugh asked him.

He paused for just a second, then handed Aunt Nancy a wrapped loaf of bread, what looked like some type of meat, and enough water for all of them. Then he pulled two more bottles out of his bag and threw that and another chunk of meat into the other cell. The Dark Fae stopped their pacing and fell upon the offering like they hadn't eaten in weeks.

"I'll try to come by again soon and check on all of you," he said, looking at her aunt. Then he folded up the bags and made to leave.

He was just going to walk away and ignore her? Oh, she didn't think so.

"So you're just going to leave us here again?" she asked loudly. "Why am I not surprised."

He stopped but didn't turn around.

"Just leave us here to be the entertainment for your sick friends," she continued to taunt. "To be treated like animals. No. Scratch that. Even animals should be treated better than this."

He spun around. Two long strides brought him back to the bars. Her aunt backed away, and if Bronaugh wasn't so angry herself, she might have also. The look on his face was enough to make anyone cower. But he didn't scare her. What was he going to do? Open the door? Good.

"I can NO' let ye out, Bronaugh. I can NO'. And it is fookin' killing me tae leave ye here! How can ye believe otherwise?"

She strode up to him, even gripping the bars in her frustration. *Iron be damned.* "Then let us out, Marc. Please! If you care about me at all…help us. We can get away, all of us…"

But he was already shaking his head. "I can no'." His features twisted with frustration. With her? Or with himself? "I can *no'*. I promised my alpha that I would get this deal done. I can no' go back on that promise. We need this pack on our side tae help us get rid of those—" He cut himself off before he could say it, but she caught the way he looked at the disturbing creatures in the next cell.

"What?" she asked. "Go ahead, say it." When he clamped his lips shut, she finished for him. "Soul suckers? Dark Fae? Or do you have something worse that you call them? That you call me?"

"Ye are no' one o' them," he gritted out with another glance at the two males.

"Not yet," she answered. "But I will be though, right?

Someday. Isn't that what you told me? So you might as well leave me in here to rot."

Bitsy piped in then. "Uh, yeah. Well, I am NOT one of them, so would you just let me out, please?"

They both ignored her. Marc reached through the bars and cupped Bronaugh's face. "I will figure something out, lass. I promise. I need ye tae *trust* me. But right now I need tae leave ye here. Just a wee bit longer. I cannae chance them finding out that I care aboot ye. And I do care aboot ye, Bronaugh. But if they found out…we would no' make it out o' here alive. I have no doubts aboot that."

She saw how much it was hurting him. It matched the pounding blow of betrayal in her heart. But if he didn't have the balls to stand up to his own kind for her…well, then there was nothing here to save. And she was an idiot of the biggest kind to ever think, even for just a tiny little second, there ever was. "Goodbye, Marc. Best of luck with all your little doggie friends."

Pulling away from him, she returned to the back of the cell just as Zach came walking through the door. "Thanks, man." He looked between Marc and the cells. "You about done here?"

"Aye," Marc said after a moment. "I'm finished." Then he nodded at Bitsy and her mom and walked out the door.

Bronaugh waited until Zach checked the locks on their cells and was about to close the door behind him. "Oh, Zach? It's Zach, right?"

He stuck his head back in. "Yeah. That's right."

She smiled. "When you have a changing of the guard again, would you please tell Jace that I'd like to see him?"

"Bronaugh, what are you doing?" her aunt hissed.

She continued to smile sweetly at the young wolf.

He narrowed his eyes with suspicion, but agreed to her request. "Yeah, I'll tell him." Then he closed the door firmly behind him.

"Whatcha doin', cuz?" Bitsy asked.

Bronaugh took a deep breath and turned to her cousin and aunt. "Plan B."

Aunt Nancy stepped forward in alarm. "But Marc said he'd help us. He seemed sincere—"

Bronaugh cut her off. "We don't need him. He doesn't care about me, about us. He's not willing to do what it takes to get us out, Aunt Nancy. But I am."

CHAPTER 20

Marc lay in bed at the ranch house late that night going over and over the things Bronaugh had said to him. The guilt from his conscience was practically eating him alive, but he had told her the truth. He'd had to leave her there in that disgusting cell. There was nothing else he could do. Not at this time. Not yet.

She would just have to be patient and wait until he finished his business here, and then he would come back and break her out after Keegan and his pack thought he'd returned to Seattle. They would never put two and two together and realize it was him if he played his cards right. He'd talk to Cedric, and he and the rest of the Seattle pack would back up Marc's story if they did happen to suspect anything.

He'd already taken enough of a risk by talking Keegan into letting him take the Fae their food. The alcohol and bandages—he'd snuck those into the bag before he'd left the house.

Then why did he feel like complete shite?

Actually, he knew why he felt the way he did. It was true he didn't want to let her out. And it was true that it was because he didn't want to fuck up what he was supposed to be doing here. But that wasn't the only reason he wanted to keep her in that cell.

If he waited a few more days or so, however long this took, he would know for sure that she wasn't going to turn from that bite.

But what aboot the other females in there with her?

Rolling over onto his side, he punched the pillow into a better shape and closed his eyes. But all he saw was her feelings of betrayal reflected in her colorful eyes as she glared at him. There was nothing he could do. He had an assignment, and that was to butter up this pack and convince them to band together with other packs for a short time and a common purpose. To keep the Dark Fae from running amok in the world and taking out the entire human population, and possibly the canine one as well. It was so much more than just what was going on personally between him and his Fae lass. Why couldn't she understand that?

Did she truly believe he didn't care about her? Well, she was wrong. He did care about her crabbit little self, more than he wanted to admit. He just needed to not ruffle any more feathers here, get the agreement from Keegan, and get out of Texas. Then he would come back for her and her family, and they could talk at length and she would see why he'd had to leave her here. Temporarily. And she would be okay until he could get her out. She would understand.

She would.

What if she didn't?

Marc sat up and threw his bare legs over the side of the bed. Walking over to the window in his boxer briefs, he pulled the ruffled white curtain aside and looked out into the night. The full moon was high in the sky, illuminating the night. He could feel it pulling him. But contrary to popular belief, it didn't call his wolf until he couldn't control the change just because it was full. However it did call to that part of his nature that longed to go run free through the night under its soft light.

Movement below caught his attention. His second-floor window looked out over the back of the property, and so he had a clear view when he saw someone leave the large barn where Bronaugh and her family were being kept. Moonlight glinted off the bright strands of hair on the male's head, and Marc narrowed his eyes. *Jace.*

Slapping his hat against his thigh first, Jace stuck it on his head, effectively hiding his features. Assuming he'd had guard duty, Marc moved to the side so he wouldn't be spotted, and watched as the arrogant male sauntered across the yard toward the house. He'd only gone a few steps when he stopped to reach down and adjust himself in his tight jeans, and even from this distance Marc could see the raging hard-on the guy was sporting. Instant fear shot through Marc, making his blood run cold. He stiffened as his eyes went from the aroused werewolf in the yard to the barn and back again.

His immediate response was to throw open the window and pounce on the eejit from above, then pummel him into the ground. His hand was already on the latch before he realized what he was doing and stopped himself. Acting that way was the very thing that would give him away, and probably exactly what Jace would love to have happen. His suspicions were confirmed when Jace looked directly up at his window just before he passed out of sight beneath the roof of the back porch. He smiled and cupped himself when he spotted Marc watching him.

Aye. He'd been right. Jace was just trying to get a rise out of him. Well, he wouldn't give him the satisfaction. Marc raised his hand in greeting and smiled back, then went back to gazing at the moon. Beneath him, he could hear Jace stomp up the steps to the back porch and slam into the house.

Marc's smile broadened, but it fell from his face when his eyes went back to the barn. Maybe he should go check on the Fae lasses. The gods only knew what had gotten Jace into such a state, though he was hoping it was nothing but wishful thinking on his part.

But the more he thought about it, the more convinced he became that he was overreacting. Wannabe cowboy or not, Keegan didn't seem the type to put up with such behavior from his pack. Rodeo, yes. Raping helpless females? No.

Turning from the window, he got back into bed. Tomorrow, Keegan was hosting another rodeo. Marc would need his sleep if he was to have any hope of controlling his wolf this time.

* * *

BRONAUGH LAY on her side near the back of the cell as her aunt fussed around her and her cousin shouted obscenities at the wolf who had just left. Her "Plan B" hadn't gone exactly as she'd hoped.

Jace had shown up as requested, and Bronaugh had girded her loins and turned on the charm.

After closing the outer door behind him, he leaned one shoulder against the bars of her cell, just out of reach of the ill-fated males next door. He touched the brim of his hat to her aunt and cousin in a show of politeness, even though the smirk on his face ruined the effect he was trying to achieve. Then he focused on Bronaugh. "I got your message. What can I do for ya, girlie?"

She sidled up to him until she was well within arm's reach. "I was wondering if I could possibly get some soap and water to clean up, and maybe a change of clothes."

He ran his eyes over her torn shirt and the good dose of cleavage it revealed. Of course, she'd helped that tear along a little bit as soon as Marc had left. Jace took his sweet time admiring the sight before saying without raising his eyes, "Now why would I want to do that?"

Exactly what she'd been hoping he'd say. "Because I'll let you watch," she told him.

That got his attention. His blue eyes shot to her face. "Is that so?"

"Sounds like a fair offer to me," she replied with what she hoped was a sultry smile.

He chewed on the inside of his cheek as he backed away a few steps and let his eyes run over her entire body. Bronaugh held her breath as he took his time deciding. She was a bit plumper than most, but from her experience, werewolves normally seemed to appreciate that in a female.

"All right, spitfire. You got yourself a deal," he agreed.

"Bronaugh, don't do this!" Aunt Nancy pleaded. Bitsy shushed her.

"It's just a little soap and water," Bronaugh told her. "He can look all he wants to. I just can't stand being this dirty."

Jace gave her a wink. "I'll be right back."

As soon as he left, her aunt rushed over to her. "Bronaugh, this is the stupidest plan you've ever come up with."

"Shhh," she whispered, and touched her ear to remind her aunt that he could hear them. Putting her mouth to her aunt's ear, she said as quietly as she could manage. "I got this. I'm getting us out of here tonight. Just be ready." Then she nodded once at Bitsy. Her cousin nodded back. Bronaugh could always count on her to be up for taking a risk.

They heard Jace sending away whichever young wolf was guarding the doorway, and a few seconds later he walked in carrying a bucket and a man's large T-shirt. Setting them both down by the door to their cell, he indicated for all of them to move to the back. He stuck the key into the lock, and the door clanked open as he said, "The water's cold. I hope you don't mind."

Yeah, she knew exactly why he wanted the water to be cold. The perv. But all she said was, "Not a problem. I appreciate it."

Holding the door shut, he looked at each of them in

turn. "Let's not go trying anything stupid now ladies, all right?"

"What could we do?" Bitsy asked. "Overpower a were-wolf while inside a fucking iron cell?" She added just enough venom to her voice to make it believable.

Jace smiled at her. "But do feel free to make use of the soap and water yourself there, darlin'."

She smiled back at him, sickly sweet. "I'd rather be covered in my own excrement. But thanks."

"Your loss, honey." Reaching over, he grabbed one of the cattle prods off the shelf, then he swung open the door and stepped inside. He set the bucket down and took the soap out from inside the shirt and set it down next to it, keeping one eye on the occupants while he did so. Hanging the shirt over one of the bars, he pushed the door shut with one booted foot but didn't lock it again. Leaning back against it, he crossed his ankles casually. "All right, spitfire. Have at it."

Dammit. Bronaugh hadn't expected that he would stay in the cell with them while she stripped. She'd fully expected him to put the stuff inside and lock them in again. Then she would get him all riled up with her little strip-and-wash show, and either she'd lure him in mid-show or he'd be so distracted when he came in to retrieve the bucket that they could shove him over to the crazies. Or Bitsy could smash him over the head with that bucket. Whatever would work best at the time. Him being inside could make things quite a bit more risky.

But then again, maybe not. She was willing to take the chance to get them the hell out of there.

"Come on, little girl. A deal's a deal. I ain't got all night."

Giving her aunt a look of reassurance, Bronaugh gripped the bottom of her shirt and pulled it up and over her head. Then she kicked off her sneakers and undid her jeans and slid them down over her hips. She reached out a hand and he automatically put his out to steady her. Bending down, she pulled off one pant leg and then the other, making sure to give him a good view of her breasts barely contained in her skimpy bra. When she straightened, his eyes were still hungrily focused on her chest.

Ah, a boob man. She could work with that.

Still in her underwear and bra, she stepped over to the bucket, but stayed facing him. There was a cloth in there for her to wash with, and she picked it up and wrung it out, but not completely. Instead she let the drops of cold water run down the front of her as she wet her face, and felt her nipples pucker in response. Bending over again, she picked up the soap and lathered up the cloth, then started rubbing it over her arms and chest.

"Aren't you going to take off your bra?" he drawled.

Bronaugh gave him a look. She could care less if he saw her breasts, but she didn't want to give it to him too easily. "Well, since I don't have a clean one, I thought I'd wash that too."

He chuckled quietly. "Yeah. Take it off."

She lifted an eyebrow at his demanding tone, but then she shrugged and reached behind her to unhook it.

Jace swallowed hard as his eyes dropped to her hardened nipples clearly visible beneath the thin, wet material.

Sliding the straps down her arms, she imagined it was Marc she was stripping for, and they were back by the creek behind the house. At the last possible moment, she pulled the garment away from her skin and dropped it into the bucket of water, then dropped the cloth on top of it. With her hands, she rubbed the soapy water over her breasts as she washed herself, getting them good and clean.

"Good gods," Jace muttered.

Out of the corner of her eye, she saw her aunt stiffen with indignation and turn away. Uh oh, had she gone too far? But when she looked, he was still leaning against the bars, albeit with one hand now rubbing his obviously swollen manhood.

"Keep going, honey." His voice was strained.

She glanced at Bitsy, her bravado not quite what it was a few minutes ago, and her cousin gave her a small nod. She was ready. Bronaugh bent over to get the cloth again. A little quicker this time, she washed her belly and legs.

"The panties go too," he ordered.

Bronaugh stilled. Peeking up at his expression, she took a deep breath.

Yeah, okay. No big deal. It's not like no one has ever seen me naked before.

Without a word, she hooked her thumbs under the sides and stripped them off, dropping them into the bucket with her bra.

"Now touch yourself," he commanded.

"Whoa, wait a minute." Casually keeping up her sponge bath, she bent down and rinsed out the rag, then started rinsing herself off. A puddle of mud was forming at her feet, and she dug her toes into the mother earth, then moved out of it and closer to Jace. "I didn't promise a sex show, just a peep show."

He pushed away from the door. "You're gonna tease me like that and then not deliver? I don't think so, spitfire."

Aunt Nancy moved to stand between them. "Leave her alone!" Over her shoulder she told Bronaugh, "I told you this was a stupid idea."

Jace shoved her out of the way so hard she cried out when she hit the bars. Bitsy rushed over to her mom to check on her.

He continued to stalk Bronaugh. She stepped back, drawing him farther into the cell. Holding her hands straight out in front of her, she let her nervousness show. "Come on, this wasn't our deal." Out of the corner of her eye, she saw Bitsy and her mom tiptoe closer to the door. Her aunt slowly and carefully pushed it open, keeping a watchful eye on Jace. But he was so focused on Bronaugh's nude, soapy body that he didn't notice what they were doing, not even when the hinges creaked slightly. They stepped out of the cell and over to the cattle prods. Easing one each off the shelf, they snuck up behind Jace.

In the meantime, Bronaugh had her hands full trying to keep herself out of arm's reach without exposing what the other females were doing or getting too close to the dark ones who were reaching through the bars toward her. Before she knew it, she had backed herself into a corner. Literally.

Maybe she should've given this plan a little more thought.

"C'mon now," she told Jace. "This isn't what we agreed on."

"You agreed that I could watch you wash up," he said. "I don't recall you adding any stipulations as to what I could or couldn't do afterward." He raised the cattle prod he'd brought in with him and touched the underside of her breast with it.

Bronaugh stiffened, waiting for the shock, but it didn't come. Exhaling gratefully, she crossed her arms, hiding her breasts from him as she tried another tactic. "Seriously, I don't think your alpha will be real happy to hear that you were abusing his newest attraction."

"Ah, honey. You're gonna enjoy what I'm about to do to you. I really don't think 'abuse' is the right word for it." Pushing her arms aside with the prod, Jace captured her wrists in his free hand and lifted her arms above her head. Setting his weapon up against the bars, he started feeling her up, roughly slapping her breasts and pinching her nipples.

The males in the next cell suddenly began throwing themselves into the bars and Jace's head snapped around just as Bitsy stuck him in the back. He let out a yell as his body jerked up against Bronaugh. Bitsy hit him again. "Get out of there, cuz!"

But Bronaugh couldn't get away. The shocks of electricity shooting through him had tightened his grip on her wrists, and no matter how she twisted and turned he wouldn't let go. Bitsy hit him again and again. His roar of pain echoed through the room and his heavy body slammed her backbone into the bars behind her. She yelled over all the noise, "Bitsy, stop! He won't let go!"

Then she heard a popping sound. With horrified eyes, she looked up to find glowing blue eyes looking back at her. As she watched, he opened his mouth. Canine teeth that hadn't been there just a few seconds ago grew long before her eyes. Sharp claws dug into the tender skin of her wrists, and the bones of his face became more prominent.

"Oh, shit. Shit!" she yelled. Looking around him, she screamed at her aunt and cousin, "He's turning! Get out! Get out! Both of you! Lock the door!"

Bitsy dropped her prod and dove under his arm. Reaching up, she tried to get him to release his grip on Bronaugh's wrists. She managed to get one arm free. "Get him, Mom!"

Aunt Nancy jabbed him in the side with her prod, and miracle of miracles, it worked! He dropped his arm, falling to his hands and knees. His back bowed and arched, the material of his shirt ripping under the strain of the breaking bones and swollen muscles.

Bronaugh wasted no time scooting around him. Grabbing the shirt he'd brought her from where it hung over the bars, she ushered her family out of the cell and slammed the door. Frantically, she looked around. "The key. Where is the key?" As one, they looked at the partially changed werewolf inside the cell.

He shook his head and sat back on his heels, breathing hard. Pulling something out of his front pocket, he began to laugh, the sound strangely distorted. It was the key to their cell. Then the strange laughter stopped as he got his anger under control and began to jerk around, his body contorting back to his human form.

"Let's go," Bronaugh said as she yanked the shirt over her head. "Now," she told them when they didn't move. "Now! Come on!" She grabbed them both by an arm and they finally got moving. Running to the door, she fumbled with the latch.

"Bro, we need to go," her cousin said, her voice frantic.

Bronaugh glanced back over her shoulder to see that Jace was getting to his feet. Turning back to the door, she finally managed to undo the latch and yanked it open.

Stone stood blocking the doorway with his feet apart and his hands on the wall to either side, effectively impeding their escape. He smiled his big smile when he saw them there. "Ah now, come on. You ladies know I can't let you just up and leave here. It wouldn't be much of a show with nothing but those two yahoos to chase around, now would it?" He pushed into the room, forcing them to back up, and shut the door behind him. Glancing down at the forgotten cattle prod in her aunt's hand, he tsked at her. "What's a little thing like you doing with that?" Quick as a snake, he'd snagged it from her hand and tossed it across the room.

Bronaugh's mind spun as she frantically tried to think of a way to get them out of this. Another look over her shoulder told her Jace was now out of the cell and standing behind them. And he didn't look happy. There were no windows. No other way out except through the large werewolf standing in front of them.

She could zap him. But if she tried to take him out, Jace would be on them in a heartbeat with the damn prod he now had back in his hand. And if he got to her with that, it would counteract her own power and her secret would be out. Her aunt and cousin didn't have the abilities that she did as a Dark Fae. They were more susceptible to the iron sickness.

Before she could make a decision, the chance was taken away from her when a meaty fist came flying out of nowhere and clocked her in the jaw. Stone hit her so hard that her entire body spun around and she fell into her aunt, taking them both down to the floor. She scrambled to her feet and shook her head, rubbing her jaw and clearing her vision. When she could see again, she reached down to help her aunt up.

Stone grabbed Bitsy and pulled her back against him with one arm around her neck and the other holding her arms down at her sides. The ever-present grin fell from his face as he cupped the side of her head in one large palm. "Now let's all just behave ourselves and get back into our cell. Either of you try anything else, and I'll rip off her fucking head."

Aunt Nancy grabbed Bronaugh's arm. "Enough, Bronaugh. We tried. I'm not risking my daughter. We'll think of something else."

"Yeah, you do that," Jace said from behind them. Her aunt yelped and stumbled forward as he jabbed her with the prod. "Come on, momma. Get moving."

Bronaugh reached out and knocked it aside. "Don't fucking touch her with that thing!" she snarled up at him.

With one long stride he was in front of her and had her by the back of the neck. Yanking her face up to his, he growled, "You still owe me, sweetheart. I wouldn't push it." Pointing at her aunt with the prod, he ordered her back into the cell without taking his eyes from Bronaugh.

Bronaugh watched her go with tears of anger and frustration filling her eyes. Once she was inside and at the back of the cell, Stone walked Bitsy over and tossed her inside to join her mother.

Jace kicked the door shut, keeping Bronaugh with him. "Why don't you go on ahead," he told Stone. "Me and this little gal still have a few things to discuss."

Bronaugh's stomach clenched as he suddenly pulled her back into him and jabbed the cattle prod into her side as his other arm wrapped around her, one large hand settling over her breast. She looked frantically at her aunt and cousin, shaking her head slightly when Bitsy made to try to come help her. Her jaw throbbed and she thought she was going to be sick, but she wasn't about to let them pay the price for her bright—or not so bright—escape plan.

"Jace, man. You know I can't let you do that."

A thread of hope allowed her to breathe again. Although Jace outranked him, Bronaugh had never seen him seriously stand up to the strange hybrid.

Jace leaned down and nipped at her cheek. "Why not? She owes me." Bronaugh could feel his hard-on pressing against her ass. "She totally dick-teased me, man. And she's all nice and clean, thanks to me going out of my way to show her some kindness. Shame for all that effort to go to waste."

"Keegan will have your hide if you break her before we can do it in the rodeo."

"We can find him another toy."

Stone laughed. "Yeah, cuz these abominations are just running free all over for us to catch. We've brought in too much money from this gig to ruin it, man. And you know it. The pack's never been in such good shape."

Jace sighed, and Bronaugh felt another sliver of hope sneak in. But it was quickly crushed when he suddenly released her and shocked her with the cattle prod. Bronaugh grunted and fell to her hands and knees, her shirt riding up her bare ass. Before she could get up, he shocked her again and her body jerked forward. Gritting her teeth, she refused to scream. A smack on her bottom was followed by another shock, and try as she might, she couldn't swallow the yelp that escaped her.

"That's enough, Jace. Put her in the cell."

After a pregnant pause, Bronaugh was lifted by the back of her shirt and dragged over to the cell. Kicking open the door, he threw her toward the back. Then he grabbed the bucket and left, slamming the door behind him. He smiled at her as he took the key from his pocket and locked the cell door.

Bronaugh moaned as Aunt Nancy fussed around her and Bitsy shouted insults at the closed door.

Where the hell was her so-called champion when she fucking needed him?

CHAPTER 21

Marc stomped out the back door, down the porch steps and out into the hot Texas sun. He'd just spent the better part of the morning pleading his case to Keegan, with no luck at all. The male was convinced the threat of the Dark Fae returning to wipe out the population was just that—a threat and nothing more. The Fae Prince was a nut job, he said. And his little game with Brock and Heather, who was one of his own kind, for pity's sake, proved it.

The problem was, Heather *had* believed the prince, and she'd convinced Cedric that they needed to be ready. But no matter how many times Marc told Keegan that, he'd refused to believe it.

So Marc had tried a different tactic. He'd suggested putting an agreement in place that *if* something did happen and the Seattle pack got word the soul suckers were indeed escaping from their prison, the Texas pack would then agree to join with them at that time. This agreement could include all of the packs on their side of the country. If and when it was needed, they would bond together in a show of unity. The agreement would be something that could be handed down through the generations. If no war was going on, they could carry on separately, business as usual.

Marc thought it was a brilliant compromise, and he was certain Cedric would give the idea his blessing. But then Keegan had tossed out an idea of his own. One that, in his mind, trumped Marc's plan by a landslide.

"I have a better idea," he'd told Marc. "One even more binding than some lousy piece of paper."

"A better idea?" Marc was almost afraid to ask.

Keegan leaned back in his hard wooden chair. "I've seen the way Corrina acts around you," he said. "It's pretty out of character for her to be so flirty. I've never seen her like this. Not with any of us. She's taken quite a shine to you, Seattle."

Marc sat silently, giving away nothing of his thoughts.

"Cor's a fine looking female," Keegan continued. "She's a good fighter and would make a loyal mate. You could do a hell of lot worse." He leaned forward and put his elbows on the table. "Think about it, Marc. You saw the way the pack reacted to your idea of an alliance. There's no way it would work. We're not made that way. There'd be a mutiny if we tried something like that. But Corrina's been with us a long, long time. If you mated with one of our own, well, that right there would make you family. And therefore, anything that threatened you and your pack would also be a threat to us."

Marc also leaned forward and stretched his arm across

the table, placing a hand on the pack master's forearm. To be considered as a mate for one as valued as Corrina was something of a shock, and he didn't take the offer lightly. "I am honored that ye would consider me a good mate for Corrina, and I agree that she is a braw and bonnie lass and will make some lucky male an excellent mate. But I'm sorry. I dinna feel that way aboot her. And I could no' take her tae be the mate of a male that does no' love her as she deserves tae be loved."

Keegan had accepted his words with a thoughtful nod. "It was just a thought. I saw the way she had her sights on you and just wanted to let you know that I would be all for a match between the two of you. I still would, if you happen to change your mind."

In the end, they'd come to an impasse about the whole alliance situation. Keegan had refused to budge from his position on it, insisting the rest of the pack would not adhere to the agreement, so what was the use?

Marc wanted to tell him that as their alpha, he could force them to accept it, but it wasn't his place to tell the pack leader how to deal with his pack. He was a guest at a rival den, and he'd already overstepped his bounds. Doing so again could very well get him killed.

Keegan had also refused to shut down his rodeo, though Marc had pled his case with care. Again, the alpha had remained steadfast in his decision. The rodeo, he'd argued, was something that brought his wolves a lot of enjoyment and gave them a safe activity where they could take out their aggressions without terrorizing the nearby towns.

Marc stomped around the side of the large barn and all the way around to the back.

Safe? Safe for whom? No' for the poor Fae creatures inside.

He stopped right about where he thought Bronaugh and her family were being held, though it was hard to tell with no windows. Pressing his hands against the side of the building, he wished he could go inside and check on her, but worried that if he did so again it would begin to look too suspicious.

Pushing away from the wall, he paced back and forth as he ground his jaw together.

Fook it.

He was getting her out. Now. Her family too. He wasn't gaining any ground with these rednecks here anyway.

Keeping to a subdued pace, he went around to the tall doors and let himself in. It was strangely quiet inside for the home of a rodeo. There was no roar of motorcycles, no whooping and hollering from a crowd of rowdy werewolves, no air horns, no announcer.

But the smells were still there: dirt and dust and sweat and engine oil.

And fear.

More determined by the moment, he strode through the empty arena and down the hall to the room that contained the cells. When he got there, he told the male guarding the door that Keegan was asking for him and he would watch things while he was gone. The pup didn't look quite convinced, but was more afraid of angering his alpha if it did happen to be true, so off he went.

Before he left, Marc asked him for the keys to the cell.

The kid frowned and told him he didn't have a key. That only Jace and Keegan had one.

"Ach. Aye. That's right. I was only going tae offer tae let them use the facilities." He shrugged.

"They have buckets."

Marc nodded. "Aye. Go on with ye, then. Ye dinna want tae keep Keegan waiting."

After giving him one last uncertain look, the pup left. Marc waited until he was out of the tunnel before he let himself into the room. He would need to hurry. But at the sight that greeted him, his entire body went rigid and his breath froze in his lungs. He rushed over to Bronaugh's cell. The soul suckers came alive from all the excitement, rising from their respective corners to rush the bars of their cell.

Marc had to raise his voice to be heard above their hisses and snarls. "Bronaugh! Bronaugh, lass. What the hell happened tae ye? Where are yer clothes?" He looked around for something more to cover her with than the large T-shirt she was currently wearing, but there was nothing, not even a blanket.

After a moment, he noticed that she hadn't responded or even so much as looked at him yet. No. His feisty lass was sitting in the corner with her head hanging forward, her blonde locks hiding her face from him. She wasn't railing at him like she normally would be. She wasn't shooting daggers at him with her strange rainbow eyes. He looked to the aunt and cousin for an explanation. Neither would look at him.

"Bronaugh?" His voice trembled like a pup, but he couldn't seem to help it. He was imagining the very worst, and not a one of them was doing or saying anything to ease those fears. An icy terror suddenly froze his blood in his veins. "Is it the bite? Are ye…" He couldn't bring himself to finish the sentence out loud. He turned to the aunt, as she was the nearest to him and had at least stood when he came in and acknowledged his presence. "What happened tae my Bronaugh?" he growled.

Her eyes flew to his face at his tone, widening in fear when she saw his expression. But she lifted her chin and answered him. "The bite is healing. She's not… She had a plan for us to escape. And it very nearly worked, but then another of the wolves showed up and—"

"Where are her bloody clothes?" he interrupted quietly.

A knowing look came into her eyes. "She's fine," her aunt told him adamantly. "She's fine. Or she will be very soon."

He didn't even hear her. Wrapping his hands around the bars, he shook the cell door in a rage born from fear. "Where are her fookin' clothes?" he bellowed. His skin began to feel tight over his growing muscles, his voice barely recognizable as human. If someone didn't ease his fears, and soon, he was going to change right there and start ripping apart anyone that dared to come near him.

The aunt stumbled away from his anger and sank down again next to her daughter, who just stared at him like he'd lost his mind. But he couldn't help it. No one was giving him an acceptable reason for what he was looking at. He turned away and strode to the door, determined to tear this pack apart piece by piece until he found out why his lass had on nothing but a male's shirt and wouldn't look at him. He had just unlatched the door to leave when he heard her soft voice.

"I'm okay, you crazy Scot. Jeez."

Marc squeezed his eyes shut, feeling dizzy with relief. Resting his forehead against the door, he felt his blood calm, his body ease. Locking the door again, he whirled around and walked back over to the cell. His Bronaugh had lifted her head and was looking at him. A large bruise discolored one side of her jaw and the skin under her eye.

At the sight of her beaten and bruised, his blood began to boil again. Spots flashed before his eyes. He fell to his knees, the fear leaving his body as suddenly as it had come on, only to be replaced with an overwhelming guilt that he had not been there to protect her. "Bronaugh…" he choked out.

She scowled. "I said I was fine. Buck up, will ya?"

"Will you please go to that male and ease his mind?" her aunt scolded.

"Yeah, Bro," Bitsy chimed in. "He looks like he's about to cry."

Marc sat back on his heels. He was acting like a right eejit. But gods, the sight of her wee face…it was killing him. His eyes burned with suspicious moisture as she rose gracefully from the dirt floor and came over to him. Kneeling down in front of him, she quirked one eyebrow and waited.

Gently, he reached through the bars and cupped her cheeks in his hands. With his thumb, he pressed lightly around her bruise, checking that no bones were broken.

"I told you I was okay," she said. "Apparently it looks worse than it feels."

"Who did this tae ye?" he growled.

Unlike her aunt, she didn't so much as flinch at the rage in his voice. "I'm not telling you that."

His eyes flew to hers. "What do ye mean yer no' telling me? I need tae know who it was!"

"Why?"

"So I can kill the fookin' bastard!"

"Which is exactly why I'm not telling you."

"So help me, lass. If ye dinna tell me, I'll...I'll..."

"Let me out of this damn cage?" she asked with a smart-ass smile. Then she winced like even that small movement hurt her.

He rubbed her bruised jaw gently with her thumb, his anger draining away. "That's what I came here tae do, actually. But the pup at the door didnae have a key."

"You did?"

He nodded. "I cannae break these bars. They're specially made tae keep ye in and others out. I need the key."

"But what about your boys' club? I mean, pack. And your all-important mission and blah, blah, blah."

He shrugged his shoulders. "It's no' going so well. These cowboys think they can handle whatever comes their way without any help from anyone else. And they dinna believe it's going tae happen anyway. Keegan thinks the Fae prince is a 'nut job' that's no' worth listening tae." He didn't bother to tell her about the mating offer. It wasn't an option he would consider, in any case.

"He's right. The prince is a nut job," she said. "But that doesn't mean he isn't telling the truth."

Bitsy spoke up for the first time. "Sorry to interrupt

this tender moment and all, but if what you're saying is true—Marc, is it?—then you guys could really use our help. That is, if you're for real about not wanting to hurt any of us."

Marc never took his eyes from Bronaugh when he said, "Aye. I meant every damn word."

Bronaugh smiled sadly and pulled her face from his hands.

What? What had he said?

"Well, I'm fine, as you can see," she told him as she scooted back over to her family.

He suddenly felt empty, like it wasn't just her physical presence she'd withdrawn from him.

"My missing clothes are nothing more than a bad escape plan gone awry. Nothing happened to me but a good punch in the jaw and a few more shocks from the cattle prod. Nothing I can't handle. But yeah, if you could help us get the hell out of here before you head back to Seattle? That would be awesome."

He didn't understand. What had just happened? "Bronaugh, I—"

"You should really go, Marc. And let these wackos calm down." With a sideways look, she indicated the males who had renewed their efforts to get to them through the bars of their cell. "Before the guard comes back and hears what's being said in here. You can't help us if they find out you're planning on breaking us out."

She was right. He didn't want to leave yet, but *ach*, she was absolutely right. He stood up and ran his hands through his hair, feeling helpless once again. "Aye. I'll go. But I'll be back, lass." He looked at each of them in turn. "I swear it tae ye all. I'll get ye out o' this place." Bronaugh just looked at him with a blank expression on her beaten face. He knew she didn't believe him. Her cousin smiled, but she didn't look like she believed him either.

He would prove them both wrong.

But her aunt gave him a genuine smile. "Thank you," she told him. "And be careful."

He gave her a respectful nod. "Aye." With one last longing look at Bronaugh, he went over and unlocked the door that led out to the arena. He had just closed it behind him when the guard returned.

"Keegan was nowhere to be found, man. Who told you he wanted to see me?"

Marc scratched his head and tried to look confused. "No shite? Huh. I must have misunderstood." Then he shrugged. "The accent and all." Smacking the pup on the shoulder, he left him to his duty.

Bronaugh's brown eyes haunted his every step all the way back to the house. He'd noticed that this time, for the first time, they hadn't changed colors when she'd looked at him.

CHAPTER 22

Bronaugh remained where she was long after the door closed behind Marc. She'd tried to hear the muffled conversation between Marc and the returning guard, but couldn't make out what was being said above all the noise from the idiots in the cell beside her.

Funny that she felt nothing for those two. No sympathy, no empathy, no other "-athy" of any sort, even though they were her kind, and could very well be her one day, as Marc so liked to remind her—maybe sooner than either of them thought.

His visit had done nothing to change the way she felt. Marc, she was quickly learning, was a lot of talk and no action. And was more concerned with what others thought of him than what he knew to be right or wrong. In spite of all of his bold talk, she now understood he would do nothing to get them out of here. It would be up to her.

Bitsy came to stand beside her. "What do you think, cuz?"

Bronaugh didn't hesitate when she said, "I think he's full of shit."

"I don't think he is, Bronaugh." Aunt Nancy's voice came from behind them where she was resting in the corner. "I think he genuinely cares about you, but he's kind of stuck between a rock and a hard place. Can you imagine what the pack here will do to him if he's caught helping us? He's already taken a huge risk more than once by coming to check on you."

"Yeah, well, I never asked him to. Besides, it's his fault I'm fucking here to begin with." She stuck out her lip in a pout.

"Bronaugh. Language!" her aunt scolded. "And how in the world is it his fault?"

Spinning around to confront her, Bronaugh spoke without thinking. "Because he didn't want me, okay? I threw myself at him, bare-assed naked, no less, and he turned me away."

The look on her aunt's face went from surprised to suspicious. "How long exactly have you two known each other, honey?"

"Just a few days before I got caught."

"A few days!" Bitsy snorted. "Bronaugh, you don't seriously expect him to give up everything—including very possibly his *life*—for a chick he's only known a few days, do you?"

She crossed her arms, her face heating. "Yeah, I kind of did. There's something between us, Bits. I can't explain it except to say that I've never felt it before with anyone else in all the time I've been alive."

Her aunt got up and came to join them. "Honey, no matter how attracted to you he is, he's still just a male. It'll take a little while for the blood to make its way back to the right head. Especially if you're prancing around with no clothes on."

Bitsy turned to look at her mother, her mouth falling open. "Mom!"

"What? I know a thing or two about males. How do you think you got here?"

"Ew, mom. TMI."

A reluctant giggle escaped Bronaugh. She dearly loved these two crazy females.

"Anyway," her aunt told her. "My point is, give him a little time, honey. He'll come around. And in the meantime, we'll keep our eyes open and be ready. Because we certainly don't need to just sit around here and wait for a male to help us."

"Damn straight, Mom," Bitsy cheered. "We're strong, independent females."

"That we are," Bronaugh agreed. She didn't want to tell them that she already had a new plan in place. A plan that terrified the hell out of her, but one that she believed to be the only way she was going to be able to get her family out of the mess she'd gotten them into.

Bronaugh took a deep breath, preparing herself to embrace the darkness that had always beckoned within her, but that she'd been terrified of knowing.

* * *

MARC MARCHED up onto the back porch, his eyes blazing with a murderous heat. He threw the back door open so hard he ripped it from the hinges, not bothering to stop to check the damage. Instead, he tore across the kitchen and into the dining area where the pack was just gathering for lunch.

Shoving chairs out of the way, he launched himself across the table. Dishes piled high with Corrina's good cooking went flying amidst shouts of surprise. Everyone scattered to get out of the way before they were wearing her latest creation. But Marc's focus was on one person and one person only.

Wrapping his hands around Jace's throat, he took him down to the floor on the other side of the table and landed heavily on top of him. He ignored the shouts around him that had swiftly turned from surprise to anger. Lips compressed with fury, he tightened his grip until the bastard's face turned red, then purple, from lack of air. Struggling to breathe, Jace bucked underneath him, but he was no match for the rage that was roiling through Marc. He felt the skin stretching across his face and the ache in his gums as his canines prepared to rip apart his prey.

"What did ye do tae her, you fooker?" His voice was nothing but a guttural growl.

Jace sputtered beneath him. His hands wrapped around Marc's wrists and he tried to get him to release him. In response, Marc sunk his elongated nails into the soft skin of Jace's throat, lifted his head, and smashed it into the hardwood floor. The violence felt good, the scent of blood pungent in his nose. So he did it again. And again.

"Stop this! Right now!" The timbre of the alpha giving a command could not be ignored. Not even by a wolf from a different pack. And yet, somehow, Marc managed to do just that.

He got in one more good head smash before he was knocked off Jace's body by nearly three hundred pounds of muscle, fur and teeth. Already partially changed, his wolf responded to the threat fast and hard. His roar of pain and rage turned to a howl as his body contorted. Bones reformed and his muscles re-knitted. Hair grew long, sprouting from his new skin. Baring his teeth, he whipped around to face this new threat and found himself face to face with the alpha.

Keegan's larger form paced back and forth in front of him. Low warning growls ripped from his throat as he eased forward with each pass until Marc was backed up against the wall. He didn't attack, but rather held him there, blocking Jace from his sight and giving Marc a chance to get a grip on himself.

When nothing but Keegan filled it, the red haze gradually faded from Marc's line of vision. Gradually, he stopped snarling and lowered his head to the alpha. Breathing hard, he bowed down in a submissive pose. This was not a challenge he wanted to make. He respected the Texas leader.

His second-in-command, not so much.

Marc shook his massive head and lowered his front end even closer to the floor. After a moment, he felt Keegan grab him lightly by the scruff of his neck with his teeth as he growled deep in his ear. Marc kept absolutely still except for the shudders that shook his fur from the adrenaline still flooding his system, knowing that any sudden move on his part would be taken as a challenge and would result in a fight to the death. One he would most likely lose.

After a few seconds, Keegan released him and stepped back. Rearing up on his hind legs, he howled long and loud, then dropped back down to the floor and turned his back on Marc to go check on Jace.

Unfortunately, Marc noticed the eejit was sitting up on his own and seemed like he was going to be fine.

Dismissed, Marc snuck away and padded up to the guest room where he was staying. It took him a few more minutes to calm down enough to change back, but he managed. He was dressed and packing his duffel bag when a knock sounded on his door. Rising from the bed, he went to answer the door, knowing full well who was on the other side.

"Come in," he told Keegan. "I was just getting packed tae go."

Keegan, also back in human form and wearing jeans and a white tee, stepped inside and closed the door behind him. "Where are you fixin' to go?"

"Ach." Marc raked a hand through his hair. "I cannae stay here anymore. No' with him. No' with what's going on here." He waved his hand toward the window, indicating the barn outside.

"What happened with Jace?" Keegan asked calmly.

Marc debated what to tell him. If he said he'd gone out to check on Bronaugh, Keegan would want to know why.

If he accused one of his pack—his second-in-command, no less—of attacking her, would he even care? Keegan seemed like a braw alpha, fair and honest. But Marc hadn't been here long enough to know how far he could trust him.

Marc's eyes dropped to the tree pendant hanging from the silver chain around the alpha's muscular neck. It was intricate and delicate and definitely belonged to a female. A Fae female, if he was to hazard a guess, for his Bronaugh had one just like it. "I just dinna care for him."

Keegan sighed and went over to sit on the edge of the bed, shoving Marc's bag out of the way. He indicated for Marc to sit also, so he grabbed the handmade wooden chair from the corner and angled it toward the bed. Sitting down, he waited patiently for Keegan to get his thoughts together.

"Jace can be a hard pill to swallow," he began. "He's hotheaded, stubborn, and thinks way too much of himself."

Marc cocked an eyebrow.

"Yeah, I know," Keegan answered Marc's unspoken words. "There's more. But he's as loyal as they come, and his cockiness is an asset when it comes to handling things for the pack. Things that others would be afraid to do."

"Like capturing innocent Fae females?" Marc couldn't help the sarcastic tone that accompanied his words.

Now it was Keegan's turn to lift an eyebrow. "Why do you care so much about those gals down there?"

"I dinna."

"You're lying," Keegan said. He said it with no menace in his voice, but rather just an honest observation.

"I just dinna like seeing females treated—"

"Yeah, yeah, yeah. We've all heard that bullshit before, Seattle. What's really going on?" Leaning his elbows on his knees, Keegan leaned forward and settled in for a chat.

Marc looked down at his hands where they twisted in his lap. This alpha was a good male, and his every instinct told him he was trustworthy. Yet something held him back from telling him the truth about Bronaugh. Besides, what was there to tell? That he'd met the Fae lass a few days ago, had a bit of a tumble with her that didn't change his mind about not wanting to get involved with her in spite of his savage attraction to her, and then let her be caught for their rodeo? Barely doing a damn thing to stop them from treating her like cattle and worse?

But then again, what would it hurt? His mind was made up. One way or the other, he was getting his lass and her family out of those fookin' cells, if he had to burn the place down to do it. He was leaving, and he was taking his female with him. Cedric wouldn't be happy that he'd sabotaged their chances to get this pack to the gathering, but he would understand. At least Marc hoped he would.

Ach. Surely, he would. Even though Marc had no intention of keeping the lass once he'd freed her. In spite of what he felt for her, she was still *an olc*, a Dark Fae.

Leveling his steady gaze at Keegan, he told him, "I'm freeing the females, one way or the other." However, he was quick to point out that he meant no disrespect to the Texas pack by doing so, it was just something he had to do.

"What about the dark ones? Are you planning on freeing them too?" Keegan asked with a hint of laughter.

Marc shook his head. "Nae, I'm no' daft. Ye can keep those two. They should still provide ye with enough entertainment tae draw the crowds. Hell, I'll even try tae send ye a few more after, instead o' sending them back when the portal opens up." He looked at Keegan earnestly. "I just cannae swallow what's going on here. No' with the lasses. And aye, one o' them has brought out...feelings in me. I dinna ken the how or the why aboot it. It just is." Keegan's eyes narrowed at that last remark, but he pushed on. "I still hope we can work this out between us, but if it's no' possible, then I'm going tae do what I have tae do. And I hope ye can at least understand the why o' it, if nothing else."

The alpha sat quietly. He would make a great poker player, Marc decided after giving up trying to read his expression. The male had no tells. Not a twitch to give you an idea of what he was thinking.

Finally, Keegan stood. "You're welcome to go in peace. But you won't be taking my gals with you."

Marc stood also. "Keegan, I beg ye tae reconsider—"

"The answer is no." His voice had lowered, the alpha timbre adding extra conviction to his next words. "The girls are MINE. You will not go anywhere near them."

Marc sat down again under the weighted pressure of the command.

Then just like that, the pleasant smile was back, and Keegan tipped his imaginary hat at him. "Happy travels to you, Seattle. Please let your alpha know we appreciate the warning. But if—and that's a big *if*—those things happen to escape whatever realm of hell the good prince had us put them in all those years ago, we'll take care of those bastards our own way." Leaving the door open, he strolled out of the room.

Bloody hell.

CHAPTER 23

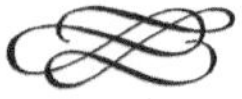

Bronaugh closed her eyes and stretched her neck from side to side, loosening the tense muscles there. Her mind was made up. She knew what she had to do. She'd already warned her aunt and cousin.

"Bronaugh, don't do this," her aunt begged her. "Please, honey. We'll figure out another way."

"There is no other way, Aunt Nancy. It's my fault you're in here. If I hadn't taken off, you wouldn't have come after me, and you wouldn't have been caught by these assholes. I'm the only one who can get us out of this place, and you know it. I'm prepared to do whatever I have to do to make that happen."

The outer door swung open, and Stone came in with a couple of the younger members of the pack. "Afternoon, everyone!" he said in a boisterous voice. "You all ready for today's games?" At their silence, he looked at each of them in turn, even smiling at the soul suckers as they threw themselves into the bars of the cell in their efforts to reach him. "Well, I can see that you two are. But it's not your turn, guys. Ladies, you might want to get a quick stretch in. You're up first. All three of you." Still grinning, he grabbed one of the cattle prods and fished the key to their cell out of his pocket.

Bitsy grabbed Bronaugh's arm in a tight grip and leaned close. "Don't do this, cousin. We don't know what will happen."

"It'll be okay." She barely spoke above a whisper, afraid he would hear as he unlocked the lock and swung the door open. "I should have enough control over myself to get you guys out. Once we're out of this horrid place though, you have to leave me, Bits. Promise me that you'll leave me."

"Enough talking," Stone told them. "Let's go."

Giving Bronaugh one last desperate look, her aunt walked through the door with her head high. She stared down Stone as she passed. He winked at her, then nodded at the two younger wolves to take her to the arena. He watched her leave, then noticed that Bronaugh and Bitsy hadn't moved.

With an exaggerated sigh, he opened the door wider. "Let's go, you two. Time's a wastin'."

Bronaugh started walking, pulling a reluctant Bitsy behind her. They left the cell and preceded him down the tunnel to the arena.

"I won't be making you that promise," Bitsy said in a low voice. She was instantly reminded by the shock of the cattle prod that talking time was over. "I won't," she hissed at Bronaugh even as her body jerked and stumbled from the electricity running through it.

Bronaugh glared at her out of the corner of her eye, but resisted the urge to argue. She needed all of her strength to do what she was going to have to do, so avoiding those damn prods was prudent to her plan.

They managed to complete the rest of their journey without getting prodded again. The roar of the crowd greeted them as they got closer to the arena, and Bronaugh could hear Keegan on the mic, working up the crowd. Aunt Nancy was already in the bucking chute waiting for them. As she and Bitsy entered, Aunt Nancy turned to take their hands. Her face was a picture of disgust as a wad of spittle landed at her feet from a nearby spectator, the others around him laughing and hollering. She didn't acknowledge the insult other than a tensing of her jaw. She stared hard at Bronaugh, and Bronaugh knew what she was asking her. She gave her aunt a nod, and with tears filling her eyes, Aunt Nancy nodded back.

Steel straightened Bronaugh's spine as air horns blared and boots stomped. The noise was making her head swim, or maybe it was the adrenaline flooding her system. Jace appeared on the other side of the gate. Swinging it open wide, he moved aside as Stone got them moving from behind. Motorcycles revved their engines from the far end, adding to the uproar, but Bronaugh refused to look to see if Marc was one of the participants this time. As she walked by Jace, he reached out and squeezed her bare ass, hard enough that she knew it would leave a bruise. She was still only wearing the over-sized shirt he'd left for her, and the feel of his hand on her stilled the blood in her veins and sharpened her mind. The idiots in the stands catcalled and whistled as he felt her up, then smacked her so hard with his palm that she stumbled.

Bronaugh felt the darkness in her rise closer to the surface. *Oh, yes.* That asshole was going to be the first one to go. She turned around and gave him a chilling smile. He must have noticed something different about her, something that spooked him, for he stopped laughing and made a show of shutting the gate.

Without looking away from Jace, Bronaugh spoke just loud enough for Bitsy and Aunt Nancy to hear her above Keegan's voice and the noise of the crowd. "Make your way over to the door on the other side of the cage, but not too close. As soon as I open it, meet me at the barn doors." They stood to either side of her and she spared them each a quick glance so they would know how much she meant her next words. "I love you both," she told them, her voice thick with emotion. "Thank you for everything you've done for me."

"We won't lose you completely, Bronaugh," her aunt said. "I refuse to let that happen."

Bronaugh smiled and touched her forehead to her aunt's, then did the same with her cousin. They each exchanged glances that said more than words ever could, and then the only family she'd ever remembered separated from her as the bikes started moving toward them and Keegan announced the first event.

Watching them go, Bronaugh hardened her heart, suppressing every ounce of emotion except the anger and disgust and pure hatred that she felt for every werewolf there. As the air horns sounded again, she heard a motorcycle heading toward her from the left, but she paid it no mind. Instead, she set her sights on Jace. The epitome of cockiness, he never left the arena while the events were taking place like Keegan did, but would stand just outside the bucking chute with his elbows and one booted foot up on the bars of the cage behind him.

Bronaugh felt a flash of satisfaction when he noticed her still standing there. That ever-present smirk fell from his face as her eyes impaled him with all of the hatred she felt toward him and everything they did here. Jace glanced around nervously, looking for someone to help him, but no one was there.

The motorcycle came closer, and then flew between her and Jace, kicking up dirt and dust as it passed. But she ignored it other than to knock away the chain the rider tossed at her so it couldn't encircle her throat.

A momentary flash of indecision at what she was about to do, what she was about to let herself become, caused her to pause for just a moment. But then, amidst all of the noise, she heard her cousin scream from some-where behind her.

Setting her jaw, she began to stalk her prey.

AFTER HIS CONVERSATION with Keegan earlier, Marc had finished packing up his stuff and left the house while everyone was out preparing for the day's rodeo. Throwing his bag into the trunk of his car, he'd driven a few miles down the main road before pulling over and parking behind an old gas station.

Turning off his cell phone, he'd put it in the glove box,

and then he'd sat for a moment, thinking hard about what he was about to do. Marc had never been the rebellious type, which was one of the reasons he'd never fought for an alpha position. He considered himself lucky he'd found Cedric as a young wolf, for he was a fair and just alpha who genuinely cared about his pack. And Marc had always been just fine following someone else's orders and going along with the flow. But up until now, "the flow" had never involved hurting a female he had…feelings for.

Sitting there in the front seat, he could still smell the faint fragrance of meadowsweet after the rain, and he breathed the scent deep into his lungs. His body reacted immediately, his muscles hardening and his cock swelling in his jeans. A low growl rumbled up from his chest. The longing to touch her again, to taste her, was nigh maddening. But it wasn't just the physical reaction he had for her. It was much, much more. He'd never met a lass who was as intelligent and brave and passionate as his Bronaugh. Gritting his teeth, he got out of the car.

Leaving the key hidden under the wheel of a trash bin near the back wall of the building just in case he no longer had his clothes when he returned with the females, he glanced around to make sure no one was paying him any mind and walked into the overgrown brush that passed for trees there. Once out of the sight of any lingering humans, Marc broke into a steady run, heading back the way he had come.

He was going to get his lass.

Sweat broke out on his brow and ran down the center of his back as the afternoon sun beat down on his head, but Marc felt no discomfort from the heat. His mind was elsewhere. As he approached the area where he and Bronaugh had argued near the creek, he increased his pace. He didn't stop to get a drink, or to wipe away the perspiration that was burning his eyes. As a matter of fact, he felt downright cold as he heard the roar of the crowd. So loud he could hear it even from this distance.

Slowing down to a jog, he made his way along the back of the building. Marc patched together a hasty plan and turned the corner, hoping he wasn't too late to blend in with the guests as they entered. If he was, he wouldn't be able to get in without causing a ruckus and drawing attention to the fact that he was there.

But the luck of the Fae was with him that day. He arrived just in time to blend in with the last group. The members of the pack who were waiting to close the doors didn't even notice him, distracted as they were by all of the commotion going on inside. Money passed from hand to hand as fast as Keegan could call out the riders and the crowd bet on who would come out on top.

Taking a seat near the end of one of the bottom bleachers, as near to the door of the arena as he dared, Marc watched as the Fae females were brought out first. His Bronaugh, he noticed, was still wearing nothing but the shirt she'd been in when he'd last seen her. A low, warning growl that no one could hear rumbled through him as Jace's eyes locked onto her. Marc nearly jumped from his seat when Jace stuck his hand underneath her shirt and grabbed her bare arse. Only the fact that the crowd around him jumped up to cheer at the same time saved him from giving himself away. They also blocked his view enough that he didn't see the smack Jace gave her, though he did see her stumble and could well guess why it had happened. Taking deep, calming breaths, he sat back down. His vision darkened with hatred and narrowed in on Keegan's second-in-command.

That wolf would be the first one to die. Consequences be damned.

Bronaugh spoke urgently with the other females, then touched foreheads with them both before they left her and made their way over closer to Marc. He watched in confusion as Bronaugh's family separated themselves from her, and she set her sights on Jace. What the bloody hell was the lass up to now?

And why did he get the feeling she had just told them goodbye?

Air horns sounded and the crowd went wild as the first event began. Marc used the commotion to make his way over to where Corrina was guarding the door to the arena. She looked from side to side nervously when she saw him, but didn't call out or alert anyone to his presence.

Over her shoulder, he could see Bronaugh stalking Jace. He didn't know what she was planning to do, but whatever it was, he wasn't feeling good about it. Not at all.

"Corrina, I need ye tae open that door and let me in tae the arena." He spoke quietly but with authority. He knew she could hear him.

She looked genuinely sorry when she told him, her voice just above a whisper, "I can't do that, Marc. You know that."

He moved in closer to her. She was a tall female, but still he towered over her. "Yer going tae just continue tae let this happen, then?" He pointed toward Bronaugh's aunt and cousin as they faced an oncoming motorcycle. The wolf riding it was not someone he recognized. He must be from a visiting pack. Marc watched in horror as the rider succeeded in roping the older of the two females and she was flipped off her feet to land face-first in the dirt. The younger one screamed as her mother was dragged away from her.

"This is madness, Corrina! Ye ken this! Please," he begged her. "I just want tae get the lasses out o' here. I will say ye resisted and I'll take full responsibility for what I'm about tae do. I'll even leave the soul suckers back in their cells. They're too far gone tae be helped anyway. But these lasses are no'! They're no' even that kind of Fae! They dinna deserve this!" At least two out of the three were not. And his Bronaugh was still good, but she wouldn't be for long by the look of her. He needed to do something, and do it fast. Or he had a horrendous feeling she would be lost to him forever.

Corrina's eyes were clouded with indecision as she glanced over her shoulder, and then back at Marc. Cracking his knuckles, he waited impatiently for her to decide what she wanted to do. He would make her open the door by force if need be, but he'd rather not hurt her if he didn't have to.

Her eyes suddenly hardened and she gave him a nod. "Make sure you hit me hard," she ordered, then pulled the key from her front pocket and handed it to him. "Go on! Hit me!"

"Thank ye." As the crowd roared, Marc hauled back and nailed Corrina with a hard left hook, wincing as he did so. She fell away from the door and stayed down. Stepping over her, he wrestled with the lock while he fought the need to let his wolf take over. He needed to stay human just long enough to grab the lasses and get them out of there.

The lock clicked and sprung open, and Marc yanked it off the bars and ripped the door completely off its hinges. Tossing it aside, he tore into the arena as the first sound of alarm went up from the onlookers closest to him.

Motioning to Bronaugh's cousin to stay where she was, he yelled for Bronaugh as he chased down the young wolf who was dragging her aunt around. Cutting him off when he turned to go back down the length of the arena, Marc jumped off a ramp and flew through the air, tackling him around the middle. The bike fell over with both males still on it, spun in a circle and stalled out.

"What the hell, man?" the male shouted. In response, Marc jumped up, tore the end of the chain from the pup's hand and ran over to pick up Bronaugh's aunt. Lifting her easily into his arms, he yelled again for Bronaugh.

Bronaugh swung around, turning her back to Jace. A blank look crossed her features when she saw Marc running hell-bent toward her with her aunt in his arms, not comprehending what she was seeing at first. Behind her, Jace locked eyes with Marc and hefted his cattle prod.

Marc tried to warn her, to reach her before it happened, but her aunt was awkward to hang on to with her chain still dragging behind them. She writhed in his arms as she tried to loosen the links from her neck so she could breathe, and Marc had no time to stop and help her. A bellow of rage tore from his chest just as Bronaugh's eyes widened with understanding. But it was too late. She had no time to see it coming.

The other rider had made his way back around and now roared up on one side of Bronaugh, distracting her as Jace came up from the other side. Swinging his cattle prod with one hand, Jace lifted it and swung it like a bat right into the back of her head. Blood spurted from the wound as her body flew forward to land sprawled in the dirt at Marc's feet. Her body convulsed alarmingly from the electrified hit. The dirt bike roared past, the thick tires coming down hard on her lower legs, leaving them twisted and broken as she screamed. The rider laughed while he did it.

Marc roared with pain and rage, and he lost what little control he'd had on his emotions. His body contorted with violent motions, and he began to change.

Bronaugh's aunt wriggled out of his arms just in time and landed on her butt beside her adopted niece. Raspy screams tore from her throat as she tugged at the chain that was still around her neck, finally managing to get it off so she could bend over her niece. Tears streaked her face and dripped into the dirt, mixing with the blood to turn it into mud.

Marc, in full wolf form now, leaped over the females. His jaws clamped down on Jace's throat, and this time he didn't hold back. Jace had no time to defend himself or even to change into his own wolf form, and Keegan wasn't close enough to save him. Tendon and muscle shredded like chopped meat under the violent assault. Marc didn't stop, not even when his teeth hit bone. Shaking his head, he tore Jace's head from his spine. And still he didn't stop. He didn't stop until Jace lay in bloody pieces at his paws.

The sudden silence was short-lived. Howls echoed through the building as the Texas pack began to turn. And they weren't the only ones. The violence witnessed against one of their own triggered the change in all who were watching.

Marc trotted back over to where Bronaugh still lay motionless in the dirt. Her cousin was there with her now also. Standing over them, he snapped his teeth at the wolves that had made their way into the arena and were now circling around them. And at their head was the largest of them all, the alpha.

Marc stayed close to Bronaugh. Lowering his body into a protective stance over her and the other two females, he bared his teeth, snarling at the wolves in challenge even though he knew his chances of surviving this were minimal. But he would not go down without a fight. And in spite of his imminent death, he felt alive for the first time in a very long time. He was taking a stand about something he knew was wrong, and he was fighting for a female. *His* female. He felt like a true male. It felt good.

It felt...right.

Keegan and his pack paced around the group, tightening the circle little by little as they moved in for the kill. Marc swung his large head from side to side, trying to watch all of them at once. A steady growl rumbled up from his chest, warning the others not to approach, but they kept coming anyway. The males outside, most now in wolf form also, clamored around the cage, searching for a way to get in and join the fight while the females yipped at their heels for them to stay out of it.

A small gray wolf came in fast from the left, and Marc reacted instantly. Rearing up, he caught the young one around one front leg and used its own momentum to throw him into the wolves coming in from the right. They scattered to avoid him, then with a barked demand from the alpha reformed their circle.

Bronaugh stirred beneath him, and though his heart rejoiced that she was alive, Marc lowered his chest down onto her in an attempt to keep her down. It didn't work. Her head rose from between his two front paws. She slowly turned her head to look at first one huge paw and then the other. Never taking his eyes from the pack that was threatening them, he gave her head a lick to let her know it was him on top of her and then went back to snarling at the other wolves.

"Marc?" she rasped, peering up at the underside of his jaw.

"Just stay down," her cousin told her from where she crouched alongside his massive form.

Marc lowered his head down to Bronaugh's again and rubbed his cheek against her like a cat, wordlessly asking her to trust him. Now that he saw she would survive, he would get them out of this. Somehow.

In spite of his efforts to keep her there, she squirmed her way out from under him and struggled to her knees. She touched the back of her head, and stared at the blood on her hand. But instead of acting like a normal female in distress, fire lit up her brown eyes until they burned with a near reddish hue as she glanced up at

Marc and then turned her wrath to the wolves still circling them.

Marc felt fear clutch his bowels. Damn bloody stubborn female. Why couldn't she ever do as he wanted her to do?

Before he could even guess what she was about, she up and disappeared. Marc blinked. She was right there in front of him, and then she was gone. Rearing up onto his hind legs, he spotted her on a large black wolf—Stone. She was on his back, her broken legs hanging limply to either side. Leaning forward, she wrapped her forearm around his throat and gripped his head, preparing to snap his neck. Leaning down until her mouth was by his ear, she whispered something to him. The wolf lowered itself down to the ground, and Marc could see shivers ruffle his fur beneath her. Her colorful eyes still glowed with that reddish haze.

She cocked her blonde head and gave him a sad smile. Her eyes were mesmerizing, bright colors flashing in and out underneath the haze of red. "I have to do it, Marc. It's the only way to get us out of here alive. They'll kill you if I don't. They'll kill us all."

She was right. But still he shook his head in denial, hoping against hope that somehow they would make it out of this alive.

Her features hardened. "Even if they don't kill us, they won't let us go. I can't stay in here anymore, Marc. We'd be their playthings until an 'accident' happens. And I can't let that happen. Not to me. Not to my family."

He exchanged a look with Keegan. The massive alpha lowered his eyes and gave another nod, wolf talk for "Let's diffuse the situation." Keegan nipped at the others around him, letting the rest of his pack know to stand down. One of them went over to block the doorway into the arena and keep the visitors out. Once they had all gone into a neutral posture and backed away, Marc began the painful process of returning to human form so he could talk to his lass.

He knew it was a risk. Changing back in the midst of this group made him unnecessarily vulnerable to attack. The werewolves could easily take him out either while he was changing or as soon as he became human. But it was an act of trust that he had to take if he had any hope at all of getting them out of this situation.

His eyes remained on Bronaugh as he willed himself to relax enough to come back from his wolf form. She watched him change, her face a mixture of curiosity and sympathy. In the silence, the sounds of breaking bones echoed and mixed with the wet sucking sounds of tearing muscle and the hissing of his breath. When he was finished he straightened to his full height, breathing hard, completely unabashed by his nudity. Her erratic eyes ran over him hungrily as he approached her, and they began to burn with a different kind of heat.

He spoke first to the alpha, his voice passionate with honesty. "I am sorry that ye lost your second, but I am no' sorry that I killed him. The bastard tried tae rape my Bronaugh." He indicated her near nakedness. "He took her clothing and left her with naught but this T-shirt tae wear. He left *marks* on her." His voice shook with rage, and he fought to calm himself. He responded to the silent question on Keegan's face. "Aye. She is MINE. And I will no' allow ye tae abuse her, or her family, anymore. Ye do what ye need tae do about that. But I will no' go down without a fight. Ye can count on it. And ye will face the wrath of my pack when they find out what happened tae me. And they will find out."

Keegan narrowed his eyes, looking first at Marc and then at Bronaugh before finally shifting his gaze to the other females. When his eyes landed on Bitsy, a low growl rose from his throat. He did not agree with Marc's plan.

"Bronaugh is mine, Keegan. And she wants her family with her. They come with me." Marc's tone would brook no argument.

CHAPTER 24

Bronaugh watched as the pissing contest ensued between the two wolves. She had no faith that Marc's plan, whatever that might be, was going to work. The Texas pack weren't about to give up their new toys that easily, and saying Marc was outnumbered was the understatement of the year.

The only chance they had was for her to allow the darkness she'd been born with to take over. For with that darkness came power—power that would allow her to get herself and her family out of here in spite of the iron cage. She could feel it writhing around inside her, begging to be released.

And it felt good.

Marc moved closer to her, his bare abs rippling with every step, effectively grabbing her attention and distracting her from her murderous plans. Apparently, the darkness derived its pleasure from other things besides fighting. Not that her libido needed any help when it

218

came to the werewolf now standing just within her reach. Her body leaned toward him of its own accord, and she touched her nose to the narrow section of soft dark hair that trailed down to the impressive manhood jutting out from between his legs. His stomach clenched at the soft touch, and she inhaled his scent deeply into her nose.

She felt so strange, like everything was moving in slow motion.

Reaching out, he cupped her chin in his large hand and tilted her face up to look at him. She heard the wolves pacing around them, scenting the air. They could smell her rising desire, and it made them restless. All except the one she sat on. He wouldn't be moving until she allowed him to do so, for she still had a death grip on his head and could snap his neck in an instant.

Marc looked down at her, his eyes darkening with need. They made her a silent promise that she desperately wanted him to keep. "Bronaugh, lass. Please. Trust me so we can all live another day."

Trust him. Trust the male whose rejection had landed her here to begin with. Trust the male who had seen her inside that cage and left her there, more than once.

Trust him, he said.

The wolves stopped their pacing as one separated itself from the rest of the pack. For the second time that day, she witnessed the horrific change from wolf to male. Keegan retrieved his jeans from where he'd tossed them minutes before and slid into them before approaching. As he did so, Bitsy and Aunt Nancy also made their way up to stand on Bronaugh's other side.

She felt a flare of possessiveness heat her blood when

her cousin ran an admiring eye up and down the back of Marc's nude form. Lifting her upper lip in a snarl, Bronaugh was about to say something to her when Keegan beat her to it.

"Don't get your hopes up there, darlin'. Seems this male is taken." Though his words were teasing, his tone was not.

Bitsy smiled innocently at him. "Oh, don't you worry, cowboy. I'm just admiring the view is all."

Bronaugh felt the tension strumming the air between them with interest. But before she could think much about it, Keegan spoke again.

"Because I think you're a good male," he said to Marc, "and that you honestly mean no disrespect...I'll give you an hour's head start." He nodded at Bronaugh. "If you can manage to disentangle her from my new second-in-command without breaking his neck in the process."

Marc turned back to Bronaugh with a hopeful expression. She found it quite amusing that all of these males thought they were still in charge of the situation. Wiggling her toes, she found her legs were healing quite nicely. The wolf whimpered under her hands as she tightened her hold. Marc and Keegan both went still, waiting to see what she would do. Her silence seemed to make them nervous. As it should.

Trust me.

"We can take him out," she heard someone whisper behind her. The words were mouthed in a near silent manner, yet she heard them. She hadn't realized that more of the pack had turned back. The darkness swirled within at the threat, fighting for dominance over the part of her that was beginning to fight back. The better part of her.

"No," another answered just as quietly. "If we do that, we'll have the entire supernatural population of the northwest down here. And it won't just be werewolves we'll need to worry about. I hear they're tight with the vamps up there too."

Keegan shot a glare over her head at the two who were speaking. "We're not doing anything. They get an hour's head start. Do you understand?"

His voice shook with the timbre of the alpha, and she could just picture the two behind her cowering in submission. It brought a smile to her face. Her fantasy was interrupted when Marc's face appeared a mere inch from hers.

"Bronaugh, I know what you're thinking of doing. I can feel the turmoil inside ye, lass. But if ye do this, ye'll be lost tae me." A suspicious moisture made his eyes shine as he stared into hers. "Dinna do that tae me. Dinna make me lose ye now. Not now, lass. When I finally pulled my head out o' my arse and figured out that I wanted ye for my own. Please, Bronaugh."

Taking her face in his large palms he opened his mouth to say more and closed it again. A look of stubborn determination settled over his handsome features. Without further ado, he pulled her face to his and took her lips in a kiss that was neither gentle nor pleading, but demanding and possessive. She moaned at the taste of him, and her fingers loosened just a tad from Stone's fur as a dull ache began to throb low in her belly.

But then he drew back. "Release the wolf, Bronaugh." His voice was deep and rough. It was not a request.

She let go of the wolf's head immediately, without thinking. Then she frowned and went to reach for it again, but Marc swooped her up into his arms before she could get a good grip.

"One hour," he said to Keegan.

Keegan ran his eyes over Bitsy, then ground his jaws together and nodded. "One hour," he agreed.

Bronaugh reached for her aunt and cousin as Marc strode past them with her still locked firmly in his arms. She noticed that he made sure that one hand held her shirt tightly over her bottom so as not to expose her, and found it hilarious since he was strutting around stark naked. Smiling, she craned her neck around, and made sure Bitsy and Aunt Nancy were following before she started arguing with him.

"Put me down, you overgrown dog."

He didn't answer, but his hold on her tightened and she saw the muscles tense in his jaw. His eyes never strayed from the doorway that was even now being cleared so they could leave.

"I said, put me down," she repeated.

"I will *no'*," he ground out without looking at her.

Bronaugh sighed and crossed her arms over her chest. He was just so damned stubborn sometimes. It looked like she had a choice to make. She could encourage her inner demons to rise and try to kill every wolf in the place, risking Marc and her family in the process, for the Texas pack would fight back and she couldn't get to all of them at once...

Or, she could *trust him*.

They passed through the open door and out of the

arena. The crowd of werewolves, some turned and some not, backed away with unhappy growls, forming a path for them all the way to the tall barn doors.

Bronaugh wrestled with her decision, but Marc's words kept echoing in her head.

I can feel the turmoil inside ye, lass. But if ye do this, ye'll be lost tae me.

And he was right. She would be lost to him. Forever. She knew this as well as she knew herself. And that was pretty damned good after all the years she'd lived so far. In all the years she'd been alive, she'd never met a male who affected her the way this stubborn Scotsman did. Did she really want to throw away what was between them before it even had a chance to start? Just because she felt the need to prove something?

Marc walked out the barn doors with Bronaugh in his arms and her family right on his heels. And Bronaugh let him.

KEEGAN WATCHED Bitsy sashay out of the arena behind her mom in typical Bitsy style. He even almost smiled when she flipped off a group of the visiting werewolves, but he caught himself just in time. Once they were all out of the building and he made sure no one had any ideas of disobeying his order to let them go, he went to retrieve his shirt and hat.

"Are we really gonna give them a whole hour?" Lorrent asked. He was young, and therefore impatient.

Keegan took his time re-shaping his hat before he

settled it back on his head. "We're giving them more than that. We're not going after them at all," he said as he picked up the microphone from where he'd dropped it.

"You can't be serious," Lorrent said with a nervous laugh.

"I'm completely fucking serious," Keegan growled. "You got a problem with that?"

The younger wolf dropped his eyes. "Nope. No problem. Just wondering is all."

Keegan waited until he was quite sure the message had gotten across, then he turned on the mic and filled in everyone else before sending them all home.

No, no one was going after Bitsy. No one except him. But he'd give her a little time to miss him first.

CHAPTER 25

Marc didn't stop until they hit Seattle.

Once he'd gotten the females out of the barn, he'd kept right on going into the cedars and brush behind the house and headed back to the car, taking care to avoid the cactus in his bare feet. None of them spoke. And if the lasses thought it strange that he was running around showing everyone his bare arse and then some, it wasn't mentioned. Modesty be damned. He wanted to get them all as far away as possible.

As soon as they were out of sight of the house, he asked the lasses if they could run. They both answered that they could, Bitsy even dragging her eyes from his arse to do so. He grinned at her and she grinned back. But the scowl that darkened his Bronaugh's face when she looked at her cousin delighted him even more than her cousin's admiration. Giving her a firm kiss on the temple, he started running, her wee weight not hindering him at all.

They reached the car in good time, and Marc told the

older female where the keys were, reluctant to let go of Bronaugh even for a moment to retrieve them himself. Shifting her weight to one arm, he opened the trunk and pulled out some spare clothes. Then he deposited Bronaugh in the passenger seat and pulled on a pair of jeans and a T-shirt. He left his boots unlaced.

When he was assured they were all safely inside, he took off like the hounds of hell were after them. He didn't stop to sleep or rest, and only grabbed food when they had to stop for gas. Very few words were spoken the entire trip as they all kept a vigilant watch that they weren't being followed.

Thirty hours later, just after sunset, they spotted the gleaming city lights of Seattle.

Marc pulled into his assigned parking spot underneath his apartment building and shut off the engine. They all sat quietly as a collective sigh of relief went through the car.

"Where are we?" Bronaugh finally asked.

He looked into her beautiful eyes, eyes that no longer had any colors other than her sweet chestnut brown. "Just north of Seattle. This is where I live," he told her. "Along with the rest of my pack."

They stared at each other with tired eyes until Bitsy noisily cleared her throat from the back seat. "Are we ever going to see this apartment? Or are we just going to live here in the car?"

Marc tore his eyes from Bronaugh to smile at her. "Aye. Come on." Getting out of the car, he was pulling Bronaugh out of her side before she even had a chance to open her door. He ignored her insistence that she was "fine" and lifted her easily into his arms. Though she now had a pair of his lounge pants on, she had no shoes, and he wasn't about to let her cut up her bonnie feet.

Without waiting for the others, he hit the lock button before shutting her door and strode off toward the elevators. By the time the doors opened, Bitsy and Aunt Nancy had caught up to them and they all crowded in.

"Marc, please put me down," Bronaugh demanded. "This is embarrassing."

He grinned at her and pulled her in closer to his chest in answer. Now that they were home and he'd had a moment to catch his breath, he only had one thing on his mind. And that was getting his lass into his home and into his bed. He'd wasted enough time fighting what was between them.

The elevator dinged and he got out. Walking down to the last door on the left, he pounded on the door.

"Ach, aye," a deep voice growled from within. The door was thrown open and Lucian stood in the opening. His gray eyes widened in surprise. "Yer back."

Marc chuckled at the lack of enthusiasm in that statement.

"Who the bloody hell is this?" Lucian asked, looking from Bronaugh to the two females standing behind him. His face scrunched up like he smelled something unpleasant.

Marc shoved past him with Bronaugh still in his arms, calling over his shoulder for her aunt and cousin to follow him. Once they were all inside he said, "This bonnie lass is my Bronaugh. And these lovelies are her Aunt Nancy and her cousin, Bitsy. Everyone, this is Lucian."

Lucian tilted his head and scowled. "*Yer* Bronaugh? What the hell is that supposed tae mean?" He sniffed the air and his face wrinkled up again. "Whoa." Lucian held his hands up in front of him like he was warding off something evil. "Wait just a minute. That lass is Fae." He looked more closely at the others. "And so are they!"

"Aye," Marc confirmed. "And be nice tae them, or ye will be answering tae me." Then he nodded to Bitsy and Aunt Nancy and left with Bronaugh. As an afterthought, he stuck his head back in the doorway and told them both, "We'll be right there down the hall. Just yell if he gives ye any problems."

Aunt Nancy smiled at Lucian. "We'll be just fine, Marc. Thank you."

Lucian's scowl deepened.

"Where are you taking me?" Bronaugh asked as Marc strode down the hall. "Come on. Put me down. My legs are fine. Don't your arms hurt? I must be getting heavy by now. Even for you."

"Ach. Yer no' heavy, lass. No' at all." To prove his point, he tossed her up into the air and caught her again. Her laughter rang pleasantly in his ears, soothing his very soul. But he did put her down when he reached his apartment. Punching in the code that unlocked the door, he pushed the door open and then ushered her inside with a hand on the small of her back. Kicking it closed again, he spun her around until her back hit the wall.

She raised an eyebrow, but her calm, cool, and collected act didn't fool him. He could hear her heart pound and could see her breasts rise and fall with her excited breaths. And that lovely scent that belonged only to her became stronger, muskier, as her body responded to his. A smile broke out on his face, and her breath caught as she stared up at him. She started to say something else, some smartass quip he was sure, but he cut her off.

"Bronaugh, lass. If ye agree, I mean tae make ye mine. Right now. I cannae wait any longer. And I dinna plan tae let ye go until I'm cold in my grave." Her luscious mouth dropped open at his blunt honesty, and he continued, "I ken I've been nothing but a bloody arse, but I mean tae make it up tae ye. If it takes me another thousand years tae do so, then so be it."

She stared up at him, speechless for once, and he used the time to look his fill of her lovely wee face. Her bruised jaw was all but healed, but then he remembered her legs and he backed away a step.

"Yer legs…" he began.

"Are fine," she blurted out. Then she wrapped her arms around his neck and pulled him back to her, pressing her soft curves against him wantonly. His body, already hard, responded to her ardor with enthusiasm.

A low growl vibrated in his throat as he slid his hands under her plump arse and lifted her up off the floor. She wrapped her shapely legs around him without needing any prompting, and he could feel the heat of her core right through his jeans and the thin material of the lounge pants she was wearing. One hand slid up to cup the back of her head, and he stilled when he felt the dried blood from her head wound still in her hair. "Shower?" he asked.

She nodded, and began to kiss his neck, nipping at his skin every other kiss or so.

He needed no more encouragement. With just a few strides they were in his bedroom. He sat her on the edge of his large dresser, pulled off his shirt, and then nearly tore hers from her body. Her full breasts tumbled out, and he was unable to resist reaching out to touch one. The rosy nipple hardened against his palm when he grazed it, begging for more of his touch, and he was more than happy to oblige. He watched her face as he pinched it between his thumb and forefinger. Bronaugh closed her eyes on a moan, and one of her hands slid down the front of her pants to caress herself.

Marc swallowed hard as he watched the movement of her hand. For a moment he could barely speak, but somehow he managed. "Ach, Bronaugh. Yer going tae unman me, lass." His heart was beating so hard he felt like it was going to pound right out of his chest. He continued to tease her nipples as she began rolling her hips in rhythm with the movement of her hand. Her breath came faster and faster. His seemed to stop altogether.

When he could take it no longer, he pulled her hand away and grabbed the waistband of her pants. With one hard yank he split them in half and tore the material all the way down her legs. Running his hands up her legs starting at her ankles, he squeezed the soft flesh on the insides of her thighs, pushing them farther apart until she was sitting there with her womanhood fully open and exposed to him, the pink folds flushed and damp with moisture. The scent of her arousal rose in the air between them, and his mouth began to water.

Falling to his knees, he licked her from her opening to her tight little bundle of nerves, giving it a flick with his tongue when he reached it. Her hips bucked forward and she widened her thighs even more to give him better access. Then he felt her hands bury themselves in his hair to hold his head there between her legs.

His lass was not shy about what she wanted.

His arms went under her rounded thighs and he pulled her hips closer to him. The soft sounds she made guided him as he laved her tender flesh, sucking the sweet bud into his mouth and flicking it with his tongue. She smelled like the musky flowers of the meadowsweet plant and tasted like honeysuckle. He couldn't get enough of her.

Very soon, her hips began to rock in rhythm with his tongue. "Marc…oh…gods…"

His cock was so hard he had to reach down and release himself from his jeans to ease the pain. With a groan of relief, he went back to tasting her with relish until she stiffened under his hands and mouth. Her cries went straight to his soul as she came, her body convulsing with the power of her orgasm, knocking over the lamp next to her.

She was still moaning when he rose up to his feet and in one motion pulled her hips forward and sank his cock deep within her wet heat. His bellow of pleasure mixed with her cries, her body hugging him tight. He'd never felt such pleasure with a female before, and before he knew it he had her off the dresser and back up into his arms. She wrapped her legs around him and hung on tight as he braced his feet apart and began to fuck her. One hand went under her sweet arse and the other held her head to his shoulder as he rocked in and out. But it wasn't enough, so he moved his hands to her rounded hips. He raised her up and slammed her back down, impaling her on him, harder and harder and faster and faster until she began to tremble in his arms and he felt his orgasm rising up his shaft.

"I'm going tae come, lass," he gritted out. "I cannae stop."

"Yes," she cried.

Using her legs, she pumped her hips even faster. Her head fell back, giving him a perfect view of her perfect breasts bouncing up and down against his chest. Her cries came faster and louder, and he had the sudden urge to sink his teeth deep into her shoulder, but she was moving too fast. And then it was too late as his orgasm hit him like a truck. He roared with pleasure, his cock pulsing inside his sweet Bronaugh at long last.

She tightened around him as she came a second time, her body squeezing every last drop out of him. When he could breathe again, he fell to his knees and sat back on his heels with her on his lap, still inside her.

For a long time he did nothing but sit there and hold her. He loved the feel of her bare back, her skin soft and supple under his hands. Loved the feel of her body encasing him in her slick passage. Loved the sound of her soft breaths in his ear as she tried to catch her breath.

"I'm sorry, lass," he said softly.

She pulled back to look at him. Her blonde hair was mussed, her lips were swollen from her biting them while he fucked her, and her skin was still flushed. She was the bonniest thing he'd ever seen in his long life. "Sorry about which part, exactly?" she asked with a twinkle in her brown eyes. "Because I sure as hell enjoyed every second of what just happened."

His chest ached at the thought of what might have happened to her. What he very nearly allowed to happen to her. "For everything," he finally said. "For turning ye away. For not taking ye out o' that fookin' place the moment I saw ye were there. For pretending tae play along with them when I should have stood up for ye and yer family." He hid his face in her neck, ashamed. "I'm so, so sorry, lass."

After a moment she said, "So, does this mean that you're not afraid that I'm going to become a soul sucker?"

He squeezed her tighter. "Just the opposite. I'm more afraid now than ever," he told her with brutal honestly.

"Then why did you do this?" she asked. "Or was this just a one-time thing? Like a 'just get it out of your system' type of deal?"

He lifted his head. She kept her eyes down, but he'd heard the slight tremble in her voice. Taking her face between his palms, he forced her to look at him. "No, Bronaugh. Dinna even think that! I was no' lying tae ye earlier. Yer MINE, lass. And I will no' be giving ye up. Not ever."

"But what about my dark side?"

"Especially no' tae yer dark side," he swore vehemently. She dropped her head back down to his shoulder and hugged him. "C'mon," he said. "Let's get ye cleaned up." Carefully, he lifted her off him and set her down so they could go take that shower.

Two hours and two more showers later, Bronaugh was sitting at the small kitchen table while Marc whipped them up something to eat. He smiled to himself when he remembered the horrified look on her face when he'd suggested that she cook them something. It was probably a good thing that he'd learned to provide for himself so he'd never have to depend on a female to feed him.

A loud knock sounded just before the front door was opened and closed again and Cedric announced his arrival. Marc stopped whisking the eggs and set the bowl on the counter before greeting him. Lowering his eyes with respect, he tried to remember all of the excuses he'd rehearsed during the ride up from Texas, but they'd completely fallen out of his head. In the end, all he managed to do was assume an even more submissive posture and hope that Cedric wouldn't choose this day to decide to slam down the hammer on his sometimes less than obedient pack members.

"Ach. Get up, Marc. Ye look like a wet kitten."

Marc ran a hand over his damp hair and lifted his eyes to meet Cedric's ice blue gaze. He couldn't read much in them. "Cedric, I—"

"I'm so verra happy that ye made it back home safe," Cedric interrupted him. "I ken that things didnae go as planned, and that was no' yer fault, Marc. Ye did yer best, I'm certain."

Marc didn't know what to say.

"Are ye going tae introduce me tae yer new lass?" Cedric asked, giving the lass in question a wink. "Lucian was sure tae call and tell me about the 'bloody Fae' ye brought into our home."

She smiled back warmly, and a low growl of possession escaped Marc before he could stop it. His eyes widened in horror and he cleared his throat to try to hide the fact that he'd just practically challenged his alpha over nothing more than a friendly smile.

"Ach. Aye. Where are my manners? Cedric, this is Bronaugh Lane. Bronaugh, this is my pack master, Cedric Kincaid."

Cedric gave her a nod. "It's verra nice tae meet ye, Bronaugh," he told her sincerely.

"Thank you," she answered. "And before you say anything else, I'd just like to say that I know you're probably all kinds of pissed off at Marc right now. But you should know that even though he messed everything up with the Texas pack, he saved me…and my family. I know we're just Faeries, but he risked his life standing up for us, and I think that should count for something."

"Messed up everything, eh?" Cedric asked. "There's no way tae make amends with them?" He looked to Marc for confirmation.

Marc straightened his spine. "They would have killed her, Cedric. Ye should have seen what those bastards were doing tae them. Tae *females*. It does no' matter that they are Fae. No female should be treated that way. I could no' continue tae let that happen. Especially after they caught my Bronaugh…" He dwindled off at the twinkle of amusement in Cedric's eyes. It was there and gone by the time the alpha turned back to Bronaugh.

Cedric cocked a brow at her. "But what aboot the havoc he's caused for me now? I assume the Texas pack will be coming after ye?"

She shrugged one shoulder, unconcerned. "Probably. But I can help you take care of them."

"No, you will NO'," Marc ordered. Ignoring her sound of protest, he slammed the bowl of eggs onto the counter and turned to Cedric with a sense of urgency. "Cedric, ye cannae let her do anything o' the sort. She will no' be able tae handle it."

"I could so handle it," she insisted.

Cedric raised a hand to quiet Bronaugh and focused his attention on Marc. "And why no'? She's a Fae. She has power. And she's offering her help. Why should I no' take it?"

Marc snapped his mouth closed. He saw Bronaugh watching him from the corner of his eye, waiting to see what he would say. Well, she was about to have quite a surprise.

He barely even stuttered when he informed his alpha exactly what kind of female he'd claimed for his own. "Bronaugh is *an olc*, a Dark Fae, Cedric. But she is no' a soul sucker. She is braw. And she is kind." He didn't need to know about the other side of her that Marc saw when they were alone—the side of her that liked to be in control, to have him at her mercy. The dark hunger and excitement that shone from her rainbow eyes when he allowed her to do so.

No. No one else needed to know about that part of her. If she felt the need to let the dark side of her nature out, she could do it with him, in private.

He was getting hard again just thinking about it.

"I can no' allow her tae fight, Cedric. Ye know what might happen if she does."

Bronaugh left her chair and hopped up onto the counter, swinging her legs over until she was sitting on the edge near Marc in nothing but his shirt and a pair of his boxer briefs. "Do I get to have an opinion about all of this? Being that, you know, it's *me* you guys are talking about?"

Marc opened his mouth to tell her no, she didn't. But then he shut it again. "Go on, lass. Say yer piece."

She looked vaguely surprised that he'd acquiesced, but quickly got over it. "Well, I'd just like to say that Marc is probably right." Smiling at the shocked look that must be on his face, she told Cedric. "Before Marc stood up to the Texas pack, I was preparing to fight them myself. They had us inside a building lined with iron, in an iron cell, and their arena had an iron cage over it to keep us inside. It sapped our power. The others more so than me because of what I am. I decided that to save myself and my family, I needed to call on the darkness inside me." Multiple colors of the rainbow shone from her eyes as she remembered. "I could feel it, churning around inside me, wanting to be released. If I'd let it out, it would have given me the power to defeat them…possibly. And to save the people who had saved me. But I never would have been the same. I'd have lost my adopted family." She looked at Marc, her eyes brightening with beautiful rainbow tears. "I'd have lost you."

Reaching out, he cupped her cheek in one large hand, telling her with his touch and his eyes everything he couldn't say with words.

"Ach," Cedric told them. "Save it for when I'm no' here, will ye?"

Marc smiled at Bronaugh and she smiled back, her eyes fading back to brown. He gave Cedric his attention as the alpha filled them in on what had gone down with the Fae prince and princess while Marc was in Texas.

At the mention of the dark princess, Bronaugh jumped down off the counter. "She's here? Princess Duana is here?"

Marc frowned down at her as Cedric told her, "Aye. She's with the Fae prince."

"No shit," Bronaugh breathed in disbelief.

Cedric smiled. "No shite," he imitated her. "I was verra surprised myself. All of the Dark Fae were sent away during the war, or so I thought. The princess has been with Prince Nada all o' this time. Her brother took her tae him for safekeeping when she was verra young. So yer not alone out here, Bronaugh. There is at least one more o' yer kind that escaped."

Bronaugh leaned back against the counter and averted her eyes.

Marc narrowed his gaze on her. He was getting to know her tells. And right now, he could tell she was hiding something. "What is it, lass?"

"Hmm?" she mumbled.

"Yer hiding something, Bronaugh," he stated. "Ye may as well tell us now." She looked everywhere but at him. "Bronaugh," he warned.

"All right, all right." She heaved a sigh. "The princess and I aren't the only *an olc* out there," she admitted to Cedric. "There's a lot more of us."

"Where?" Cedric demanded.

"Everywhere," she answered. "Most of us were young then. We hid anywhere we could find during the fighting, and scattered to the winds when it was over. Some, like me, were taken in by other Fae. By *na maithe*, the Good Fae."

"And the others?" Marc asked.

"Some of them turned, like the ones back in Texas, and are even now wreaking havoc in different parts of the world. You heard about the people on bath salts running around naked and eating other people's faces, right?"

They both nodded, and Cedric said, "Aye. I've seen something about that on the news."

"Yeah, not bath salts," she said. "Those are *an olc* that have gone to the dark side."

Marc raised a hand in front of him. "Wait just a minute," he said. "So, they're *eating* people now?"

Bronaugh just looked at him and said nothing.

"The one at the rodeo," Marc said with a look of dawning understanding on his face. "It bit ye…"

"I didn't believe the rumors until I saw it with my own eyes," she told them. "Or should I say felt it…"

So not only was there a chance that she would go dark and suck out his soul, but now he had to worry about her *eating* him as well? He scrubbed his face with his hands. When he dropped them back to his sides, his eyes landed on the sweet curve of her thigh and then wandered up over her full hip. His blood surged and his cock began to swell. He hadn't even touched her and he was wanting her.

Completely worth the risk, he decided.

Cedric interrupted his daydreaming. "We need tae tell the others. Can ye both be at my place in an hour?"

Marc tore his eyes from his mate to give Cedric a distracted, "Aye."

Cedric rolled his eyes and headed for the front door, telling them, "Ye can have two hours. But no more."

The front door slammed behind him and Marc turned back to Bronaugh only to be greeted with the flurry of colors burning in her eyes. Reaching behind him, he flicked off the stove. "We can eat later," he growled.

"Aye," she breathed.

Bronaugh walked into Cedric's apartment with Marc, trying to appear a lot more confident than she felt. He gallantly ignored the fact that she was holding his hand in a death grip. She couldn't help it. Not only was she about to walk into a roomful of strangers wearing nothing but his borrowed clothes. But she was about to walk into a roomful of werewolves.

Her insides churned as the group came into sight. They were lounging around in the living area, and although they looked like your normal group of guys just hanging out watching the game, Bronaugh half wondered if she was going to be sick. She knew it was really kind of silly to be nervous, being that she was just in an entire arena full of a hell of lot more of them just a few days before. But this was different. These were Marc's friends, his family. What if they didn't like her?

As they left the entryway and the galley kitchen came into view on her left, Bronaugh stopped short, her mouth falling open in surprise. Marc, halfway into a hug of greeting with one of the guys, turned to her with a question in his eyes. But she was too busy staring in shock at the scene in front of the stove to notice.

Her Aunt Nancy and her cousin Bitsy were…cooking. Like, with pots and pans and ingredients and everything. Well, they were attempting to cook anyway. But by the sound of the arguing that was going on, it didn't seem like things were going very smoothly.

A large male with brown hair and dancing green eyes loomed over them, and Bronaugh felt a tug of fear in her gut for her family until she heard him say, "Nae. Ye dinna put the flour in the pan until ye mix it with the melted butter first. Otherwise, yer gravy will be full o' lumps." Reaching around Bitsy, he grabbed some kind of wire-looking thing out of a drawer and started briskly stirring whatever was in the pan. "Dinna fash yerself, lass," he told Bitsy when she let out a discouraged sigh. "We might be able tae save it yet. Just need tae whisk it a bit." Her cousin looked like a child standing in front of his massive body, but his tone was kind and his body language was completely respectful of her and Aunt Nancy.

Just as Bronaugh began to relax, he caught her watching them, and gave her a saucy wink. Her eyes widened, but she couldn't help but smile back at him. He was a very good-looking male.

A menacing growl sounded beside her. "Watch yerself, Duncan," Marc threatened.

Bronaugh stiffened, still not used to the possessiveness of her werewolf, but Duncan just threw back his head and laughed. "Dinna worry, lad. I'm just being friendly is all.

Ye should ken that by now, Marc. Ye have been around me for a long time."

"Aye, I do. So I would appreciate it if ye dinna flirt with my lass. Bronaugh is—"

"Ach. Aye. She's yours." Duncan waved his hand at him and turned back to the stove. "Besides, by the way she is gazing at ye with her colorful eyes, I dinna think ye have anything tae worry about."

Marc glanced down at her, his own brown eyes darkening when he saw the way she was looking at him. It wasn't the time or the place, but she couldn't help it. She'd never had anyone act so protective of her before.

She kinda liked it.

Before he realized what she was doing, she'd pulled Marc into the guest bath and slammed the door behind them. She could hear Duncan's boisterous laugh on the other side of the door, but she didn't care. Reaching up, she pulled Marc's head down to her and kissed him hungrily.

A low growl of a different nature rumbled in his chest, and she ran one hand down the front of his soft T-shirt to place her palm over the vibration. But that wasn't enough, so she started yanking his shirt up out of his jeans. She needed to feel his warm skin. And it was so very warm. Hot, silky satin over hard, ridged muscle.

He bent lower and gripped her around the back of her thighs, lifting her up. He seemed to like having her wrapped around him like that. Walking forward, he sat her on the edge of the small sink and wedged his hips between her legs. Talking between kisses, he said, "Ach, lass…I want tae be alone with ye…but we need tae…go out there…for our meeting."

"But I'm aching for you, Marc," she breathed. "I need you." He nipped at the muscle between her neck and shoulder and she groaned as her body responded with a surge of wet heat between her legs.

"Bronaugh…" His voice was little more than a rasp.

Taking matters into her own hands, she pulled her borrowed T-shirt up and off. Marc leaned back so he could see her, going completely still at the sight of her naked breasts. She squeezed them as he watched, then plucked the nipples until they were as hard as little stones. "Give me your hand," she told him.

In somewhat of a daze, he obliged, and she brought it to her mouth and sucked in two of his fingers. Closing her eyes, she ran her tongue lightly around them, then sucked again, imagining it was his cock in her mouth. When she opened her eyes, Marc had stopped breathing. Removing his fingers from her mouth, she slid his hand down her throat and all the way to her breast. She made him squeeze it, then she trailed his hand down her stomach to the place where his hips were pressed against hers.

"Undo your pants," she demanded.

"Bronaugh," he moaned, but did as she ordered. His cock sprung out, falling long and thick against her belly. A drop of come seeped from the tip.

She licked her lips. She wanted to taste him. Pushing him away until he was forced to take a step back, she dropped to her knees in front of him and took him in her hand. He was so large her fingers couldn't reach all the way around him. With the tip of her tongue, she licked the head of his cock, moaning hungrily.

His hands slid into her hair even as he made a sound of protest, holding her head to the front of his hips. He exhaled a harsh breath of air, and she smiled and licked him again, with more pressure this time. His hips bucked forward, but she pulled away before he could slide into her mouth, teasing him. His hands tightened almost painfully, and then immediately released her when he realized what he was doing. But she didn't mind. She thoroughly enjoyed pushing him until he lost control.

With that in mind, she took him into her mouth fast and hard and pulled him out slowly. She repeated the process until he was shaking with the effort to hold back his orgasm. But Bronaugh wasn't known for showing mercy. Instead, she sucked him in and out again, then ran her tongue on the underside of his cock from his balls to the tip and around the rim of his head while she slid her hand up and down his satiny hardness.

"Bronaugh, lass. I'm going tae come in yer mouth if ye dinna stop."

Yes. Yes, you are.

Bronaugh took him into her mouth again, as far as she could, and pumped him in and out with short, fast movements. Gripping his hips with both hands, she took him in as far as she could and released him slowly, scraping her teeth along his shaft as she did.

Marc let out a muffled shout as he came hot and fast, his cock pulsing in her mouth and his hips thrusting in her hands. She took it all, sucking every last drop out of him.

Leaning over, he grabbed her around the tops of her arms and pulled her right off her feet and up to his chest where he wrapped his heavy arms around her and hugged her to him hard with trembling arms. "Just give me a moment, lass. And I will return the favor." His chest heaved against her as he fought to catch his breath.

The sounds of everyone talking and visiting in the other room came through the door, and she could hear someone asking where they were. "I think we need to get out to the party," she told him.

He stared into her eyes for long moments. She wondered briefly what was so damn fascinating until she realized that they were probably going all rainbow on her. They did that whenever her emotions were high, whether it be lust or fear or hate.

Or love.

The realization hit her like a bucket of ice on her ardor. It must have shown on her face, for Marc's heavy brows came down in concern. "What is it, lass? What's wrong?"

"Nothing," she told him, and tried to smile. "We really should be getting back out there."

"They can wait," he insisted. "Now tell me why the colors suddenly left yer eyes and ye look like ye just saw a ghost."

She smiled. "It's nothing. I just heard everyone out there and realized that I just took complete advantage of you in full hearing of a roomful of werewolves."

He narrowed his eyes at her. It was clear he wasn't buying it.

"Put me down," she said. "And let's get out there before

someone comes banging on the door and catches you with your pants hanging open."

"Ach. We're wolves, Bronaugh. They see my bare arse all the time."

"Yeah, but they'll also be seeing my bare tits." She almost laughed at the speed at which he dropped her and grabbed up her shirt from where it had fallen to the floor. He fumbled with it until she took it from him and pulled it back over her head. She was still braless, but the shirt was Marc's and therefore huge on her. It could practically be a dress. But it was thick enough and dark enough to cover her, and he'd promised her they'd get some new clothes later that day.

When she was dressed again, she shooed him out to the other room, telling him she'd be out in just a minute. Locking herself in, she slowly turned around and leaned back against the door. Bronaugh let out a shuddering breath.

She was falling in love with her werewolf.

Well, what the hell did she think was going to happen after he'd saved her and her family and claimed her as his own? Actually, if she was completely honest with herself, she'd known from that first night that he was much more than one of her normal playthings. She just hadn't wanted to admit it.

Pushing away from the door, she used the restroom and washed her hands. By the time she came out, she was feeling better about things. She'd just needed a few moments alone to come to terms with it all.

Marc was waiting right outside the door. His eyes searched her face, but she must have passed his inspection, because a second later he grinned at her and leaned down to kiss her on the head. "Ye all right, then?" he asked in a rough voice. "I was worried ye had changed yer mind about being here with me."

She took his hand. "Nope. I'm still here. Besides, where am I supposed to go dressed like this?" With a wave of her hand, she indicated the big shirt and boxers and bare feet.

Of course, they both knew no one would have to see her at all if she wished it so.

Marc tucked her in against his side and as they turned toward the rest of the group, he whispered, "Just tae my bed, I hope."

"There you are!" Aunt Nancy exclaimed happily before Bronaugh could respond. She had a stack of plates in her hands. "Dinner is ready. Why don't you come help me, Bronaugh?"

She automatically went to help her, but Marc pulled her back. He gave her aunt an apologetic smile. "I just need tae introduce her tae everyone first."

Aunt Nancy shook her head at herself and waved Bronaugh away. "Yes, of course. I can handle it."

The crowd parted and Bronaugh's attention was immediately caught by the aura of an unknown female who was sitting on the couch. Not because of the kindness that radiated from her light brown eyes, or the lovely smile lighting her features, but because she was a Faerie. Beside her sat a ruggedly handsome male with hair as long as hers, a close-cut beard, and twinkling blue eyes. His arm was around her and she was curled up snugly against his chest.

When she saw Bronaugh, she smiled and jumped to

her feet, banged her knee against the coffee table and fell into the lap of the male. He caught her and grunted playfully, then steadied her to her feet again, and with a smack on her behind, sent her on her way.

The female was tall and voluptuous, but Bronaugh hadn't realized how different they were in size until she stood up, for her mate made her look tinier than she was. "Hey, Marc!" She greeted them, and then she stuck out her hand to Bronaugh. "I'm Heather. I'm Brock's mate." She glanced over her shoulder at the male with the gorgeous hair. He was still watching her. Were all wolves so obsessed with their mates?

Not that it was a bad thing.

Bronaugh craned her neck back to smile timidly up at her. She was at least five or six inches taller than Bronaugh, and built like the majority of Fae woman: a bit heavier than was considered attractive by the humans these days. Bronaugh liked her immediately. She took her hand and shook it firmly. "Bronaugh Lane. It's nice to meet you."

"Bronaugh is also Fae," Marc offered. "She is no' used tae being around so many werewolves."

She noticed he left out the "dark" part.

Heather grinned down at her. "Don't worry about these guys. They're all a bunch of big teddy bears once you get to know them."

"Sure, to you," Bronaugh said. "You've got that one to protect you." She peeked around Heather's arm at the male she'd been sitting next to. "He's huge." Looking at the rest of the towering wolves in the room, none shorter than six foot three or so, she clarified, "Then again, I'm thinking maybe there's something in the water here."

Grabbing her hand, Heather pulled her over to Brock. He stood when she approached, unfolding to his full height of six foot seven inches, and Bronaugh felt a twinge of fear due to his sheer size in spite of Marc's reassuring presence at her back. But then the male smiled, and her stomach did a little flip for an entirely different reason.

"How ya' doin'?" he said in a pleasantly deep voice. "I'm Brock Hume." He threw an arm around Heather's shoulders, all casual-like, but Bronaugh got the distinct impression he didn't like his female being out of his reach. She wondered what had happened to make him so protective. "I'm sort of new here, too," he added.

Marc took her around the room then. She said hello again to Cedric, who was just as large as Brock. Duncan kissed the back of her hand and gave her a smile and a wink, much to her amusement and Marc's ire.

Last was Lucian. Only slightly shorter than the others, he looked very Scottish with his shock of russet hair and pale skin. And when she said hello, he glared at her with eyes as stormy and gray as the Highlands. It seemed her welcome was over.

"Lucian, don't be like that, man. Say hello to the lady," Brock said from behind her.

Lucian turned his cold gaze on him. It warmed only slightly when it landed on Brock. He was a friend, then? Bronaugh would hate to see how he acted with his enemies.

"This female is no' just Fae," Lucian informed him.

"She's *an olc*—the Dark Fae." His glare turned to Marc. "He brought a dark one here, into our verra home!"

"Lucian. Haud yer wheesht!" Cedric ordered. "I dinna want tae hear anything more aboot Bronaugh. She is Marc's, and therefore one o' us now, and ye will respect her as such."

Without taking his eyes from her, Lucian responded, "She will never be one o' *my* pack."

"Then may I suggest ye find a new pack," Marc growled without hesitation.

Bronaugh looked around. It wasn't only Lucian who was against her being there. Brock, Heather, and Duncan were all looking at her differently now, too. The welcoming expressions were gone, replaced with faces filled with fear and surprise. And when it came to Lucian —pure hate. Which she immediately resented. What the hell had she ever done to him?

Aunt Nancy and Bitsy, having heard the raised voices from where they were setting the table, shoved their way into the circle that had formed around her and Marc. They immediately took up protective stances in front of Bronaugh.

Aunt Nancy defended her adopted niece to Lucian. "My Bronaugh is a good girl." She stood before the huge werewolf without fear, even though she was half his size. She even stuck a finger up in his face as she told him, "You can just take that look off your face right now, young one. Dislike us all you want for what we are, but I'll not have you so much as looking at my niece in such a threatening way. Do you understand?"

Lucian's eyes flicked over to Aunt Nancy and back to

Bronaugh again. His lip curled in disgust. "Look at her eyes. Having her here will do naught but bring trouble tae this pack."

Everyone except Marc turned to stare at her again. Bronaugh dropped her eyes, knowing they reflected her emotions and probably looked like something out of a carnival funhouse right about now.

Marc stepped in front of her and tucked her in behind him. "Ye will shut yer bloody mouth right now, Lucian." His voice was rough, and Bronaugh could see his muscles straining against his clothes. He was on the verge of changing to protect her. She didn't know whether to cheer him on or run away so he wouldn't have to fight his family for her. He was a wolf, and wolves needed a pack. Even she knew the odds were against him surviving without one.

Lucian stepped up to the challenge, and Bitsy and Aunt Nancy jumped to the side to avoid getting squashed between the two males. "I will no'! She does no' belong here with us!" His upper lip was lifted in a snarl, exposing his growing canines.

Bronaugh placed her hand on Marc's back, hoping it would calm him. His muscles rolled beneath her palm as they twitched and swelled beneath his skin. "Marc..."

Cedric shoved himself in between the two males, facing Lucian. He too seemed even larger than before. "Ye will back down, Lucian. And ye will do it now. I will no' have ye two smashing up my place again." He paused. "Unless ye wish tae challenge *me*..." He let the words hang in the air.

After a tense couple of seconds, Lucian's eyes flicked

over to the alpha. The muscles jumped in his jaw as he clenched his teeth, but in the end he submitted to his leader and backed away.

"If anyone else has a problem with Bronaugh, ye will have a problem with no' just Marc, but with me." Cedric speared each of them in turn with his icy blue gaze. "So do any of ye have a problem?"

One by one, the wolves and even Heather fell into submissive stances amongst mumbles of "No problem here", "Of course not" and "Why would I want tae chase off another bonnie lass in our pack?" This last, of course, from Duncan.

Cedric turned to Marc. "Stand down, Marc. 'Tis over. There willnae be anyone threatening yer mate. I promise ye that."

Bronaugh kept her mouth shut and stayed behind Marc. She still had her hand on his back, and she could feel the muscles slowly calm down and go back to normal size with his every breath. Marc gave Cedric a nod.

She wondered what was up with the alpha, that he was standing up for her like he was. Or was he just trying to keep the males of his pack under control? Even for someone who was unwilling to discriminate, it seemed a bit much, considering what she was.

"Um, speaking of Bronaugh's eyes," Heather said into the heavy silence. "There's something that you all should know."

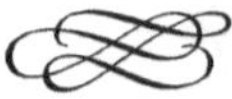

CHAPTER 27

"Why didn't you say anything before now?" Brock asked Heather after she had told the group what she knew. They'd all sat down again in Cedric's living room after eating the fine meal that Duncan had coached the Fae females into making, Marc seating Bronaugh near Cedric and grabbing chairs from the kitchen table for him and Duncan.

Heather looked over at Cedric and opened her arms out in front of her. "I honestly just forgot. With everything else that happened and then getting moved into our place and all...I really wasn't trying to withhold information or anything." Her eyes pleaded with them all to believe her.

"It's okay, sunshine," Brock told her. "I know you'd never do that."

"It just came to me again after meeting Bronaugh. No offense," she told her.

"We're good," Bronaugh answered.

"Aye," Cedric added. "Dinna fash yerself, lass." He

smoothed his black hair back in its ponytail, his brows lowered in thought. "So, yer sure that the prince does no' ken that one o' the dark ones has somehow wormed his way into his inner circle?"

Marc had yet to meet this prince, but from what he'd heard, he sounded completely daft. "And how do ye ken that he does no' want ye just tae *think* he doesn't ken what Frank is?"

Heather wrinkled her forehead in confusion. "What?"

"Maybe he does ken," Marc clarified. "Ye said yerself that he likes tae play games. What if this is just one o' his games?" It didn't sound like the idea was so farfetched to him. The prince had already sent Brock and Heather off to fight their way out of some far off who-knows-where with no extra clothes or supplies, just for fun. Brock had told them all about it. During the week he and Heather were there, the prince had even made them toss a coin numerous times to find out what was going to happen next. They'd either gotten something good or a battle for survival, depending on how the coin landed.

And sometimes the battle for survival was the better of the two choices.

Heather looked thoughtful as she glanced at Brock. "I guess that could very well be the case. But I didn't get that feeling when I was there with him."

"Actually, there are a lot more of us still here than you all realize."

All eyes turned to Bronaugh once again, and Marc leaned closer to where she sat at the end of the couch and kept a close eye on the rest of them. Other than Lucian, they seemed to have come to a kind of a nervous acceptance of her.

"What do ye mean?" Duncan asked.

Cedric leaned back and crossed his arms over his chest with a sigh.

Bronaugh glanced at Marc and he gave her an encouraging nod, taking her small hand in his. It was so wee and fragile-feeling. He carefully gave it a squeeze.

"Many of us *an olc* who hadn't succumbed to the human addiction escaped the enslave— roundup," she quickly corrected," of our kind. I've run into a few here and there."

"Why did ye no' stay with them?" Duncan asked. There was no menace in his tone, just an honest curiosity.

She gave a small shrug. "Aunt Nancy, Uncle Ken, and Bitsy were my family. We moved around a lot to avoid any of you finding out about me, so I never really had the chance to get to know any of the others."

"We like to travel anyway," Bitsy said with a smile at her adopted cousin.

Cedric sat up again. "There's an uncle? Ye never said anything aboot a male." He looked between Marc and Bronaugh in question, then over to her aunt and cousin.

"We don't know where he is," Aunt Nancy answered. "We were separated in Austin." Bitsy reached over and took her hand when her voice broke. She smiled at her daughter, though it was obviously hard for her. "I'm sure he's fine. He'll find us."

Marc slapped himself on the forehead. "I totally forgot aboot yer uncle!" he told Bronaugh. Then he turned to her aunt. "Do we need tae call him? Go back and look for him?"

She shook her head. "There's no need. We've been together for a long time, and have a Fae bond. He will find me anywhere if he is still…" She looked away, unable to finish what she'd been about to say.

"How many?" Duncan asked. All eyes turned to him in question. "How many like you have you seen?" he asked Bronaugh.

"At least fifty," she told him. "Give or take. Some were in groups. Some by themselves. Some were adopted by other Fae as I was. And those are just the ones I happened to run into. There are more."

Cedric exchanged a look with Brock and Heather.

"What? What is it?" Marc asked them. "I thought ye said there was no' a problem with my Bronaugh being here. This should no' change anything…"

"There is no'. No' with Bronaugh," Cedric assured him. "No' with us."

"Then with who?" he asked. "The bloody prince?"

A loud knock sounded on the front door. They all looked at each other in surprise, and then Cedric got up to answer the door. When he returned, he was with a tall gentleman with long silver hair. The man was dressed impeccably in a three-piece suit that looked tailor-made to fit him. The look was topped off with silver-toed boots and a silver cane.

Prince Nada smiled as he looked around the group until his eyes landed on Bronaugh. "My ears were ringing so loudly that I decided to come over and join the party."

"At least ye had the courtesy tae knock this time," Cedric remarked.

"Yes, well. I know how strange you wolves are about all of that. So I 'whooshed' on over here, as you like to say, but only to the hallway. I didn't want to spook you." His eyes had never left Bronaugh the entire time he was speaking. "Aren't you going to introduce me to your new guest?"

Marc started to stand up, but Bitsy beat him to it. With a hand on his shoulder as she passed, she pushed him back down into his chair with a strength he wouldn't have expected from her. "Hiya, your highness. Remember me?"

"Bitsy." He acknowledged her while still staring at Bronaugh. "And your mother, Nancy. I trust you both are well?"

"Yes, your highness," Aunt Nancy answered. "We are doing just fine. Thank you."

He smiled. "Good, good. And you've added another to your little family. *Introduce me.*" It was not a request.

All this time, Bronaugh had sat frozen to the couch, her back to the prince of *na maithe* tribe. But now she popped up and turned to face him.

Marc grabbed her arm and tried to stop her. "Ye dinna need tae talk tae him, lass." But she just patted his hand, gave him a wink, and strode up to stand before the prince.

Marc stood also and stayed close to her, just in case. He didn't care who this fancy pants was. He'd be damned if he would let him or anyone hurt one little hair on her blonde head.

She curtsied low before the prince, still managing somehow to look proper and graceful in her oversized T-shirt and boxers. "Prince Nada, it's an honor to meet you." She stayed as she was until he bade her to rise.

"Bronaugh, I presume?" he asked.

She gave him a nod. "Bronaugh Lane, of *an olc* tribe."

The prince looked her over from the top of her head to the tips of her toes. Nothing he was thinking showed on his face, yet Marc could feel the little hairs rise on the back of his neck at the way he was looking at her. Then he smiled happily and told Marc, "She's very pretty."

"Aye," he agreed.

"Seriously?" Bronaugh asked them both. "That's all you have to say about me? That I'm pretty? Not smart? Or brave? Or dangerous, even?"

"Oh, I know exactly how dangerous you are," the prince said as the smile fell from his face. "I know more so than anyone here, including these silly wolves. Except perhaps Lucian." He nodded in Lucian's direction.

Marc frowned over at his pack brother, but Lucian would not meet his gaze.

"And Brock, of course," the prince added.

"Oh no. Uh uh. Leave me out of this," Brock told him. "What's in the past is in the past."

The prince tilted his head, curiosity clouding his features. "Is it? Truly though? After all, her family killed yours."

"What the hell are you talking about?" Bronaugh asked.

"Aye. What the bloody hell are ye talking aboot?" Marc repeated.

Prince Nada walked around Bronaugh and Marc, unbuttoned his jacket, and made himself comfortable in the oversized armchair that Brock and Heather had vacated when he came in. Setting his cane carefully against the end table, he crossed his legs and laced his fingers together over his stomach and looked out the window while he waited.

Cedric rolled his eyes and went to join him. A moment later, the rest of the group followed suit and retook their seats.

Bronaugh scooted up to the edge of the couch, leaning toward the prince. "Why would you think something like that about my family?" Marc could tell it was taking her every effort to stay composed.

"Oh, I don't think, young Bronaugh. I know. For I was there, you see. I saw it all happen. Your mother, father, and brother attacked the pack that Brock and Lucian were born into. Fortunately, these two were playing down by the loch and so escaped having their souls sucked out by a rabid group of *an olc*."

Marc saw her stiffen beside him out of the corner of his eye. "You're lying," she accused.

The prince smiled kindly. "I never lie, my dear. Although I do enjoy my fun now and then, I would never tell you an untruth. It's entirely too hard to keep track of what you told whom when you get to be my age. Eventually, someone calls you out on the untruth." He leaned forward also until he was mere inches from her face, like he was telling her a secret. "Plus, it's just so very uncouth of one to do. Don't you agree?"

Bronaugh leaned back, putting some distance between them. "I haven't lied to anyone here. They all know who and what I am."

The prince winked at her and resumed his own comfortable pose. "I never said that you had, dear."

Bitsy spoke up from the other side of the room where she was seated on the fireplace with her mom. "What are you going to do about Bronaugh?"

The prince furrowed his brows and tapped one finger against his chin. "Now *that* is a good question, daughter. What am I going to do with this one?"

Her aunt opened her mouth to speak just as an animalistic growl filled the room. "Ye will no' be doing anything with my lass," Marc gritted out. "She stays with me."

Cedric had sat quietly observing the conversation this entire time, as had the rest of them, but now he spoke up. "With all due respect, prince. Her tribe aside, Bronaugh, from all I've seen and heard, is a braw lass. She has no' done or said anything tae make me think otherwise. And more importantly, she has been claimed by one o' my own pack, and that makes *her* one o' our pack. I would truly hate for this tae cause a rift between us, just when things are going so well." Though his words were light, his tone was ominous. So much so, the prince narrowed his gaze in surprise at the alpha wolf. Cedric didn't so much as flinch as he met that gaze with a warning look of his own.

Marc felt a flood of gratitude for his pack leader. However, from what little he'd seen and heard of him, he didn't think the Fae prince would take well to threats, so he sought to try a different tactic. "I dinna think we've been properly introduced," he said to the prince. "I am Marc Kincaid, and I would just like tae say—"

"So sorry," the prince interrupted cheerfully. "But we really need to go now. Don't worry, I won't keep her long."

Marc frowned and exchanged a look of panic with Cedric. The alpha stood up. "Yer no' taking anyone anywhere…"

A gust of wind that appeared to come from the closed windows blasted through the room. Marc raised one arm to shield his face while reaching for Bronaugh with his other hand.

But she was gone.

The wind died down as quickly as it started, and when the dust settled, the prince was gone. And so was Bronaugh.

A roar of rage rent the air as Marc reacted instantly to the absence of his mate, followed by the sounds of tearing flesh and shifting bones. His emotions high, Marc's change was nearly instantaneous. Within moments, the huge brown werewolf flew out of the room and crashed through the front door, knocking over furniture on his way.

BROCK PRESSED a quick kiss to Heather's lips, ripped off his clothing and started to change, as did Duncan. Grunts of pain and the howls of wolves echoed in the otherwise silent room. Shaking off what remained of their clothing, they bounded out of the apartment after Marc. Heather watched them go, knowing nothing she said would keep Brock from helping a member of his pack.

Cedric threw up his hands as one them landed on the kitchen table, splintering the wood into twenty different pieces. "Dammit, ye eejits! I just replaced that table!"

Hands on his hips, he shook his head, then noticed Lucian still sitting. "Well, let's go! We cannae have them starting a war with the Good Faeries without us now, can we?"

Spinning on his heel, he stalked out after the others. Lucian followed reluctantly behind him, muttering under his breath about "Fookin' daft Faeries."

Heather exchanged wide-eyed looks with Bronaugh's family, and then they all sank back down onto their respective chairs to wait.

"Maybe we should go after them?" Heather said.

Bitsy popped back up off the couch. "Maybe we should not depend on males to handle everything, and help by conducting our own search." Then she ran out the broken front door.

Aunt Nancy was right on her heels, and with a shrug, Heather followed.

"No one actually told us we needed to stay here," she commented to the empty room on her way out.

CHAPTER 28

Marc threw his head back and released a howl into the misty night sky. An answering howl echoed through the hemlock trees, followed by three more. It was Cedric and the others. They were less than a few miles away, fanning out into ever-expanding circles as they searched.

The wolves had been out for two days straight looking for Bronaugh. And although they hadn't found even the slightest hint as to where the prince might have taken her, Marc's heart nevertheless swelled enormously for his brothers. Even for Lucian, who, in spite of his obvious feelings for Bronaugh and her kind, had shown a surprising amount of stamina and loyalty during their vigil. Although if what the prince had said about his family was true, Marc couldn't say he blamed Lucian for how he felt. And that just made him appreciate his help even more. The fact that it was under the alpha's orders didn't matter in the slightest to him.

Cedric had led them first to the little house by SeaTac airport, but it was empty. It still contained all of their stuff however, including a set of obnoxious thrones, so it didn't appear that Prince Nada and company had abandoned it entirely. Thank the gods.

They'd left the house and searched the neighborhood for any scent of the Fae, hoping to be able to find what direction they'd gone, but with the way the Fae "whooshed" in and out of places, there was no trail of them once they'd left the boundaries of the property.

Out of options but needing to do something… anything…the wolves were now searching every inch of the mountainous terrain around their apartment. The prince could've taken her to any number of different places, none of which were reachable by any other than the Fae, but Marc couldn't just sit around and wait.

Though it was still late summer, the winds howled through the mountain passes and cold rain drizzled down upon Marc's shaggy back. Exhausted, his legs trembling from running for days without stopping, he sank down onto his haunches beneath the shelter of one of the towering trees and cried out into the night for his lost lass. The sound, eerie and forlorn, rose through the trees and faded into the night. A gaping hole of isolation tore through his chest, and his massive head dropped forward to hang between his front legs. He stayed like that for a long time.

The rain began to let up, and Marc raised his head and took a deep breath of the damp forest air. He shook his head. He would not give up. Now that he'd found his Bronaugh, the mere thought of living the rest of his seemingly endless life without her was too much for him to bear.

No. He would not accept that she was gone.

Mentally and physically as prepared as he was going to get, he was about to continue on when one ear twitched to the side. He became still, listening. Something was off… Something… A sound over to the right. It reminded him of the creak of wet rope. Like a swing…or a noose.

Shaking *that* horrifying thought out of his head, Marc trotted off the trail he'd been following and forged ahead through the wet undergrowth, chasing the sound. He should alert the pack, in case it was something dangerous, but for some reason he couldn't bring himself to sound an alarm. Though the fur stood up on the back of his neck, he had a feeling that whatever was there, he needed to see it alone.

Pushing his nose through a row of wet sword ferns, he saw he had come to a small clearing. A single old maple tree with leaves bigger than his paws stood in the center, partially hidden by the mist. The ground around it was covered in thick green moss and a few leaves that were just beginning to fall. The strange sound was coming from the other side of the tree.

Much as he wanted to, Marc did not rush into the clearing all willy-nilly, but instead stayed within the cover of the forest for a few moments—waiting and watching. Scanning the trees that surrounded the clearing, he watched for any signs of danger. Cocking his ears, he listened. But all he heard was that fucking creaking sound. He sniffed the air…

Meadowsweet after the rain.

His heart thumped within his chest so hard he got lightheaded. Keeping to the edge of the clearing, he crept through the wet foliage, staying just out of sight. His frightened eyes never left the tree, and as the other side of its trunk came into view, he finally saw what was making the noise.

Two pieces of thick rope were hanging over one of the large branches high above. They swung back and forth in tandem, creaking on the wet bark. At the ends of the rope, a makeshift swing was attached.

And in the swing sat his Bronaugh. She was leaning forward with her arms looped around the ropes, barely keeping her from falling face-first onto the damp ground. Her blonde hair swung forward, hiding her face as she spun the swing back and forth with her bare toes. She was wearing a gauzy white shift of a dress, and her arms and shoulders were bare. As he watched, she sniffed and shivered and pulled her arms into her body without releasing the rope.

Marc stared, afraid to trust this fairytale-like image he saw before him. The after-shimmers of something magical still hung in the heavy air, causing the fur to ripple on his back and the adrenaline to rush through his veins.

Bronaugh suddenly raised her head and looked straight at him with forlorn brown eyes. She blinked, and the sadness was replaced with disbelief. "Marc?" she asked. "Marc, is that you?"

He glanced around again, still not trusting his very own eyes. It looked like Bronaugh. Her smoky voice sounded like his Bronaugh. His heart told him it was his

Bronaugh, but his fatigued mind was having a hard time believing it.

"It *is* you!" she exclaimed. Then she rubbed her eyes and looked again, like she was also having trouble believing it was so. But when he was still there, a bright smile lit up her bonnie face. She hopped down off the swing, but when she saw that he made no move to come toward her, she stayed where she was. Uncertainty crossed her features. "Marc, what's wrong? Why are you just standing there?" She took a hesitant step. "It's me," she told him softly. The excitement suddenly fell from her face, to be replaced with the forlorn expression he'd first seen. "I guess that's still the problem, huh?"

He stayed where he was, afraid to believe that she was actually real and not just an illusion. Or worse, a trap. Lowering his head, he growled low in his throat as he checked the clearing again.

She took a step back. No fear showed on her face, just that heart-wrenching sadness. Then her eyes started to dance with angry color. "Buck up there, wolfman," she spit out. "Nothing's going to fucking bite you."

Marc let out a sort of yelp that didn't even begin to describe everything he was feeling, and then he sagged to the ground. It *was* her. Reaching deep inside himself, he found the strength he needed to change back. It took him a while, but eventually he managed. Once it was done, he could do nothing but lie limp on the damp moss for a few seconds, breathing hard. Even then, he couldn't take his eyes from his lass. Not certain if he could stand just yet, he gathered his legs under him until he was on all fours and started to crawl toward her.

Her bare feet disappeared from his vision, only to suddenly appear again directly in front of him. She dropped to her knees, staining her white dress on the ground. "Marc! What's wrong with you?" Her voice was filled with panic as she gathered him up in her lap. "What happened..." She pulled away to look him over. "Wait, *did* something bite you?"

Joy rose up inside him. Recovering quickly from the trials of the last few days, Marc barked out a laugh and pulled himself up onto his knees until they were face to face. Sitting back on his haunches as she was, he took her face in his hands. "Nae, lass." Then he got serious again. "Where the bloody hell have ye been, Bronaugh?" he asked. "We've been searching for ye for days!"

She reached up and pulled his hands away from her face. "Yeah, Bitsy told me."

Marc was confused. "Bitsy?" Unable to help himself, he ran his hands down her arms and legs, searching for injuries. But his Bronaugh appeared to be braw and healthy.

She slapped his hands away. "I'm fine, Marc. Bitsy, Aunt Nancy and Heather found me," she said. "Well, found me and the prince. They convinced him to let me come back."

"Found ye where?" he asked. "We've been looking for ye for days," he repeated. This entire conversation was leaving a sour taste in his mouth. Five brawny werewolves had set out to save her and it was the females who rescued her?

That just wasn't right.

But his Bronaugh was here with him, and she was safe, so did it truly matter?

Aye. It does matter.

No, it does no'.

Ach. His head was beginning to pound.

Bronaugh's voice pulled him away from his internal argument. "It's okay, Marc. Prince Nada and I had a good talk. I agreed to help him and he agreed to let me stay. He even took me to see Princess Duana. She was thrilled to see one of *an olc*, and was reluctant to let me leave."

"But where were ye, lass? Where did the bastard take ye?" he demanded. For some reason, it seemed important that he know. Not that he meant to ever allow this to happen again.

"He took me somewhere you couldn't have followed," she finally admitted.

"But yer family could," he practically snarled. "Because they're Fae, like ye."

"Not like me, no."

She dropped her eyes, and Marc suddenly felt that aching emptiness again. He could feel her leaving him. Not physically. Physically she was still sitting right there in front of him. And yet she was leaving him.

He could not let that happen. "Bronaugh, lass. What is it?" When she didn't respond, he hooked a finger under her chin and lifted her face until she looked at him. "Why are ye hiding from me, lass?"

Clenching her jaw, she tried to pull away, but Marc wouldn't allow her.

"Talk tae me, lass." Her colorful eyes clashed with his,

shining with so many conflicting emotions it took him aback. He dropped his arm. "Bronaugh?"

"Why are you here, Marc?" she asked.

Confusion creased his forehead. "What do ye mean, why am I here? I told ye. I've been looking for ye for days, lass…"

She shook her head. "Yes, but why?"

"Why? What kind o' bloody question is that?"

Her head fell forward, her blonde hair hiding her face again. She twisted her hands together in her lap. "I saw the way you reacted when you saw me here. You're afraid of me…"

"Nae, Bronaugh," he said.

"You are," she argued. "You always will be. Because of what I am, because I'm *an olc*." She sniffed, and when she raised her head again, she gave him a sad smile. "It's okay. I understand why you feel the way you do."

Marc had heard enough. "Ye dinna have a bloody clue how I feel aboot ye!" he growled. "Dinna sit there and assume ye ken…"

She started to stand up. "Marc, it's okay. Really, I understand."

Grabbing her by the wrist, he pulled her back down. "Ye understand nothing, Bronaugh. Nothing. Do ye hear me?" Holding her jaw in his large hand, he made her look at him. "I love ye, Bronaugh Lane. I dinna care if ye are Dark Fae or no'. I'm no' afraid o' ye. For two long days, the only thing I've been afraid o' is that I had lost ye." His voice broke on the last few words, and he had to take a moment. Releasing her jaw, he cupped her wee face in his hands. "I cannae lose ye, Bronaugh, lass. No' when I only

just found ye. Please, do me the honor o' staying with me."
His eyes were wet with unmanly tears, but he didn't care.
He only cared that she believed him. "I want tae be with
ye, Bronaugh. I dinna care where. If we have tae leave,
we'll leave. And I will protect ye from all that would do ye
harm. I swear it tae ye, lass!"

As he sat trying to think of what else he could say or
do to convince her of how he felt, Bronaugh's eyes went
from blues to greens to pinks. Then the colors began to
rotate in and out, spurred on by flashes of yellow. It was
the most beautiful thing he'd ever seen. Like a sunset over
the ocean.

"You love me?" she whispered in awe.

"Aye." There was not one ounce of hesitation there.
"Aye, Bronaugh. I love everything aboot ye, lass. With my
whole heart."

She continued to watch him with those striking eyes.
"I thought, when you saw me here and didn't come to me
right away…I thought you had changed your mind again. I
thought, maybe, that when the prince took me, it had
given you time to think about what it would mean to be
with me—"

He interrupted her. "It did. It gave me a chance tae
imagine my life without ye, lass." He shook his head as
some of the moisture in his eyes leaked out and trailed
down his face. "That's a life I dinna want tae live,
Bronaugh."

"Truly?"

"Truly, lass."

Her lips turned up, hesitant at first, but gradually blossoming into a wide smile. "I want to be with you, too. I love you, Marc..."

With a predatory growl, he pulled her in and took her lips in a hard kiss. Her hands came up to grip his shoulders, and Marc moaned at the feel of her cool skin touching his. He wanted to renew his claim on her, right here, right now. But there were things that needed to be discussed first. .

Breaking off the kiss, he smiled when she let out a disappointed sigh.

All in good time, lass.

"So yer family found ye?" he asked.

"Yes. And they brought Heather with them." She smiled again. "You should have seen her face! She'd never been to the Fae world before, apparently."

"Brock will no' be happy aboot that," he told her, distracted by the way her smiling face lit up the night.

"Probably not," she agreed.

Then something came to him. Something he was almost afraid to ask. "What is it exactly that the daft prince wants ye tae do, Bronaugh?"

She looked everywhere but at him. "Nothing, really..."

"Bronaugh, lass, dinna play with me," he told her sternly. "I want tae ken what it is, and ye better be telling me..." His words tapered off to nothing when he noticed that her eyes, those bonnie colorful eyes, were zeroed in on his cock.

And his cock couldn't have been happier about it.

She ran the tip of her little tongue over her bottom lip, and when she raised her eyes to his again, they were different than they were before. Now they were like the birth of a new star. Never had he seen such a multitude of colors within them.

"Can we talk about this later?" she asked. Without waiting for an answer, she pushed her dress off her shoulders and shimmied out of the top half of it, exposing her bare breasts to his hungry gaze.

He swallowed hard. "Nae. We need tae talk aboot it now," he protested. And he meant it.

"Why?" she asked. One wee hand ran down the muscles of his chest while the other wrapped itself firmly around his swollen shaft.

He knew she was trying to distract him. Marc dug his fingers into the tops of his thighs, fighting the urge to touch her. If he touched her, he'd be lost, and they might never get back to this conversation. "Because o' what I said earlier..."

"But I don't want to talk about it," she told him. "I want to push you back onto all this soft moss and put you inside me." She stroked him with her hand as Marc watched, fascinated by the sight of her wee fingers gripping his wide girth. Sliding her hand to the top, she gave the head a squeeze. A drop of come appeared as he moaned. "I've missed you," she said in a soft voice.

"Aye," he breathed, reaching toward her bare breast. Then he scowled and clenched his hand into a fist before it could touch her warm skin. "Nae, Bronaugh. We need tae talk first."

Rising up onto her knees, she shimmied the rest of the way out of her dress. Leaving it pooled around her knees, she put her hands on his shoulders and leaned forward to kiss him. He caught sight of her dangling breasts, the nipples hard and begging to be touched, just before her luscious mouth landed on his. Her warm tongue probed at his lips, demanding entrance.

He groaned. He had no choice. He let her in, and he was lost.

Marc gave up the fight. It was a fookin' unfair battle anyway. Without breaking the kiss, he wrapped his arms around her and pulled her down on top of him as he lay back in the moss.

Her soft belly pressed into his cock as she rocked her body on top of him. His groan mingled with hers as he held her body tight to his. Sliding her knees up alongside his hips, she lifted her bottom up and forward, sliding his cock between her warm folds until he felt his head at her entrance. Unable to wait, his hands gripped her round arse and held her immobile as he lifted his hips and slid inside fast and hard. Bronaugh's cries were muffled by his kisses as her body accepted him. She was tight and wet, and more than ready for him.

Before he could do anything else, she nipped his bottom lip, put her hands on his chest and pushed herself into a sitting position.

Then she started to move.

Marc's eyes nearly rolled back in his head. But he quickly opened them again, not wanting to miss anything.

His Bronaugh sat above him, riding him like a bull. Her head had fallen back and her full breasts bounced deliciously with her movements. Slowing things down, she lifted her hips until he was barely inside, moved them in a circle, and then sat down on him hard.

Marc tensed, his body already on the verge of release. "Bronaugh…"

Lifting up again, she slid him out of her body, and then ever so slowly lowered herself back down. Her fingers dug into his chest as she lifted her head. Their eyes locked, and she smiled a vixen's smile.

"We'll talk about it later," she told him firmly.

"Aye," he breathed.

And she started to ride.

* * *

Thank you for reading! I hope you loved meeting Marc and Bronaugh. The next book in The Kincaid Werewolves series is
<u>The Alpha's Redemption.</u>
Keegan wants Bitsy back, but not for his rodeo. Find out if this alpha wolf can ever possible redeem himself after what he allowed to happen to her.

<u>READ THE ALPHA'S REDEMPTION NOW</u>

"Keegan and Bitsy's story is one that will have your emotions all over place, mine were. I loved this book!!" - Amazon Review
"Keegan, Keegan Keegan. He is MINE. I mean I guess Bitsy was ok.. Fine they were perfect and I loved them together.. but whatever. " -Amazon review

THE
KINCAID
WEREWOLVES
BOOK THREE
The Alpha's
Redemption
L.E. WILSON

ABOUT THE AUTHOR

L.E. Wilson writes Paranormal Romance starring intense alpha males and the women who are fearless enough to tame them — for the most part anyway. ;) In her novels you'll find smoking hot scenes, a touch of suspense, some humor, a bit of gore, and multifaceted characters, all working together to combine her lifelong obsession with the paranormal and her love of romance.

Her writing career came about the usual way: on a dare from her loving husband. Little did she know just one casual suggestion would open a box of worms (or words as the case may be) that would forever change her life.

Peach tea and her tiara are a necessary part of her writing process, though sometimes you'll find her typing away at her favorite Starbucks. She walks two miles to get there, to make up for all of those coffees. On the weekends she likes to hike, garden, cook vegan food, and have date nights with her favorite guy.

On a Personal Note:
"I love to hear from my readers! Contact me anytime at le@lewilsonauthor.com."

Keep In Touch With L.E.
lewilsonauthor.com
le@lewilsonauthor.com

www.ingramcontent.com/pod-product-compliance
Lightning Source LLC
Chambersburg PA
CBHW061612190726
48288CB00007B/2292